CRUEL SUMMER

WESLEY SOUTHARD

DEATH'S HEAD PRESS

Houston, Texas
www.DeathsHeadPress.com

Copyright © 2020 Wesley Southard

All Rights Reserved

ISBN: 978-1-950259-38-0

First Edition

The story included in this publication is a work of fiction. Names, characters, places and incidents are products of the author's imagination or are used fictitiously. Any resemblance to actual events or locales or persons living or dead is entirely coincidental.

Without limiting the rights under copyright reserved above, no part of this publication may be reproduced, stored in or introduced into a retrieval system, or transmitted, in any form, or by any means (electronic, mechanical, photocopying, recording, or otherwise), without the prior written permission of both the copyright owner and the above publisher of this book.

Cover Art: Alex McVey

Book Layout: Lori Michelle
www.TheAuthorsAlley.com

PRAISE FOR *CRUEL SUMMER*

"If Peter Benchley, Poe, and Lovecraft drank too much and got into a bar fight, *Cruel Summer* would be the novel they'd hash out whilst waiting for someone to post bail. It begins as a domestic thriller and suddenly detours into aquamarine demi-god insanity. Cinematic and brutal, this is without a doubt Southard's best work to date.

—Aaron Dries,
author of *A Place for Sinners*, *The Fallen Boys*, and *House of Sighs*

"Wesley Southard has masterfully crafted a high-intensity, emotional gut punch of a fantasy-horror tale set against the backdrop of the Florida Atlantic coast. This is sun-drenched, vacation-themed horror at its beachy best.

—Kenzie Jennings,
Splatterpunk nominated author of *Reception* and *Red Station*

"There's nothing like an idyllic family vacation . . . and this, packed with toxic relationships, secrets, aquatic mayhem and unnatural menace, really is NOTHING like an idyllic family vacation!

—Christine Morgan,
Splatterpunk Award-Winning author of *Lakehouse Infernal* and *The Night Silver River Run Red*

For Mom and Dad,
Thanks for cleaning up that cabana urinal. I have since learned to pull instead of push.

"Time and Tide wait for no man."
—St. Marher, 1225

"What would an ocean be without a monster lurking in the dark? It would be like sleep without dreams."
—Werner Herzog

"Peace starts with suffering . . . "
—Medusa

THE OCEAN WAS nervous. Though the briny water ebbed and flowed, weeds and debris floating like stardust, the beasts that called it home remained perfectly still. Even the breath of the wind above could not disturb their pause. Shad and herring, barracuda and grouper, mako and marlin—the very essence of kill or be killed—froze in place. Instinct told them to flee or to fight. Nature warned them otherwise. Their bodies grew cold and weak.

From far below, it rose.

The crisp cyan water darkened around them. The coral reef wilted. Peripheral eyes widened.

The massive shape lumbered through the still waters. A cloud of hate and reckoning clung to its unnatural bulk. Gingerly giving it berth, the sea life watched, following its slow, antediluvian drive. Long after it moved on, they remained in place, unsure what to do. They knew it would only be a matter of time before they, too, would be called upon.

And when that time came, they would have no choice but to obey.

SUNDAY

" **LOOK, MOM, HE'S SLEEPING!**"

Melissa Braun snapped awake from a nap she didn't realize she was taking. It had been a painfully silent ride, save for the awful country music that twined through the car speakers, and the consistent rhythmic melody of the SUV's wheels must have lulled her to sleep somewhere near Macon. She barely remembered sitting in Atlanta traffic—a city stretched to its utter limit—and was amazed there always seemed to be construction on I-75 going both ways. In her thirty-one years, whatever problem they were repairing never seemed to have been fixed. She wept for its residents.

Adjusting her sunglasses, she sat up against her belt and turned around in her seat. "What's that, hon?"

Patrick looked up from his handful of Magic the Gathering cards and grinned sheepishly at his mother. "Out there," he nodded to the window. "That deer is sleeping."

At first Melissa wasn't sure what he meant. She scanned the shoulder of the interstate for a moment before she found what he'd been referring to. The brutal southern Georgia sun revealed a deer lying on a patch of kudzu, its antlered head facing their vehicle as they raced by. The creature's upper half appeared untouched, but down past its abdomen was the wreckage of a brutal hit and run from an eighteen wheeler. Its hindquarters were nowhere in sight. A buffet of sunbaked innards fed the local scavengers.

Melissa grinned, remembering their longstanding game. "That's right, hon. He's sleeping peacefully."

"He should probably move off the road and sleep somewhere else, huh?" Patrick asked, playfully.

"Absolutely. Seems pretty dangerous to take a nap this close to traffic."

Hoyt spat into the conversation, and the air conditioned interior immediately warmed. "You two are fucking disgusting." He scowled behind the wheel. His handlebar mustache curled over his corn-colored teeth. "Seriously, we've been in the car for seven hours, and you're starting on that shit again?" He shook his head.

Melissa rolled her eyes. "He's twelve years old. Why can't you just let him have some fun?"

"You find it fun pointing out dead animals on the roadside?"

"Yes, as a matter of fact we do. It might be a little weird, but it's been our thing since Patrick was little."

Hoyt's neck popped as he turned his head. "How about it, PB? You like dead animals? That shit get you going?"

Patrick's smile instantly dissolved. He buried his face back into his perfectly sleeved deck of cards.

Hoyt's voice dropped to a semi-serious growl. "Hey, boy. You answer me when I speak to you. Understand?"

CRUEL SUMMER

Keeping his eyes down, Patrick nodded.

"What's that, PB? As you can see I'm driving, with little-to-no help from either of you two dummies. I can't see it when you nod your little shaggy-ass head."

Melissa grunted. "Come on, Hoyt. Drop it. We're just passing the time."

Hoyt turned down the radio to a whisper. "No, Mel. The boy's got to learn some respect. If I'm ever going to be his daddy and teach him to be a man, then he's going to have to start addressing me like he's got some nuts. They have dropped by now, haven't they, PB? They're not still hidden up in your stomach, are they?"

"Yes, they have," Patrick whispered.

"Yes what, PB?"

He sighed. "Yes, sir."

Satisfied, Hoyt turned his attention back to the road. Melissa gave her son a tight-lipped smile, her silent reassurance it was fine and he should ignore Hoyt when he was in one of his foul, sleep-deprived moods. Patrick didn't return the gesture. He kept his glassy eyes on the cards in his hands and sucked his lips in-between his teeth. She patted his leg and turned back in her seat.

The radio found volume again, and now it was the find-and-replace vocals of Luke Bryant who was singing about some long-legged girl in short-shorts on a tailgate. No matter how hard Hoyt pushed it on Melissa, she could not find an appetite for country music. She was a rocker through and through, and right then she would have killed for some Foo Fighters or Silverstein—anything that didn't include fiddles, banjos, or put-on southern accents. The problem was he rarely allowed her access to the radio, even when *she* was driving. Inside the car, *he* was master and commander. Other than the window buttons—and sometimes not even those—all functions were under his control. The few times she had been allowed to listen to her "shitty liberal music" it was met with exaggerated eye rolls, sneers, and unrolled windows. So she didn't bother anymore. Her tastes were her own and they were kept loud and raucous when he wasn't around.

Slumped in the driver's seat, Hoyt Rainey was beginning to look like the living country stereotype he idolized. A black wife-beater and torn jeans, his 'Don't give a fuck' appearance radiated like August heat off of a blacktop. His thinning brown hair gleamed in the mid-day sun, slicked back with more than enough pomade to grease an engine. At thirty-seven, he was embarrassed he was losing his hair, a hereditary fact that, according to him, bit him in his mid-twenties and really began to chew with fervor in his early thirties. He didn't discuss it and refused to be 'hat guy.' Melissa didn't mind his hair much. It was his choice in facial styling she didn't care for. He could have grown a goatee or a full beard, which she liked. Instead, he chose a handlebar mustache to look like Sam Elliott.

"By the way," he groaned. "Thanks for staying up and navigating like I asked."

Melissa sighed, knowing he was ready to pick a fight. "Hoyt, I told you back in Chattanooga, when we got onto I-75 South, it was a straight shot down into Florida. Plus, you have GPS on your phone. Use it."

"And I told you, Melly, I needed your help to stay

awake. I'm dog-fucking tired. I didn't get any sleep last night."

She hated being called *Melly*. She hated all of his appointed nicknames, including *PB*, which she assumed was an initialism of Patrick's name. "Whose fault is that? You're the one who had to stay up for the end of the boxing match. You knew we were getting an early start on the drive. And please stop your cussing. I don't need my child repeating any of that foul language."

"Goddamn it, I don't know where I'm going! I've never been to this fucking place!"

"For Christ's sake, you literally have to stay on the same interstate for, like, four hundred and fifty miles! A monkey in a hard hat could probably do it with no problem. I'm sure I would have woken up before then."

Hoyt shook his head. "And what if I had fallen asleep, *hmmm*? We'd all be like that deer back there. Would you be cracking jokes then?"

Probably, she thought. *At least you'd be quiet then, you goon.* She should have stayed awake—maybe then he wouldn't have a reason to bitch and complain like a petulant child. She should have done lots of things. She should have driven, should have gone on this vacation with just her son, should have dropped Hoyt's worthless ass years ago. But here she was, stuck with a man she could stand no longer. Where had the time gone? Three years ago, she was a single mother, heading up a large non-profit who provided basic needs and services for low income families in the Southern Indiana region. The money wasn't great, but she was fulfilled and happy. Patrick was happy . . . or at least thought he was happy. Nowadays he seemed quiet, aloof. He no longer had that same childish spark. He kept to himself, the friends he grew up with now a sigh and a shrug away. Much like Melissa, he knew what the problem was, and the problem had a receding hairline.

It seemed like a lifetime ago. Before Hoyt, Melissa had been single for so long she had honestly forgotten what it was like to be in a healthy relationship. By her mid-twenties, she wasn't looking for anything past casual sex. It wasn't as though she'd been in anything long term, at least not since Patrick's father, Jordan, and *that* was all the way back in high school. She was perfectly fine not having anyone count on her but her son. She'd had Patrick at such a young age, much younger than she had ever wanted, and he had become the only male she wanted to support.

But there were times, long, sleepless nights, with Hoyt snoring up a storm next to her, she thought of Jordan and what could have been . . .

"Are you listening to me?"

Melissa shook away her daze. "What?"

Sighing, Hoyt rapped his tattooed hand across the steering wheel. The black, tattooed letters **DAREMETO** were spread across his eight knuckles. "I asked you why are we going down here?"

"We've been over this. We go to New Smyrna Beach every year for vacation. Well, almost every year. It's a place my family has been frequenting for decades. Patrick and I haven't been in a few years because we haven't had time. We love it down there."

"Why not Daytona or Panama City? What's so special about New Saburna?"

CRUEL SUMMER

"New *Smyrna*. It's just a nice place. The beaches are quiet, the city is clean, and we know where all the good restaurants are. Even though we haven't been there in like four or five years, I can still probably navigate my way around without even thinking about it."

Hoyt chuckled. "You know what quiet and clean means, right? It's boring. Sounds like geriatric central."

"It's really not." She rolled her tired eyes. "It's just a nice family place to vacation."

"Any bars?"

"A few, yes."

"Any titty bars?"

"Christ, Hoyt, no! I don't believe so. It's a pretty clean place. Heck, they don't even have any chain restaurants on the beach side. It's all mom-and-pop run places. If they don't allow Big Macs, I'm sure bare breasts are prohibited as well."

He grinned. "Oh well. Who needs to buy the cow when I can get the milk for free?" Wiggling his eyebrows, he reached out and squeezed Melissa's left breast.

She quickly smacked his hand away. "Will you grow up? There's a child in the car."

"Who? PB? He's practically a teenager. I'm sure he's seen some titties before, ain't that right, PB?"

In the back seat, Patrick's face turned the same shade of red as a sunburn. He lifted his handful of cards to shield his obvious embarrassment.

"I said *ain't that right, PB*? Have you already forgotten how speak to me?"

Patrick groaned, "No, sir."

"*No, sir?* Don't lie to me, PB. I've been on your laptop. I've seen your browser history. I take it you're finally finding out how to pull your pud?"

"Hoyt!" Melissa yelled. "Stop embarrassing him!"

"Hey, at least we know he's not a faggot."

"Damn it! I said *stop!*"

Hoyt laughed. "Language, Melly! *Not around the child!*"

Frustrated, Melissa threw her head back and sighed. Even when playful, it was impossible to break one of his moods without it becoming a rapid problem. He knew just the right way to press her buttons. Best to let it ride out, or hope he got his mind on something else entirely.

"Speaking of questionable internet searches . . . Why don't you help daddy stay awake over here." Shifting in his seat, Hoyt patted his crotch. His denim bulge twitched in response.

"Absolutely not!" she whispered loudly. "What the hell is wrong with you? My son is in the backseat."

"Jesus, Melly, I'm just screwing with you. What—too good for it now? Shit, it's not like you haven't done it before."

Sadly, he was right. Back when they first met, she wouldn't have had any issue making a fun evening out of a joy ride in his Mustang. At times she even enjoyed it—the thrill, the thrum of her heartbeat. But now the thought of getting anywhere near his dick made her stomach churn.

"I'm not discussing this any further, and you will not speak to me like that in front of my son—now or ever. Got it? Now drop it."

Hoyt snickered. "I'm sure he's seen worse on PornHub."

CRUEL SUMMER

"I said drop it!"

He turned back to the road with a grimace. "Some start to this vacation. You used to be fun, you know that? You used to be a firecracker, doing shit that would have put some of those internet sluts to shame. You're a fucking *bore* now, just like this town we're going to."

Screw letting it ride out. Melissa exploded. "Why? Because I won't suck you off in front of my child? You're a disgusting pig."

"You know, if we're ever going to be a family, you're going to have to start watching how you talk to me. Unless you've forgotten, I make the money in this relationship. This little Florida vacation here? All paid for by me. The food? Me. The gas? Me. I suggest you start showing me some respect." The middle and ring fingers on his right hand flexed on the wheel.

Melissa glanced at his hand and shivered. Her throat tightened. She let her retort hiss out unspoken through her teeth. How much longer was she going to put up with this? It wasn't fair to her or to her son. Part of her, some ignorant sliver of her teen self, still believed she could turn the bad boy into a loving family man. But three years later her bad boy still sat high and mighty on his beer-stained throne of narcissism. She wanted him to be good to them, to be the father Patrick never truly had. The closest Hoyt had come to being a father figure was giving her son a nickname she wasn't fully convinced by. More than anything she wanted this vacation to be a new start. She didn't want this relationship to end in a tire fire. She just had to get them to New Smyrna in one piece.

If all else failed, Jordan lived a few miles down the road from their condo.

2

A FEW HOURS LATER, they arrived at their hotel in Jacksonville. Their condo room at the beach wouldn't be available until sometime Monday morning, so much like Patrick's grandparents parents before him, they had secured a place to stay for the night before driving the rest of the way down.

It was not as secure as they had hoped.

"What the *fuck* do you mean you can't find it?"

The short Hispanic woman behind the Holiday Inn front desk jumped as Hoyt's voice broke through the silent lobby like a shattering vase. It was nearly nine PM, and they were all excruciatingly tired and hungry. Patrick's stomach growled hard enough to make his shirt ripple. They hadn't eaten since before Tifton, Georgia, and the only thing currently sitting in his stomach was a Hardee's cheeseburger and a small can of gas station Sour Cream and Onion Pringles. All he wanted was the pizza his mother promised and a full night of uninterrupted sleep. It didn't look to be going in his favor. Beside him, his mother shifted uncomfortably as she leaned on the suitcases she had no help bringing in.

"I'm sorry, sir. I can't seem to find a 'Rainey' in the

system." The woman's name tag read 'Valeria.' Her hands shook, and she took a deep breath to calm herself. "Are you sure you made the reservation at *this* particular Holiday Inn?"

Hoyt's knuckles whitened on the ledge of the desk. "First off, don't take that smart ass tone with me, lady. If I wanted any shit from you I'd pick it out of your teeth. Second, I didn't make the reservations, my girl did. Are you saying she fucked up?"

"No, sir, not at all."

Hoyt leaned in closer. "Are you saying she's a liar?"

Patrick's mother finally spoke up. "Hoyt, please stop."

"No, sir," Valeria answered.

Hoyt said, "Then why does it feel like you're calling us liars, *hmmm*?"

Much like the terrified woman, Patrick shrunk at Hoyt's rising temper. He'd been this way for as long as Patrick could remember. Waiters, cashiers, hotel clerks—if they wore a uniform, they would eventually be hit with harsh words and harsher breath. He did this so often Patrick was afraid it would become a normal thing that would seep into his own mannerisms. He refused to let that happen. Hoyt made him feel weak, spineless, and insecure, but one thing he wouldn't do was make him hurt others. He'd seen the way it affected his mom. Someday, he hoped, she would see the same thing he did.

A monster.

"I asked you a question, bitch!" Hoyt yelled. "Do we look like liars?"

"N-n-no, sir! That's not what I—"

"That's not what you what—*what*?"

"I-I-I—"

"Speaka any English, *puta*?"

Patrick's mother quickly stepped away from the luggage and stood next to Hoyt, attempting to wedge herself between the two. "That's enough, Hoyt! You're being completely ridiculous."

"*I'm* being ridiculous?" he screamed.

"Yes, you are! Now calm down. I'll handle this."

Hoyt leaned past her to growl at the shaking woman. "Fucking beaners! Coming here and taking jobs from hard-working Americans. I'm sure you lost our reservation, same as you lost your green card."

His face as red as a bell pepper, Melissa carefully pushed her boyfriend away from the counter and an escalating situation. "Hoyt, enough!"

"This is why we need the wall!"

"Outside! *Now!*"

Bouncing back and forth on his feet, Hoyt glared and snorted at Melissa before stomping past Patrick through the sliding glass doors. The hotel lobby immediately cooled.

"I'm so, so sorry, ma'am," Patrick's mother said, embarrassed. "It's been a very, *very* long day. Indiana and Florida are not nearly as close as we'd like them to be." Her eyes glassed up. "I'm—that's not usually him. He's just tired because he's been driving all day. He's not usually so . . . terrible."

Patrick sneered, wishing his mother wouldn't lie like that.

"It's perfectly alright, ma'am." Valeria wouldn't look at her.

"If our reservation has been lost, then what can we do?"

CRUEL SUMMER

Valeria stepped back to her computer. "There's not much I can do. Every hotel is booked up. There's pre-season football tonight, and there's a large banking convention in town that's taking all available rooms. I'm sorry, ma'am." The woman then turned and left, leaving them both alone with their thoughts.

His mother looked helpless. He knew she did not want to face Hoyt with the real possibility of having to drive further for somewhere else to stay the night. This time Patrick would help her take the luggage back to the car.

―⁓―

They drove for another two hours in absolute silence. Melissa couldn't reason with Hoyt, and even if she tried she was positive it would go in one ear and out the other. There was a time when he may have valued her opinion, may have cooled his jets and listened to her reasoning, but those days were dead like disco. They were tired and starving, and his refusal to even stop for a bathroom break was nothing short of maddening. The trip had barely begun and it was already a failure.

The only reason they even stopped in the small town of Deland, a mere thirty minutes from their final destination, was because they simply ran out of fuel. Lucky for them the closest hotel was directly across from the gas station. Unlucky for them the hotel was an absolute dump. Much like their tiny parking lot, the building's exterior was a maze of foundation cracks and graffiti so old it could have been painted by prehistoric cavemen. Overgrown bushes and grass which had not seen a whirling blade in two summers. She didn't bother talking Hoyt out of it. He finally appeared to have calmed down, and if he got even a few hours of sleep maybe his attitude would incrementally improve.

As they trudged to their third floor room, Melissa broke the silence. "Do you know why it's called Deland? Because it's nowhere near Desea."

Patrick smirked. Hoyt did not.

The room was as bad as she had feared—various shades of stains blotched across the floor, beds that weren't even washed or made, and the faint smell of old sex and marijuana. Without a word, Patrick took the smaller of the two beds and hopped in fully clothed.

"Goodnight, honey," she said.

Her son didn't respond, only turned his back on her to face the wall.

Melissa sighed and lugged the rest of their bags into their meager room and placed them on the single dresser that she didn't dare open. Hoyt peeked out the window, walked away, then peaked out again, presumably to check on their vehicle. Satisfied, he took off his wife beater and went to the bathroom to wash his face. Melissa badly wanted to kick off her sneakers and socks, but she was afraid of what the carpet contained, so she kept them on. It would be an easy decision whether or not to sleep on top of the blankets.

As she searched for her toothbrush, Hoyt walked out of the bathroom, water dripping down his face. He stared at her for a long time. She felt his red-rimmed eyes roaming her body, and it made her skin crawl. "What?" she asked.

"I'm tired."

"Then go to sleep."

"No. Not that. I'm tired of that mouth of yours."

Melissa stopped searching and stood up straight to face him. "Excuse me?"

He took a small step forward. "Back in Jacksonville. I'm tired of you correcting me in public. You embarrassed me in front of that woman."

If she wasn't so tired she would have laughed. "*I* embarrassed *you*? Please. You embarrassed yourself, Hoyt. You have no idea how to control your temper in public—or in private, for that matter. I'm sick and tired of not being able to go anywhere with you."

For a moment he looked genuinely hurt. "You're tired of me?"

She immediately regretted it. "No. I mean you don't know how to act around people. Let's just drop it, okay? I just want to freshen up and go to sleep. I'm done fighting for the day."

Another step forward. "Who's fighting?"

"You are, bozo. I just—"

Before she could finish, Hoyt rushed her. She opened her mouth to yell, quickly realizing her mistake. She should have seen it coming. Like a lightning strike, Hoyt clutched the back of her head with his left hand, and with his right he shoved his middle and ring fingers down her throat. Her eyes went wide, her hands grasping at his muscular wrist. His middle fingers stayed rigid and tight on her tongue while his other three gripped her cheeks like a bowling ball. Heart thrumming, she tried not to scream or panic. She forced herself to breathe steady. This was not the first time.

He leaned in to her face, his sour cheeseburger

breath hot on her teary eyes. "You see, just like that. You calling me a bozo? That's not going to fly anymore." He pushed her back against the dresser, in turn shoving his fingers in deeper. Melissa gagged but didn't dare throw up. "If we're ever going to be a family—and if PB over there is ever going to be my son—then you're going to have to start showing me some fucking respect. Got it?"

Melissa did her best to nod, though he did most of the rocking of her head for her. He pressed his shirtless chest again hers.

"I'm not going to put up with it anymore, you hear? I'm the man in this relationship—not you. You may think you've got some big balls, thinking you're in charge just because of that hairy slit between your legs, but I've got some news for you, *Melly*. You ain't shit without me or my money. You'd be a good-for-nothing bitch with a spoiled-ass bastard kid."

Where had it all gone wrong? Three years ago, she never would have called Hoyt a 'sweet guy' or the type you brought to your parent's for dinner, but he still had manners. They were both set up through mutual friends, and though the immediate attraction wasn't there, there was still a spark that continued to ignite her interest. He was a few years older than her, which she didn't mind, and he still held on to a bad boy persona that should have been shed by his early thirties like snake skin. To be honest, he intimidated her, and some part of her—a voice that continued to scream, "You should have listened, bitch!"—felt drawn to him. He was the complete opposite of what she typically looked for in a man. The thrill he gave her was unlike anything she felt with normal guys who played it safe. He drove fast, played loud, and screwed her in ways she'd only seen those porn guys do. He was exciting. Dangerous. And like a dumbass she thought she could eventually make him into something he wasn't. The three of them moved in together, and against her better judgement, she quit her job at his request because his concrete pouring business was expanding and booming. That's when the trouble began. After a contract dispute, his business partner packed up and left town, and Hoyt was forced to run the company on his own. His demeanor changed, and he grew into a caricature of his former self. He became hateful and abusive—though rarely physically—and the few times her and Patrick tried to leave, he developed his own way of punishment. The type that didn't leave marks. The type that got him exactly what he wanted.

The word **DARE** was in and around her mouth.

"You need me, Melly. And right now—" he leaned in to softly kiss her cheek, "—I need you."

Melissa shuddered as she felt his tongue flick her cheek. Her body wanted her to pull away, but her brain warned her of the last time she tried that.

"You know what I want," he breathed. "Are you going to give it to me?"

Her eyes flicked to her son on the other bed.

"Don't worry about PB. He's asleep."

Tears rolled down her face.

His thick fingers still jammed down her throat, he turned her body and forced her backwards into the bathroom. When the backs of her legs hit the toilet bowl, Hoyt kicked the door shut behind them. His grip on the back of her head loosened, but the other hand stayed put. Slowly his fingers went in and out of her mouth, gently prodding the back of her throat. He pressed his mouth against her ear. "From here on out, you're going to be better to me, aren't you? I love you, Melly."

She didn't respond.

In the other room, Patrick cried himself to sleep. He smushed his fingers into his ears, trying to block out the soft weeping coming from behind the closed bathroom door.

He wanted to go home.

MONDAY

3

MUCH LIKE THE DRIVE down to Deland, the ride toward the beach was just as soundless. Melissa didn't sleep, and neither did Hoyt, but her reasons were far different than his. In their stiff, unforgiving bed, she kept as close to the edge as possible. Hoyt, too, tried to sleep, but his shifting under the blankets and his systematic scanning out of the grimy window to check on their car made for another long night. As far as she could tell, Patrick slept peacefully. What she wouldn't give to be twelve again.

Melissa stocked up on cold bottled water from the gas station before leaving town. She hoped it would alleviate the rhythmic throb in her throat, but it did little else than temporarily sooth the burn. The other burn in her sex would have to go away on its own. He wasn't as rough as he had been in the past, but his misplaced anger prevented him from stopping long after he should have. She hated it the first time; she loathed it the last.

As angry as she should have been, the gorgeous, cloudless sky shined bright on a brand new day. The closer they got to the ocean, the better she began to feel. Hoyt thankfully let her roll down the windows. She could practically taste the salt in the air, could smell the sweet Zoysia grass that grew between the sand. The sensations instantly brought her back to her childhood. The intense warmth of the southern heat through her Jellies sandals. The sweet, rich flavor of the sugar-dusted brownies from the local French bakery. The cool caress of that first dip in the Atlantic. Despite the circumstances, she missed this. She needed this—*they* needed this—more than she realized. Her sense memories took over, and she couldn't help but smile.

Highway 44 took them straight to the outskirts of the city, and before long they had reached the South Causeway. The bridge sat high over the Indian River, which separated the mainland from the coastal barrier island. Down below, millionaires flaunted their massive homes and condos which lined the outer rim of Bouchelles Island. If their lavish boats weren't docked they were being guided through the calm, teal colored waters by their bronzed, middle-aged owners without a care in the world. Beyond that, teens sprinted along the shore of Chicken Island, nets in hand, ready to catch blue crabs. Melissa beamed. It was easy to forget her perennial vacation destination was a place where normal people like her lived their day to day lives. Tropical surroundings were merely background noise to those who knew nothing else. She dreamed of living down here, of raising her son here. Maybe someday.

She knew of at least one person who had made this place home.

The South Causeway now behind them, they

touched down on A1A and the island of New Smyrna Beach. Waves of nostalgia washed over her. All of her favorite restaurants flew past. She noticed the big one her parents loved had built a tree top bar outside the building, which she would have to text them about later. The closer to the beach they got, the more tourist shops began to pop up. Glass front buildings full of boogie boards and tie-dye NSB T-shirts she swore she would never buy yet somehow stocked up on by week's end. On her right, the Bob Ross Art Workshop & Gallery provided a haven for those wanting to learn about and celebrate the former Volusia County born artist. Maybe they could take a class sometime that week?

Before reaching the condo they quickly stopped at the realty headquarters where she signed off on the room and picked up their keys. Despite still being in pain, she jittered with excitement.

A1A stretched as far as the eye could see, but there was no need to travel any further. Just down the street, across from shopping plaza, was their condo. They hung a left and found the nearest parking spot against the building. Melissa couldn't get out of the car fast enough. Behind her, Patrick followed her across the sweltering blacktop. Beyond the thick patches of overgrown grass and the wooden steps that led down to the beach was a sight she had missed more than anything in the whole world. Brilliant morning sun glimmered over the crashing waves. Though it was still early, beachgoers were already picking their spots, piercing the gray sand with their umbrellas and low riding lounge chairs. Bestsellers were cracked open and ready to be devoured. She reached out and took Patrick's hand as her sunglass-covered eyes flickered across the horizon. Despite their current quandary, he gave her a hint of a smile back. This felt right.

"Are you two shits going to stare at the water all day, or are you going to help me carry up our bags?"

And just like that it was gone.

Hoyt popped the back lid of the SUV and stepped aside as they approached. She told Patrick to get them a luggage cart from the hallway, and when he came back they took to loading it to the max. Once finished, they locked up and pushed the cart across the mostly empty lot to the interior hallway toward the elevator.

Hoyt grunted as they approached. "What the hell?"

A small laminated disclaimer taped to the wall informed them the elevator would be under maintenance until further notice.

"Christ, what a shock," he lamented. "What floor are we on again?"

Melissa scratched her head. "Uh, third floor, I think. Room 307."

"Fucking figures. A dump just like I thought it would be."

Melissa sighed and helped Patrick wheel the overstuffed cart to the enclosed stairwell. The cart would not fit through the doorway, so they each grabbed a suitcase and began to climb. Despite the mid-eighties temperature that early September offered outside, the stairwell was absolutely sweltering. Their footsteps echoed up, coming to a halt at the third floor. Hoyt led the way, only carrying a small backpack, while Patrick lugged Hoyt's overstuffed suitcase. Behind them, Melissa carried their pillows and two of her son's bags.

Grunting at the weight, Patrick slipped on the last step before the second story platform and dropped Hoyt's suitcase. The vinyl case flipped head over tail, tumbling past Melissa until it hit the bottom floor with a deafening crash. Patrick yelped as his knee hit the concrete, but Hoyt's gasp echoed much louder. He rushed to Patrick and pulled the boy up by his shirt with both fists. Before Melissa could properly react, Hoyt had her son pressed against the handrails.

"Goddamn it, PB!" he screamed. "What the fuck is the matter with you?"

"Hoyt!" Melissa yelled. "Let him go! It was an accident."

Hoyt, in fact, did not let go. He only gripped him tighter. **DAREMETO** was wrapped up tight in Patrick's black Jurassic Park T-shirt. "You clumsy little shit!"

Wide eyed, Patrick leaned backwards, trying to pull his face away from Hoyt. "I'm sorry!"

Melissa dropped her armfuls of items and rushed to her son. She grabbed the sleeve of Hoyt's shirt and pulled. "Leave him alone, Hoyt. He didn't do it on purpose."

Hoyt focused on her son. "That was my bag you dropped, you dumb prick! I have something very expensive in there."

"Let him go, Hoyt!"

"If you broke it, I swear I'm going to wring your scrawny little neck."

Tears burst from Patrick's eyes. His chest hitched.

Despite not having much upper body strength,

Melissa drew back and punched Hoyt's arm. "I said stop it, goddamn you!"

Hoyt laughed, barely registering her blows. "Look at this. Little pussy boy is crying. Typical. Little PB pussy boy. No wonder your daddy didn't want you."

Pussy boy. PB. It all made sense now. A grenade erupted in her head. Melissa screamed and hit Hoyt as hard as she could, her closed fist connecting with his stubbled chin.

Hoyt shook his head and then slowly turned to face her. In a flash, the back of his right hand collided with her cheek, sending her falling back against the blistering, concrete wall. She yelped, completely taken off-guard. Up until this point in their failing relationship, he had choked her, demeaned her, even spat on her more than a few times, but this was the first instance he had ever struck her. Eyes blurry, her ears rang like Sunday church bells.

Patrick bawled as Hoyt lifted him up and dipped his back over the railing. "No, no, no!"

Hoyt laughed coldly. "What? You think I'm going to drop you?"

Melissa pulled herself up, holding her chin. "You son of a bitch!"

Something changed. Hoyt shook his head, as if clearing a spell of dizziness. His face dropped, and he turned to Melissa as if he had no idea what was happening. He turned back to Patrick, who he still had pressed against the railing, and slowly let him go. Patrick hurriedly pulled away and took the stairs two at a time until he exited the bottom floor door. Heart thundering, Melissa glared at her boyfriend, the man she trusted to never hurt her family, and waited to see what he'd do next.

He sighed, "I'm very tired. Give me the room keys."

Without hesitation, she pulled the keys from her pocket and threw them up to the second floor landing. She left Hoyt to go find her son.

Patrick was already down the creaky wooden steps and sprinting toward the water before his mother caught up with him. Sand flew out behind him, dusting the insides of his brand new Adidas sneakers. Screw them. Screw Hoyt. Screw his mother. Screw all of it. For a fleeting moment, he thought of throwing himself into the salty water and drowning so he didn't have to put up with another day of their fighting and abuse. The late summer heat warmed his tears.

He wasn't strong enough. Maybe he *was* the pussy boy Hoyt had branded him.

A hand fell on his shoulder. "Patrick, slow down!"

He shrugged her off. "No! Let me go!"

With two hands, his mother stopped him in his tracks. "Please, honey! Just stop running and talk to me."

Patrick spun and swiped at her arms. "Why?" he cried, not caring who was watching. "So you can make more excuses for him?"

"Patrick, I'm not going to make excuses for what he did. He . . . he's tired and cranky—"

"You just said no excuses! Those are excuses, Mom!"

She hung her head and glanced about. "Look, I don't want to do this right here."

"No!" he yelled, pointing to the ground. "We do this right here, right now. Let them all hear us!"

His mother bit her lip. He had never spoken to her this way, never dreamed of it, but enough was enough. At that moment, he wasn't a pussy. "Why, Mom?"

"Why what?"

"Why do you keep putting up with him? Why do you keep him around and let him treat us like this?"

His mother, struggling for something to say, turned her tired, misty eyes toward the horizon. "Patrick . . . "

"What, Mom? You're going to say I'm too young? That I won't get it? I get it, Mom. I totally get it. He's a bastard!"

He almost saw her nod.

"And you're weak for staying with him this long."

Her eyes darkened, and she turned back to him with a scowl. "Now stop right there! I can *almost* excuse you talking about *him* like that, but not about me. I am the mother, and you are the child. I did *not* spend the last twelve years busting my butt and sacrificing everything for you so that you could berate me in public. I will not have you speak to me that way. Are we clear, mister?"

He croaked out a laugh. "Yeah, as crystal clear as mud. He hurts you, Mom! He calls you names—he calls *me* names—and he hits you!"

"That was only one time!" she yelled, pulling her voice back at the end.

"What about last night?"

She paused. Patrick could see he struck a nerve. Maybe he was stepping out of line, but for the moment it felt nice to finally step up to someone, to show he actually had some balls, even if it was to the one person who didn't deserve it.

After a few uncomfortable moments of silence, she met his eyes. "It's complicated, hon. I don't expect you to understand what being in a relationship is all about."

Patrick threw his hands up. "What's so complicated about it? Just dump him! Let's leave him down here and drive home right now, pretend he never existed."

She snorted a small, humorless laugh. "If only it were that simple."

"It could be," he pleaded. "We could smother him with a pillow like Chief did to McMurphy!"

She grabbed his hand and started to kneel but stood when she realized he wasn't as small as he used to be. "Listen to me. I'm not going to apologize for his actions. They were his own, and I suspect that in time he'll regret them and come to you with his heart on his sleeve. But I will tell you this. I'm sorry for what I've done to you. I'm sorry that you've had to put up with this mess for so long. I'm—" She started to cry. "I'm sorry I haven't been a better mother to you, and that I haven't given you a real, honest to goodness father figure to be with you when you needed him. I thought Hoyt might be it . . . but that's obviously not going to happen."

Eyes threatening to let loose again, Patrick said, "You're not a bad mom, Mom. Don't say that."

"Yes, I am. I should have known better." She laughed dryly. "Your mom's not very smart."

"Alright, stop it."

She wiped her eyes with the backs of her hands and sniffled. "Look. I know this hasn't been the best start to our vacation, and I know Hoyt has been belligerent and hateful, but I say we start over. Right here, right now. No more fighting, no more yelling. We're going to have a great time. We'll swim all day, we'll go shopping, and we'll eat great food. Hey, cheesesteaks from Famous Philly's! You still like those, right?"

"Never stopped."

Patrick watched her curiously as she stared over his head down the beach, as if looking for someone. He turned around but didn't see anything. "Here's what I can promise you. If things between Hoyt and I don't improve by the end of the week, I'll cut him loose. I . . . " She paused, considering her words. "I might have something for you sometime in the next few days. Maybe. We'll see. I think this week will get better for the both of us." She met his eyes. "You have my word."

She reached down and scooped up a handful of sand, then put her arm out. "Shake on it."

Patrick rolled his bloodshot eyes. "You're weird, Mom." He scooped up his own sand and shook hands with his mother. Hot grit poured from their grips. It was good to see her smiling. He wanted to see more of it.

He fingered the tear near his shirt collar. "He ripped my favorite shirt."

She examined it. "It's a Jurassic Park shirt, honey. We'll get you another. They're not hard to find these days." Sighing, she turned to face the water. "It's beautiful, isn't it?"

Feeling a little better, he hugged his mother hard. She equaled his squeeze.

"I don't know about you but I'm starving."

Patrick pulled away. "God, I thought we'd never eat again."

"Tell you what, let's go put the stuff back up in the room, then we'll go get some dinner. Your choice. Then ice cream at the boardwalk on Flagler. How's that sound?"

"Sounds like we're eating at Blackbeard's tonight," he laughed. Then he asked, "Is *he* coming too?"

She guided them back to the parking lot. "Nope. It's just the two of us tonight."

4

THE SLIDING GLASS BALCONY door was wide open when they stepped back into the condo, filling the room with a sweet bouquet of salty brine and fresh cut grass. Arms full of groceries and bellies full of food, Melissa nudged the front door open and let Patrick step in around her to off-load his plastic bags. For the rest of the day he had been a joy to be with. He smiled and laughed and went on and on about the upcoming Marvel film he had yet to see but somehow knew everything about. Even though he was only eight months away from being a teenager, for those few Hoyt-less hours he was her little boy again. His face dropped when they entered the kitchenette.

She sat her two bags on the counter. "Can you put this all up?"

He nodded. "What are you going to do?"

"I'm going to have a little chat with Hoyt."

"Please be careful."

She could tell he meant it.

"Don't worry." Melissa smiled and flexed her arm muscle.

She could smell the alcohol before she saw it. The moment she stepped out onto the balcony it hit her like a white-capped wave. It was past nine PM, and though nearly every light on the property had been put out, she could still make out a dozen empty Miller High Life bottles strewn about on the table and floor. Most of the PVC lounge chairs were empty, but the forth was occupied. In the dark corner by the edge of the glass doors, Hoyt sat with a cardboard case of beer in his lap. An empty box laid on its side on the floor. He must have walked across the street to the liquor store in the shopping complex. Melissa slid the door shut behind her.

Face plastered in darkness, Hoyt shifted in his seat. "I—"

"Nope," she immediately stopped him. "Absolutely not. You do not get to speak. The moment you manhandled my son and then smacked me, you lost your speaking privileges." It took everything in her not to take one of his dead soldiers by the neck and smash it over his thick skull. Even keeping her voice at a reasonable volume was proving to be difficult. "It's my turn to speak. You will not say a single, solitary word until I say you can. Do you understand?"

At first he didn't respond. He stayed sitting straight up.

"I asked you if you understood me!"

She couldn't see his face but she saw him nod, so that was good enough.

"Let me make something very, *very* clear to you right now, and this goes into effect the moment this conversation is over. You will never *ever* lay a hand on me or my son ever again. Not in anger or in love. Not unless *I* say it's okay. What you did today was utterly inexcusable and loathsome and downright disgusting. I will never, ever forgive you for laying a fucking hand on either of us." The swelling in her jaw throbbed. "If you ever touch either of us like that again, I'll kill you. Not an 'I'll leave you' or 'I'll call the cops' sort of way." She leaned in close, nailing every word to his ears. "I will fucking *kill* you. Do you understand me?"

She was close enough to see his eyes, to smell the sour beer on his breath.

"Speak!" she yelled.

"Yes," he slurred.

"Good. Now listen here. It's taking everything in me to not leave your sorry, worthless ass here in Florida and drive back home. I don't need this shit anymore, Hoyt—*we* don't need it. We have no use for your hateful words or your choleric temper fogging up our lives. You're such a bitter, angry person now, and I don't know what to do with you anymore. You used to be a pretty decent guy. You used to be fun and witty and fairly charming, but now you're this-this-this endless pit of bigotry and misery. I want to love you, Hoyt, I really do, but you give us nothing in return. Well, that's not true. You give us bruises."

Hoyt turned his head, his dark eyes searching out over the moonlit water.

"You're toxic, and I won't let this continue. I'm giving you an ultimatum, Hoyt. Are you listening?"

He didn't respond.

She swept the nearest empty bottle off the table, sending it flying through the air. The bottle crashed and shattered against the wall near Hoyt's head. He didn't flinch, only slowly turned back to her.

CRUEL SUMMER

She growled, "I asked you a question!"

"Yes," he sighed, taking a pull of his beer. "I'm listening."

"Good. Here's what I'm going to do. I'm going to give you a chance to change. To make yourself well again. I'm giving you until the end of this week to get yourself together and make things right between the three of us. Even though you don't deserve it, this is the best I can do. I don't expect you to be perfect—hell, I'm not perfect—but I do expect to see a very different Hoyt Rainey by week's end. If I don't . . . if I see the same insufferable attitude by the time we leave Florida to go back home . . . I'll leave your ass. No ifs, ands, or buts. If you love us or have even a shred of respect for us, you'll straighten up. I really don't care if you drink. I don't care if you're wasted from today until the moment we drive back home—it's your vacation, too. But you *will* be different. Have I made myself perfectly clear?"

Fists ready, Melissa expected him to be silent once more, or even to get lippy with her. She was waiting for it. She even had a response for it, like a comedian with a heckler.

He sat forward in a small sliver of light. Tears rolled down his cheeks. "Yes. I'm sorry. It won't ever happen again. I promise."

"See that it doesn't. And keep your tears. I don't want them."

"I'm sorry for . . . today. I never meant to hurt either of you."

"But you did. Hoyt, you say you want to be a father, but you're still a child yourself. Patrick needs a man in his life, not a goddamn bully. You want to be *that* man, pushing little kids around to make yourself feel better?"

He shook his head.

"Good. Then man up and show me what you've got."

She turned to leave, but he stopped her. "Can you tell him I'm sorry? I have something very expensive in my bag and I thought he broke it."

Melissa shook her head. "Not tonight. I don't have the strength to lie for you. Tell him tomorrow."

He nodded. "I've booked us a deep sea fishing excursion for tomorrow morning." She turned back to protest, but he interrupted. "It'll be a good time, I promise. It'll be a great way for the three of us to have fun and do something together."

Thinking about it, she started to nod. "Okay. Fine."

"Did you guys bring back any food?"

"There's sandwich meat and bread in the fridge. Ice cream in the freezer. Chips on the counter. Help yourself." She opened the sliding glass door and stepped back into the living room, then turned back to face him. "Clean that broken glass up before you come back in. And also, don't bother coming into bed with me. Your place is on the couch this week." She slid the door shut.

"I love you," he said to the glass.

Melissa didn't respond.

TUESDAY

5

THE SAVORY SCENT OF frying meat rose Melissa from her bed like a zombie from the grave. Even with the bedroom door closed, it invaded the room, working better than any alarm clock. For the first time in years she felt rested. She hadn't had to share the bed with a man, so she didn't spend the night having to fight for space or half of the blankets. She quickly used the attached bathroom, then threw on a T-shirt before making her way to the kitchen.

Unlike the darkened bedroom, the plastic curtains were pulled back, and the early morning sunshine filled the living room like an over-lit movie set. Outside beyond the balcony, the ocean waves roared and beckoned.

"Hey there!"

She turned to find Hoyt working away in the kitchen. He had three different pans going on the stove top, each one frying its own fresh meat. He hopped back and forth to each one with a spatula. On the counter behind him was a bowl full of steaming scrambled eggs and next to that a plate of buttered toast. Even though she wasn't terribly hungry, her stomach rumbled and she let it guide her to the bar chairs on the other side of the kitchen counter.

"What's all this?"

"This," he said with a smile, flipping the sausage patties, "is your free continental breakfast, m'lady."

Melissa shook her head, trying to both wake herself and wrap her head around Hoyt's unexpected chipperness. His shiny demeanor was almost brighter than the sunlight. Beneath the waft of food, he smelled freshly showered and shaved. Not a hint of alcohol or resentment coming off him. "I, uh . . . where did all this food come from?"

He turned to pull the steaming buttered bread from the toaster and proceeded to cut them into triangles. "I got up bright and early and walked across the street to the grocery store. I thought maybe we should start the day with something a little more filling than Cocoa Puffs."

"Bright is certainly right."

He eyed her. "Is that okay?"

"Yeah." She shrugged. "It's just a little off-putting is all."

"Why's that?"

"First off, I hadn't expected this this morning—this radiant ball of positivity. I figured you'd be sleeping it off for the rest of the day. Second . . . you cook?"

Hoyt chuckled, something Melissa hadn't heard in quite some time. "Yeah, it's been a while. I'm not great at it, but it's hard to fuck up breakfast food." He looked at her and clicked his tongue. "I didn't sleep much last night. That couch is uncomfortable as hell—I'm not complaining, I swear—but what I did do was a lot of thinking."

"You didn't hurt yourself, doing all that thinking?"

"Har-har," he mocked. "Seriously though. I took everything you said to heart. I never meant to hurt you. I'm sorry about what a shithead I've been lately. I love you."

"What about Patrick?"

Hoyt nodded. "Him, too."

"You need to tell him that."

As if words provoked action, the bedroom door behind them creaked open, and her bed-headed son poked his face out.

"Speak of the handsome devil," Melissa said. "Good morning, hon. Hoyt has graciously cooked us breakfast."

Eyes squinted, Patrick appeared hesitant but then slowly joined his mother at the counter.

"Sleep well?" she asked.

He kept his head down and shrugged.

Melissa rubbed his back. "It's okay, hon. Actually, Hoyt has something he would like to say to you. Isn't that right?"

Hoyt nodded, maybe a bit too enthusiastically. "Yes! Absolutely!" He grabbed a plate from the cabinet and scooped up a generous portion of eggs, several strips of bacon, two wedges of toast, and a cold glass of already poured orange juice, and placed it in front of Patrick. He started on another plate. "I have something I want to say to the both of you. I understand that neither of you are too keen on me right now. I, uh . . . I haven't been a great guy to be around lately."

"Lately?" Patrick mumbled.

Instead of arguing, Hoyt simply nodded. "You're right, Patty. Not just lately. I've been a bit of a hard on for quite some time. I could stand here and give you both excuses until I'm blue in the face about how stressed out I am about how the company back home now that I'm fully in charge, but I'm not going to do that. I could throw out excuse after excuse as to why I'm a dickhead, but I'm not going to do that either. What I am going to do is this." He placed a glass of milk and a plate similar to Patrick's in front of Melissa, with sausage instead of bacon. "I'm going to say that I'm sorry. I'm sorry for being such a jerk when I should be more . . . levelheaded, I guess. I know I've got a bit of a temper, but I'm going to do my best to work on it."

Melissa wanted to interject but she bit her tongue, eagerly waiting to see where this was going.

"Patrick," he continued, "I'm sorry that I treat you the way I do. I know I can be quite the asshole to you. I've never spent much time around kids, so it's a little hard for me to figure out how to communicate with you."

Patrick cocked an eyebrow and pursed his lips.

Hands up in defense, Hoyt laughed. "You're right, you're right. You're not a kid anymore. You're almost a teenager—almost a man! Although I may be hardest on you, I just want you to be tough and harden up. It's a messed-up world out there, full of badasses like me. You've got to be able to stick up for yourself. I know you've never had a man around to teach you these things, and if your mother will allow it, I'd like to be that guy."

Though he could have maybe said a little nicer, Melissa was impressed with his attempts at reconciliation.

"I guess what I'm trying to say is, much like your mother said to me last night, I want us all to start over. Today's a new day, a new week, and we're going to spend the day out in the sun on a deep sea fishing excursion, catching all kinds of slimy creatures." He picked up his own plate and saluted them with it. "To new beginnings."

Smiling, Melissa said, "Very good."

They quietly began to eat their food, and Melissa did her best to keep chewing when she bit into a fragment of egg shell.

6

IT COULD HAVE BEEN the rhythmic rocking of the boat, or the crystal clear water that sloshed against the hull, or even the undercooked bacon he ate a few hours prior—either way, everything from his stomach was now dripping down the side of the boat in mushy brown chunks. Heaving until he felt woozy, Patrick held fast to the side railing as he leaned over the edge. It took them nearly a half hour to reach their destination—wherever that destination was—and the entire ride was spent puking his guts up from sea sickness. The Dramamine they brought wasn't working. He hated throwing up, but he hated doing it in front of everyone even more. He would have preferred the small bathroom below deck, but the boat's captain was currently occupying it with his own sickness.

Rubbing his back, his mother said, "It's alright, hon. It'll pass."

But it didn't pass. Another wave of nausea crashed and found its way out of him.

"Holy shit!" Hoyt laughed, rounding the corner of the boat, his arms full of fishing poles. "We aren't even going to need chum anymore to attract the sharks!"

CRUEL SUMMER

"*Sharks?*" Patrick moaned.

"Don't speak," his mother said. "Just save your strength."

Hoyt dropped the poles on the deck next to them. "You okay, bud? You look as pale as a ghost."

No, he thought miserably. *I'm not freaking okay.* This was the last thing he wanted to do, being stuck in the middle of the sea, not a shred of land in sight. He loved the ocean, but only fifteen or twenty feet out from the beach. He would have rather been back at the condo with his mom, taking a dip in the pool or maybe playing on the shuffleboard court at the edge of the property. Instead he was stuck on a forty-two foot fishing yacht for the next several hours, *bonding*. And *fishing*. He hated fishing. Although he'd never been fishing, he had no desire at the age of twelve to suddenly learn how. He preferred his fish battered and deep fried, not wriggling on a hook and struggling for air.

Hoyt leered at him over his mom's shoulder. Patrick turned away as he forced himself to swallow. Now it wasn't even the waves that made him sick. He thought back to Hoyt's half-assed apology and his 'Believe me, I'm a changed man' breakfast. Maybe his mom was fooled, but he wasn't as easily duped. This little excursion, this sudden change in attitude, did nothing but make Patrick hate Hoyt more. He would never ever wish his mother pain, but part of him—some nasty little devil inside—wished Hoyt would hit his mother again. Then—*then*—it would finally be over. For now, though, he was forced to continue his suffering in silence.

"Captain Rob's been gone quite a while," his mom said.

Hoyt snickered. "Poor bastard. Been working on a boat his whole life and had no idea he was allergic to shrimp."

"I know, right? How many did he say he ate? Like fifty?"

"Something like that. Hell of a way to find out after an All You Can Eat contest."

"Why didn't he find someone else to take us out? Seems pretty silly to spend the whole time down in the bathroom."

Hoyt shrugged. "There is no one else. It's his boat. Guy like that doesn't get sick days. This is probably his only income."

"I should go check on him and make sure he's not drowning in his own barf." She pulled a face at Patrick. "Sorry. That was a terrible joke."

Patrick rolled his eyes.

"Nah," Hoyt said. "Patty's got the right idea. Just think of it as recycling. You're feeding the hungry fish. You're giving back to the world."

She laughed. "Stop. That's terrible."

Patrick found his lips curling over his teeth. *Goddamn it, don't make her laugh! You don't get that privilege anymore!*

His mother moved away from the railing. "Yeah, I'm going to go below and see how he's holding up. You two need anything from the kitchen?"

Hoyt wagged his half-empty beer. "Could you bring me another sixer from the fridge, my dear? Only one left out here after this one."

"Sure. Patrick, hon, you want me to bring you anything? There might be some Sprite or some crackers in the cupboard."

Patrick slowly shook his head, careful not to make himself sick again. "No thank you."

"You sure, hon?"

"Positive, Mom. Thanks."

"Okay. Just yell for me if you need something."

Hoyt stopped her. "Hey!"

She turned, eyebrows up.

"I love you."

Patrick seethed when she smiled back at Hoyt. She turned back and disappeared through the deck door.

Downing his beer and grabbing another, Hoyt joined him at the railing. His bare, sweaty arm suddenly dropped on Patrick's shoulder. His arm pit reeked of hot perspiration. "It's beautiful, ain't it?" he asked, nodding at the endless water. When Patrick didn't answer, he said, "You know all that stuff I said earlier this morning? I really meant it. I wasn't bullshitting you two."

Patrick sighed. "Okay."

"No, really. I know I'm a dickhead—I get it. I'm hard as hell on you. I had some siblings, but I didn't spend much time with them. All my cousins lived hours away and I never got to see them. The only real family I had was my Uncle Coop. I guess what I'm trying to say is I'm bad around kids."

Kids? Patrick thought. *I'm almost a freaking teenager!*

"I don't know, man. I guess I should try a little harder with you. I try so hard to see myself in you and I come up empty. You and I were nothing alike when I was growing up, man. You're a sensitive guy. When I was twelve I was out chasing girls, trying to get my fingers wet. You . . . you just sit at a comic shop, playing card games with other nerds. I don't know. I don't get it. To each their own, I guess."

Stomach tightening, Patrick gripped the handrails until his hands turned white.

Hoyt squeezed his shoulder. "I just don't want to see you get punked on in school. I mean, for Christ's sake, do you even have any friends?"

For a moment Patrick envisioned sweeping Hoyt's arm away from him and clocking him right on the chin. He wasn't that much taller than Patrick, but what he lacked in strength he more than made up with imagination. He saw himself, blow after blow, bloodying his mother's boyfriend's face until his hands could take no more. He saw himself pick the older man up over his head and chuck that hateful bastard into the deep blue sea, and he and his mother could move on without him. But this was real life. Much like that stupid Rolling Stones song his mother loved, you can't always get what you want.

He simply answered, "Yes, I have friends."

"Well, you could have fooled me." Hoyt chuckled. "Anyway, I'm your friend, right? Yeah. I think from here on out we're going to be best friends. What do you think about that?"

Patrick quickly swallowed another bout of vomit. "Sure."

Hoyt clapped his back, a little too hard. "Excellent! And I can be sort of a father figure to you, too. I think that's your biggest problem, man. Lack of a male role model."

Yeah, that's it, he thought, rolling his eyes.

"I'm going to be like your best friend and your

dad! This will be great for you, Patty. I'm going to teach you to man up and do big boy shit, like how to fix a car and how to chase pussy, and we're going to start on all of that here today. Lesson number one: How to fish." Hoyt sat his beer on the deck and grabbed a large white fishing pole from his bundle.

Patrick noticed Hoyt's demeanor had shifted dramatically. He was excited, almost giddy for this moment. Some little part of Patrick wanted to be excited, too, that an older man wanted to show him something new, but he just couldn't stand it.

Hoyt stepped over to the stained plastic troths filled with chum. "Now I'll bait this first one for you, but you've got to toss it out and catch it yourself. *Capisce?*"

Patrick nodded. "Okay."

Hoyt lifted the lid. The smell was immediate. Fresh blood and meat wafted through the salt air, covering the deck like a warm blanket. Hoyt didn't appear to be bothered by it. He reached in and snagged a fist-sized wad of fish and baited the sizable hook. Satisfied it was properly hooked, he handed the pole to Patrick. The pole was massive, easily a foot and a half taller than he was. The rubber handle and reel felt awkward in his hands.

Hoyt stepped up behind him and reached around to position Patrick's hands the correct way. "Now, you drop the line a little bit with this button here. Yep, just like that. See, that gives you some slack when you throw it, creates some weight with the bait so it goes further. Now spread your feet apart a little bit. A little more. Yep. Now you're going to put the rod over your shoulder, and make sure to keep the button pressed until you cast it. You ready?"

"I guess so . . . " Patrick said.

"You guess so or you know so? Come on, man. No more of these half-assed answers. It's either yes or no. Understood?"

"Yes."

"Louder!"

"Yes!"

"Now call me a dickhead."

Patrick paused. "*What?*"

Hoyt snickered. "I said call me a dickhead. I know you want to. Just fucking yell it. Say 'Yes, dickhead!'".

He wasn't sure what to do. Was this a trick?

Hoyt stepped back and crossed his arms. "I'm waiting."

Screw it. With all he could muster, he screamed, "Yes, dickhead!" and threw the pole over his shoulder. Keeping a tight grip on the handle, he released the button and watched the gleaming chunk of meat go soaring through the open air. About twenty feet out it hit the water with a splash.

Clapping his hands, Hoyt laughed heartily. "There you fucking go! Could have maybe gotten it a little further out, but either way that's nice work, my man."

A little flutter in his stomach called pride made the corner of Patrick's mouth curl up. He hated to admit it, even though he'd done nothing else but cast a stupid fishing line into the water, he kind of liked the feeling of accomplishing something he had never done before. Too bad his mom wasn't there to see it.

Hoyt grabbed his own pole from the deck. "Now all we have to do is wait and—"

The pole jolted in Patrick's hands, and he had to react quickly. He gripped the handle and held it tight against his chest. "*What do I do? What do I do?*"

"You definitely don't let go! Those aren't our poles." He dropped his own pole on the deck and stepped behind Patrick to help him steady himself.

The white fishing line zipped back and forth in the water. The pole lurched in his grip, and Patrick yelped as he struggled to keep the thing in his grasp. "I don't know what to do!"

"Reel the damn thing in! A little at a time. You don't want to the break the line."

"What's going on out here?" His mother came back out onto the deck, her arms cradling Hoyt's beer.

"Patty's got a bite!"

She sat the beer down and quickly stepped up next to her son. "Patrick! You've caught something?"

"Not yet," Hoyt said. "He's still got to reel the thing in."

"Does he need help?"

"No!" Patrick yelled, suddenly feeling confident. "I've got this." *I think.* He took a few steps closer to the railing and placed the toes of his shoes against the bottom. Whatever was on the other end of his line was getting closer and before he knew it, Hoyt was leaning over the railing to lift his sea beast over the edge of the boat—and what a beast it was!

A three foot Mako shark dropped onto the boat deck with a wet slap. Patrick and his mom stepped back and gasped as the creature flopped in place and smacked its tail. Its obsidian eyes roamed the deck as its large mouth snapped at the air. Patrick had never seen a shark in person, at least not outside of an aquarium, and though it was small, it was still quite impressive. *He* reeled that thing in. *Him.* The friends Hoyt didn't think existed were never going to believe him.

"Oh my God!" his mom yelled. She put her arm around him and squeezed. "You caught a shark! I'm so proud of you, hon! Oh darn. I didn't even think to record this."

A wave of guilt suddenly washed over Patrick. Out of its element, the poor creature looked undeniably terrified. The large hook used to reel it in was now jutting out of the side of its face, dark blood dribbling out of the ragged split in its rubbery gray skin. The shark's movements were slowing. Its serrated mouth opened and closed. No, he didn't like this. The adrenaline of inexperience gone, all Patrick wanted to do was help the suffocating shark back into the water.

Hoyt stepped over to the far side of the boat and grabbed something long and chrome from a holster attached to the railing. He stuck it out to Patrick.

A baseball bat.

"What's that for?" Patrick asked.

Hoyt laughed. "What the hell do you think it's for?"

"You want me to . . . "

"You've got to finish it, man. This was your catch. Now it's time to put it out of its misery."

His mom shook her head. "Hoyt, that's terrible! You can't do that."

"Oh, I'm not going to do it. Patty is." He shook the bat at Patrick.

"Are you even supposed to do that? Aren't we supposed to, like, drop it back into the water or something?"

"Christ, no!" Hoyt said, his voice thickening. "They do this shit all the time. Why else do you think they keep a fucking bat on the boat? For an impromptu home run derby?"

Patrick stepped away from Hoyt and shook his head. "I don't want to do this anymore."

Hoyt's face shifted into an incredulous sneer. "What? Why?"

"I just don't. I don't like this. At all. Can we please just throw the stupid thing back into the water?"

Baseball bat still in his grip, Hoyt took a step toward Patrick. "*Throw it back in?* Are you kidding me? Why the fuck would we do that?"

His mother interjected. "Hoyt, calm down. He doesn't want to kill the poor shark. And I for one don't want to see it dead. Let's just put it back where it belongs. It's probably got a family that's worried about it."

Hoyt's eyes and mouth simultaneously narrowed. "*A family?* What in the blue fuck are you talking about? We're a fucking family, and that stupid fucking thing is a fish that's about to have its brains become part of that chum bucket over there."

Patrick's stomach lurched.

"Calm down, Hoyt," his mother growled. "We've been having a lovely day so far. No need to ruin it."

"Who's ruining what? I'm trying to teach your goddamn son how to be a man! Get over here, Patrick, and finish this."

Before he knew it, Patrick was already against the railing, as far back as he could go. His heart raced. Sweat stung his eyes—at least he told himself it was sweat.

Hoyt gripped the bat tighter and took another step toward him. "Get your ass over here, PB."

His mother screamed, "What did you just say?" She stepped up in front of Hoyt, her finger jabbing his chest. "Did we not just have a talk about this last night—and this morning too, no less?"

"What? What did I say?"

"You called him that God awful name again! I told you never to talk to him like that again, did I not?"

Rolling his eyes, Hoyt stood his ground. "Well, goddamn it, Melly! He's got to grow up and take some fucking responsibility for his actions! He caught the thing and now he's got to kill it. I'm not going to take no for an answer." He then shoved her aside and grabbed Patrick by the wrist. Patrick yelped as he was pulled forward toward the dying shark. The creature was barely moving, its mouth and tail had all but stopped thrashing.

"Damn you, Hoyt!" his mother said. "Leave him alone!"

Hoyt grabbed him by the back of the neck and held him in place. The bat was thrust toward him. "Do it, PB. Do it and prove me wrong." The metal bat gleamed in the sunlight, making the old dark splotches riddled across its surface stand out like birthmarks.

"Let me go," Patrick groaned.

He heard his mother take a few steps toward them. "Please, Hoyt, just stop this!"

"Just let him be!" Hoyt screamed at her. Then to Patrick he whispered, "Do it, PB. Your mother's watching. Do it and impress her. Be a big boy and not a pussy boy."

Tears welled up. "Please don't make me do this."

The grip on the back of his neck dug deeper, Hoyt's unkempt nails creating divots. "You're making me look bad, you little shit. Bash that fucking thing's brain in or so help me—"

CRUEL SUMMER

Patrick quickly spun and broke Hoyt's grasp. He leapt away and bounded to the other side of the boat.

Hoyt didn't move. Glaring, he grit his teeth and white knuckled the weapon with both hands. He lifted the bat—"Goddamn pussy!"—and proceed to smash the metal rod over and over into the shark's skull. His mother cried out and backed away. Patrick clamped his eyes shut, wincing as the appalling noise slowly went from metal to cartilage then metal to metal. The coppery tang of blood fanned across the back end of the boat. When all that was left was Hoyt's gasps, Patrick slowly opened his eyes.

Bright red blood speckled Hoyt's shorts and white tank top. It dripped from the end of the bat. Patrick refused to let his eyes move down to the mess the man had made. It was enough he could practically taste it.

"There you go. Now you see how a real man handles his shit."

"You're a damn psycho!" his mother screamed. "Obviously, nothing gets through with you."

Hoyt dropped the bat, and it clattered away and rolled toward the railing. He stepped toward her. "This wasn't supposed to happen this way."

She stepped up to Hoyt until she was right under his chin. Patrick admired her bravery. "That's it! I've had it with you! You're unhinged and always at the breaking point. I refuse to put myself and my son through this any longer."

Biting his lip, Hoyt looked as though he were about to cry.

She continued, "I'm going to get Captain Rob, and I'm having him take us back to shore. Then Patrick and I are going home."

"You're leaving me?" Hoyt asked.

"Not only am I leaving you, you moron, I'm taking the SUV with me. You can find your own way back to Indiana."

Hoyt shook his head as if he couldn't believe what he was hearing. "I don't understand. You and I—"

"What is there to not understand, Hoyt? There is no you and I—not anymore! You blew it! I told you never again, and you went and screwed everything up! Come on, Patrick."

She turned to leave but Hoyt quickly seized her arm. "No! This isn't supposed to happen this way. This was supposed to be a special day. We were going to fish—"

"Let me go!"

"—and have fun—"

"You're hurting me!"

"—and I was going to give you this!" Hoyt pulled a small black box from his cargo pocket and presented it to her.

She stopped yelling and stared at it. Patrick's mouth went bone dry, and his hands grew clammy and cold. *Oh no*, he thought. *No, no, no . . .*

"What is that?" she asked, her voice squeaking.

Hoyt laughed nervously. "What does it look like, dummy?" He let go of her arm and both of her hands shot up to cover her mouth. Before she could say anything, he dropped to his blood-caked knee and cracked the box open. When he realized the box was backwards, he quickly turned it around.

"What the hell are you doing?"

"Remember when I freaked out when Patrick dropped my suitcase? I thought he broke this. I've been saving for months, and I've been planning this for just as long. Look, I know this day has already devolved into a shit show, but I think, maybe, we can salvage it."

Despite the ninety-five degree heat, Patrick started to shiver. It started in his midsection and raced into his extremities. The muscle at the corner of his left eye twitched. His tongue felt too big for his mouth. It was everything that terrified him—his very worst nightmare. His mother appeared shocked and disoriented, and Hoyt, spattered in blood, looked like a psychopath. Patrick watched on with bated breath.

Hoyt laughed nervously. "Well . . . Are you going to keep making me look like a fool, or are you going to say yes?"

His mother's eyes flitted over to Patrick. He knew the answer was no. She knew the answer was no. For Hoyt, that would not be the right answer. Eyes wide, Patrick subtly shook his head, hoping his mother could read his frantic thoughts.

She looked back at Hoyt. Her hands dropped. "Get that damn thing away from me."

Patrick could almost see the launch sequence activate. There was seven or eight seconds of silence, the gentle crashing of the water against the hull the only sound—then *bam!* It happened so quickly. A growl wound up Hoyt's throat, and before Patrick could react, Hoyt dropped the ring box and dove head first into his mother. Arms around her waist, he took her legs out from under her. She screamed a moment before her skull bounced on the deck. Patrick screamed, too, but found he couldn't move.

Hoyt crawled on top of her, **DAREMETO** now

fully wrapped around her neck. "You fucking bitch!" he screamed. "How fucking dare you!" Eyes now open, she gagged and beat at his arms. "I gave you the best years of your life, you ungrateful whore! And this is how you thank me?"

Panicked, Patrick had no idea what to do. He couldn't let Hoyt hurt his mom, and if Hoyt really wanted to he would probably kill her. Patrick wanted to fight him, but he knew that wouldn't work. There had to be another way—

The baseball bat!

"I should have done this years ago," Hoyt growled. "Doing the world a favor by taking the trash out."

Patrick searched frantically for the bat. It wasn't in the holster, nor was it near the animal Hoyt had beaten to death.

Turning blue, his mother gagged between breaths, "Hoyt . . . please . . . "

There! By the far railing.

Hoyt continued, "You're nothing without me! You're just a lousy lay, a worthless, lazy bitch, and a shitty mother!"

Patrick swiped the blood-stained bat, took a deep breath, and stalked up behind Hoyt.

Realizing he was right behind him, Hoyt cocked his head back and glared. "What do you think you're going to do with that, Pussy Boy?"

Patrick ground his teeth. Bat over his shoulder, he growled and swung—

Never again!

—and Hoyt easily deflected the bat aside. The bat flipped out of his grasp, and before Patrick could react, Hoyt's grip left his mother's throat and grasped onto Patrick's genitals. Patrick screamed and shot up on his toes. Hoyt slowly stood and, with Patrick firm in his grip, backed him against the railing. The ocean below lapped at the side of the boat.

Hoyt growled, "What—did you actually think you were going to hit me, you little fucker?"

The pain was so intense Patrick couldn't even cry. Short, muted gasps escaped his mouth. Hoyt was crushing him, and there was nothing he could do about it. His brain screamed at him to fight back, but his arms did little more than curl up against his chest.

"You've ruined everything, PB. *Everything!*"

Patrick felt himself being raised higher until his ass was nearly sitting on the railing.

"How about a little dip, pussy boy?"

The vision around Patrick's eyes grew black and fuzzy, but near the center, just behind Hoyt's back, he saw a red, angry face. Bat held high, his mother screamed and brought the weapon down on Hoyt's skull.

The metallic *clang* was like a gunshot. Hoyt's eyes went wide with confusion, his mouth forming soundless words. Blood dripped from his nose. Patrick gasped for air as Hoyt's hands fell from his groin. Hoyt collapsed on the deck with a grunt.

Bat still in hand, his mother pulled Patrick away from Hoyt. "Are you okay, hon?" Tears dripped down her cheeks.

He didn't speak, could only cough and hold himself. She hugged him hard.

Behind them, Hoyt unsteadily climbed to his feet, leaning against the railing for support. He groaned, both hands holding his bleeding head. "I'm impressed

. . . bitch," he wheezed. "Someone finally . . . grew some balls . . . " Hoyt snarled. "But your son . . . is still . . . a Pussy Boy."

Before he could stop himself, Patrick wrenched the bat from his mother's hands and ran full force and swung the aluminum stick. Metal against bone, the bat cracked against Hoyt's chin, and the force of the blow sent the bigger man flying backwards. Feet over head, Hoyt rolled over the railing and tumbled into the bright blue water below with a splash. Patrick screamed and dropped the bat. His mother ran up behind him and put her arms around his shoulders.

Hoyt disappeared beneath the waves.

Feeling sick again, Patrick leaned over the railing and puked once more.

7

"**How many times do** I have to tell you? I didn't see a goddamn thing!"

Over the course of the last hour, Captain Ron's voice had gone from comforting and reassuring to downright manic. The slickly sheen of green he'd worn earlier that morning had considerably darkened since they had made it back to shore. Dark sweat stains on his shirt and pants, the man looked absolutely wretched. Melissa felt every bit as bad as he looked, though she did a better job at keeping her composure.

"Mrs. Braun?"

Melissa snapped from her daze. She turned away from Captain Ron screaming at a police officer to face two more staring her down. The taller of the two, Detective Holzer, was a thin, athletic woman whose brown hair was tied back as tight as her pursed lips. The other, another woman named Detective Andrews, knelt down and held Patrick's shaking hands in her own.

Melissa finally broke her stupor, her own voice quavering. "It's *Ms.* Braun."

The detective nodded. "My apologies, but the

quicker we get on with this, the sooner we can start looking for your partner. There's a lot of water to cover, and we don't have much time."

I don't think you're going to find him.

Even though she wanted nothing more than to crawl on top of the highest platform she could find and dance until she collapsed in hysterical laughter, she forced every nerve ending in her body to evenly shudder. Her face, only a moment away from tears of joy, streamed Florida gator-sized tears of pain. She never wanted it to be this way. She only wanted her and her son to leave this failed trip—this failed semblance of a relationship—and get on with their lives the best they could. But with two thick, tattooed hands around her throat, Hoyt sealed his own fate. She refused to feel sorry for him, refused to give him any more power, even in death. Even though she struck him first with the bat, she wished she had delivered the final blow that sent him over the edge and into the water. She never wanted that feeling in her hands and fingers to go away. The strength of never being hurt again.

"Just go over it again for me please? Slower this time."

Melissa forced more tears from her eyes. "We were all fishing, just like I said. Captain Ron was below deck the whole time, sick. I don't think he came up to the deck even once before the . . . incident." She paused dramatically. "Hoyt was showing Patrick how to bait a hook—my son had never been fishing in his life—and before we knew it, he had a bite. But whatever Patrick had caught was far too big for him to reel in on his own. Hoyt . . . Hoyt took the line and worked on bringing it in himself. Whatever it was, it was too strong, even for him." Melissa wiped her eyes with the back of her trembling hand.

"Take your time," Detective Holzer said.

Nodding, Melissa continued, "He tried and tried to reel the fish in, but he wasn't getting anywhere with it. He crawled up on the railing and tried to brace himself, but . . . It all happened so fast. He . . . lost his footing a-and he screamed! Before I could grab him from behind and help brace him, the line pulled tight, and he was pulled over the side and into the water. We tried to help him, I swear it, but he was already under the water and gone before I could find the life ring. We screamed and screamed for him, but he never resurfaced! Oh God . . . " Her eyes were beginning to burn from exertion.

Holzer stared at her, unblinking. "Why were you not wearing life jackets? It's state law for everyone on any type of boat to wear protective flotation devices at all times."

Melissa shrugged. "Captain Ron never mentioned it. Like I said, he was sick the entire time we were with him. He didn't really give us much information before we took off. He hit the bathroom as soon as we dropped anchor."

The detective turned to Andrews. "We'll have to have a talk with him about that."

It made Melissa feel ill to throw Captain Ron under the bus—he seemed like a nice enough man—but she didn't really have a choice. From the time Hoyt went under, Melissa had quickly went to work. She had thrown Hoyt's fishing pole overboard, and then went to work on cleaning up the dead shark he had left on the deck. She scooped what she could into a bucket and tossed the remains as far out as her arms could throw. Within minutes, multiple large fins cut through the water and fought each other for the biggest pieces. She prayed they would swim a litter deeper and take some fresh meat right off the bone. After that she sprayed the deck with the hose from the water reserve tank. The bat was nowhere to be found.

Once she finished cleaning, she forced Patrick to repeat their new story over and over until he had it down, but he had barely responded. The boy was so distraught he barely even blinked. He had sat on the deck of the boat and stared at his hands, as if they were to blame. Melissa wanted so badly to comfort him and tell him everything was going to be okay, but in order for that to happen she had to make sure it really *was* going to be okay.

Sitting next to her on the bench, her son had turned very pale and appeared somehow smaller than before, and though the detective crouched before him was holding his shaking hands, he still stared at them as if they were going to answer him back.

Andrews asked him, "Patrick, hon?"

After a few moments, he slowly looked up, but his distant eyes seemed to look right through her.

"Patrick, can you tell me what happened?"

He began to turn his head toward Melissa but Officer Andrews stopped him. "No. Don't look at her. Look at me."

"She's not going anywhere," Holzer added. "You look at us, okay?"

Please don't look at me, hon. They'll know you're lying.

CRUEL SUMMER

Fortunately, Patrick did as he was instructed. He kept his focus on Andrews, occasionally giving Holzer a quick glance. "He . . . "

Andrews let go of his hands and squeezed his shoulder. "It's okay, Patrick, I promise. You've been through a lot today. Just like your mom, take it slow. Take all the time you need."

"He . . . " A small groan escaped his lips.

Melissa was certain he was going to break.

"Go on, Patrick," Holzer said.

"He . . . " Patrick closed his eyes and trembled. "Fell. He fell over the side. Pulled in."

Melissa inwardly sighed in relief.

Andrews nodded, her short, ear-length hair bobbing. "Is that all?"

"Yes. Big fish. Then he was gone." He looked up to Holzer. "Is he really gone?"

The taller woman gave him a small shrug. "Not sure, kiddo. We've got the Coast Guard skimming the area you all were stopped at as we speak, looking for him. If anyone can find him, it's them. It's what they do." She stood there for a moment, her eyes darting back and forth between mother and son. Then she said, "Listen, you two. Your story seems fine. Just fine. It's not as if this hasn't happened before. People are lost at sea more often than you think. At least a third of my cases are dealing with this very thing. My other time is divided between drunk and disorderlies and animal attacks. We don't have a lot of problems on the beach side. We like to keep it that way. I did a small background check on you and Mr. Rainey after the call came in. I understand you've been down here before. Many times, in fact, yes?"

Melissa nodded. "Yes."

"Mr. Rainey has not. He's a bit of an interesting character. Some past on him. Some rough stuff. Doesn't exactly seem like your type, Ms. Braun."

"What exactly is that supposed to mean?"

"I don't know? But those bruises around your throat look awfully fresh. Care to tell me where those came from?"

Melissa's faux sadness was draining away to anger. "Look, officer—"

"Detective."

"*Detective*. My boyfriend is out there missing, and I have no idea if we're ever going to see him again. Are you seriously sitting here questioning some—some damn marks on my neck? Go do your job and find him!"

"Ma'am, right now my job is here with you and your son. Now, I sympathize with you and your situation, I really do, but I'm here to get down to brass tacks and find out what happened on that boat today. Other than the two of you, we have no eyewitnesses. And to be perfectly frank, Ms. Braun, I'm having a difficult time believing that a six foot man in fairly good shape could have been pulled over the side of a boat by any fish. Even the biggest Makos in this area only get to around seven feet—strong, yes, but not nearly enough to rip him from the boat. Why didn't he just drop the line?"

"I don't know," Melissa growled.

"How much did you both have to drink?"

"What? I don't see what—"

"Did he hit you, Ms. Braun?"

"No!"

"Did he hit your son?"

"What is the matter with you?"

Before Melissa completely blew her top, a short blonde officer named Leonard came up and said to Holzer, "Found this just a few minutes ago." She handed Holzer a small black box and walked away.

Melissa's heart thumped.

The ring.

Detective Holzer opened the ring box and turned it to face Melissa. "Care to comment?"

Panicked, Melissa did the only thing she could do. She grabbed Patrick, pulling his head to her chest, and wept. "Oh my God!" With her right hand on the nape of his neck, she gave Patrick a small pinch.

Patrick responded and began to cry, as well. "He was going to . . ."

Melissa nodded against him and forced every tear out that she possibly could, even though it felt every bit as ridiculous as it probably looked. But she kept it going, hoping Patrick would continue to follow her lead.

She felt Holzer's and Andrews' eyes on them, and after a few minutes, Holzer finally said, "Alright. Fine. We've got work to do. Ms. Braun, when do you leave town?"

Melissa broke from Patrick and wiped her hot, reddened eyes. "This weekend."

"More specific please."

"Sunday."

"Good. We'll do our best to find Mr. Rainey, or whatever's left of him. In the meantime, don't leave town. I mean it. Do not cross over the Causeway, either of you. There's gas, food, and groceries on this side readily available for you."

"I understand."

"I hope so." She pulled a card from her front pocket and handed it to Melissa. "That's my number. I already have yours. We'll be in touch."

She and Andrews began to walk away, then Holzer stopped and turned back. "Oh, one last question, if you don't mind? Did you happen to catch anything before Mr. Rainey was pulled overboard?"

Melissa stared at her.

"Anything at all?"

Melissa narrowed her eyes. "No. We didn't."

"Maybe something big enough to have to . . . I don't know . . . incapacitate?"

"Why do you ask?"

The detective shrugged. "No reason. Just trying to take account of everything on board, that's all." Without another word, the two walked away toward the boat.

They left Melissa and Patrick alone, and the two sat there shaking on the Marina bench as the evening sun kissed the horizon.

3

THIS WASN'T THE FIRST time Hoyt Rainey had found himself drowning.

Back in his early teens, when life had yet to smack him around like an angry, short-changed pimp, he had spent many of his summers living with his Uncle. Cooper Rainey, a lifelong native of Kentucky, owned a farm ten miles southwest of Henderson, in Corydon. From late May until early September, Hoyt would be left with his Uncle Coop, while his mother traveled the country as a groupie with various music acts— typically rock bands—and would come back home with a new tan and a swollen belly. By the time he had hit double digits, Hoyt had lost track of how many brothers and sisters he had running around the mobile home. Even during the school year, he spent very little time at home, instead sleeping on couches of those few he called friends, and when those friends dried up, he'd curl up in the jungle gym at his school, typically inside the crawl tunnels, away from rain. He never got along with his mother, and his father, for all he knew, was some beer-gutted Brooks and Dunn roadie. He didn't even know his father's name, and that was just fine by him. He had enough things to hate in his life, and adding his old man to the ever-growing list didn't need to be one of them.

One thing he didn't hate was Uncle Coop. Though Hoyt wasn't much of a farmer, his uncle made damn sure to give him every blister and sunburn to match his own. Every day, Hoyt would wake at the ass crack of dawn to help Uncle Coop with tending the fields, cleaning up the various animal stables, and canning and cleaning those various vegetables he helped grow. Coop had a team of locals he employed who did the majority of the work, but Hoyt enjoyed his uncle's shadow, always staying close by and learning the ropes. There was something about hard work and seeing it pay off at the local market that made him feel like he was actually doing something with his life. Fuck all those teachers who called him trailer trash and a lowlife. What the hell did those fruits know?

When the brutal Kentucky heat faded away with the long days, that's when the real fun began. Every year during the month of September, he and Uncle Coop and his crew would start their plans for Halloween—more specifically their famous corn maze. It was the biggest corn maze in Henderson County, and over the course of the two and a half months they were open to the public, thousands of people from all over the Tri-State area would come to drink fresh cider, pick pumpkins, and get bounced around on a tractor-led hay ride. Hoyt was always too young to work the post-Labor Day festivities, but the year his mother didn't return from the road and Uncle Coop didn't force him to go back to school, he stayed put at the farm. And what a year to do it.

A few of Coop's regulars had quit during the late

summer to go back to college, and his uncle was forced to use Hoyt as a worker. Uncle Coop had never taken Hoyt's corn maze designs, but this was the year he was granted that duty. He spent weeks tackling the project, long hours slaving over a note pad with a sharpened pencil in his grip. Thankfully, Coop was happy with his rendering, and within the next two days they created Hoyt's giant winged serpent in the corn field. The overhead shot was gorgeous, and Hoyt knew one day when he could afford it he would tattoo this kick ass dragon on his back. He wanted lots of tattoos.

By the time fall became winter, and the crowds decided to stay huddled inside their own homes, the last of the corn was torn down and stored in the giant silo near the main barn. It was a hard time for Hoyt. Another year gone, another year older. The magic of this place was waning. He knew his mother would be back soon, and he knew she would want him around to help raise his siblings.

The closest he had to older siblings were the men who worked on the farm. Though a few didn't pay him any mind, most treated him like a younger brother, and with that came the older sibling torment he didn't receive at home. He didn't mind it. Hoyt loved the attention and would do anything to keep it. Even stupid shit like jumping into several tons of loose corn.

Hoyt had helped them dump the last of the corn into the seventy foot silo, and after they were finished they sat atop the giant metal tube and drank cold beers until the sun went down. While they traded stories, an older man named Luke had told them about a friend of his who had died drowning in a silo just like the one they were perched on.

"Nah ah!" Hoyt retorted. "You can't drown in corn. It's not water."

Luke shook his head. "You absolutely can. It's like quicksand, little dude. It grabs you and pulls you down. Encases you like a shell, no pun intended."

Hoyt laughed. "No fucking way, man! I don't believe you."

"It's true," one of the other men, Donald, added. "I've seen it. Scary shit. That's why you don't go messing around on these things. Unlike the corn, you're not going to get shit out whole."

Hoyt refused to believe it. It was far too ridiculous. He sat there with them, watching the sun go down beyond the field, a cold Ski soda in his fist, and he just couldn't get it out of his head. You can't drown in vegetables. That's just stupid.

He got an idea.

"I think you guys are pulling my pud, and I'm going to prove you wrong."

The two men stared at him, half-smiling. Luke asked, "Oh, yeah? What do you have in mind?"

Hoyt stood and walked to the other side of the platform and yanked up the overhead door of the silo. "Dare me to jump in and prove you wrong?"

Luke quickly put his beer down and stood up. "Get away from the damn door, you dumbass! You're going to hurt yourself."

"Dare me to?"

Donald, still grinning, snorted a small laugh. "Fifty bucks says you don't jump."

Luke yelled, "Donny! Don't encourage the fucking kid. Coop will—"

But Hoyt was gone, his body plunging into the

darkness of the silo. It felt like he was going to fall forever, but soon his feet hit the corn below. Deep down he knew he would land on top of the grain and wait patiently for the other two to come down and open the side door for him. He was eager to collect his fifty bucks, money he was itching to spend on a couple of new shirts at the mall. But when his shoes sank, and his ankles began to submerge, he knew he had fucked up royally.

Hoyt kicked his legs, his arms reaching out for anything to grasp. The corn below seemed to fall away, and above it ran through his fingers with no purchase. His chest was swallowed up, and soon his screams were, too, as his whole head submerged.

The dried corn kernels filled his mouth and ears. He couldn't yell, the pressure too great on his diaphragm. His ribs ached. His arms and legs frozen in place under the weight. It was so dark—

He didn't remember much after that. He was obviously pulled out, probably by Uncle Coop. He didn't remember. But he *did* remember his mother's anger. He remembered never visiting the farm again. Most of all he remembered the fear.

But he wasn't afraid now. Not even in the least.

He was angry. Furious.

Much like the corn in the silo, the water grabbed at his body and pulled him under, but it wasn't a gradual process. His body hit the cool, clear water like a stone, and he immediately began to sink like one. Up or down was irrelevant. The blazing midday sun quickly disappeared and became an endless shroud of waving, bubbling black. Hoyt could barely keep his eyes open, not for the burn of the saltwater, but the throb of his swollen face. His heart raced, making every pulse of pain along his cheek and chin a chilly reminder he was still alive. But for how long? When he wasn't holding his face, his arms thrashed at the nothingness surrounding him. His chest burned from holding his breath, but he was only a scream away from filling his lungs with brine. His legs kicked, touching nothing below.

He continued down.

It was hopeless. There wasn't an uncle or farmhands to save him now. He was going to die, and it was all that bitch's fault. Her and that goddamn kid. After everything he gave them, all the time and money and passion, *this* was how it ended? He should have killed that stupid cunt when his hands were wrapped around her throat. What was the boy going to do? Hit him? Unlikely. She should have said yes. A simple yes and none of this would have happened. It was the boy's fault. Patrick was the one to blame, the little fucker. What he wouldn't give to have thrown him off the ledge instead—

Hoyt screamed in anger, and his broken mouth instantly filled with water. The cold, inky black rushed down his throat, filling his taut, aching stomach. His sinuses burned as the salt invaded his airways, and the harder he pushed it out the more they filled up. Face forgotten, his hands clamored for anything around him, anything to kill the pain—

Then it stopped.

Eyes closed, he realized his plunge into the murky depths had ended . . . yet his feet did not touch the ocean floor. His body felt weightless, suspended in place. The pain was gone. Even though his body was full, stomach and lungs bursting with water . . . he felt no need to breathe. He let his limbs float lifeless about him and let his head drift with the current. He slowly opened his eyes.

Hundreds of eyes stared back.

His vision blurred by the salt, Hoyt stared at the uncountable numbers of fish that surrounded him in the darkness. They were all shapes and sizes, and their shadowy figures went on past his eye sight. Not ten feet before him, dozens of baleful-looking sharks gliding slowly, staring him down. Hoyt stared them back, and for some unexplainable reason he was certain they weren't going to attack. Nothing surrounding him had made a move. The silence was deafening.

Then, slowly, the fish parted in front of him, and the heavy blackness behind them crept forward. Its shape was indiscernible, and the closer it moved toward him, the further the sea life moved away. But they didn't retreat. They continued to stare.

The blackness stopped some feet away. Hoyt's body flushed cold, and his vision blurred further.

"*Eísai thymoménos?*"

Hoyt stared blankly at the shapeless black as it spoke to him, its voice a whisper to his ears.

"*Noli odisse vos?*
"*¿Estás enojado?*
"*Hal takarh?*
"*Bist du böse?*
"*Tsi ir has?*
"*Nǐ zài shēngqi ma?*
"*Do you hate?*"

The icy cold gripping his joints, Hoyt blinked and gave the blackness a quick nod.

"Do you hurt?"

Yes, Hoyt thought, just knowing the blackness could hear him.

"Do you desire hurt on others?"

Yes! Yes!

"Then let me in . . . "

Before Hoyt could answer, the blackness revealed its true shape. It enveloped him. And allowed his hate to thrive.

WEDNESDAY

3

AS TO BE EXPECTED in early September, the Florida sun was brilliant and warm, the clouds surrounding it drifting lazily with the ocean breeze. Outside, a lawnmower was being led across the property, the landscaper trimming the thick St. Augustine grass under his feet. A woman in an emerald bikini was laid out on a plastic reclining chair, creased book in hand, while a man hung on the pool's edge, chatting with her. An older couple was quietly playing shuffleboard at the edge of the property in their matching Panama Jack straw hats. Children baked on the beach as they unsuccessfully tossed an emerald Wham-O Frisbee back and forth. A teenage boy sat in the sand on his cell phone.

This was exactly why Melissa wanted to be here. This wasn't an angry place. This wasn't a place of hate or separation. She came here to mend, not to break. And yet . . . with the swing of a bat, she broke everything she had.

There was a quiet, somber feeling in the room when she woke up. Outside, the waves crashed against the shore, and Melissa lay there, wondering if she really *had* hit Hoyt with that aluminum bat. She did and she could still feel the cool metal in her hands. The sound it made when it rang off Hoyt's skull. The way the bat vibrated afterwards in her grip. Over and over she saw Hoyt roll backwards off the boat. Gone. She killed him.

They killed him.

Melissa leapt out of bed and ran to the bathroom before the contents of her stomach missed the toilet. She heaved and heaved into the open bowl, tears and snot dripping from her face. When she finished, she sat back against the tub and closed her eyes. *I am not a murderer. We didn't murder him. We were defending ourselves. He would have killed both of us first.* But . . . would he? He'd hurt her before—both of them—but he'd never taken the extra step, at least not until now. She kept telling herself had they not done the right thing—the *only* thing— it could have been the both of them sinking to the bottom of the ocean. There was always something terrible simmering beneath the surface with Hoyt, and Melissa spent years thinking she could put out that fire and discover the good man somewhere in there. Turns out he didn't actually exist.

No, she refused to feel guilty about what they did. To hell with Hoyt. Never again would she allow herself to be hurt by a man, or allow anyone to lay their fucking hands on her child. There were still too many years left in her young life to waste another minute on the dead. It was far too beautiful outside for mourning shark bait.

Patrick was a different story.

His mother had spent the morning as if nothing

had happened. She had gotten up sometime before him and drove down the street to the French bakery for breakfast. He awoke to the smell of warm brownies and fresh croissants. She called for him from the kitchen, but he wasn't hungry. In fact, he didn't want anything, food or otherwise.

He just wanted to die.

And her nonchalant attitude was making it worse. Despite his protesting, she had dragged him out of bed and forced him to eat. The food was bland and gummy, and it went down his throat like thick lumps of fat. He used to love breakfasts from the bakery. Now, he only wanted to throw it against the wall.

She drove him over to Flagler Avenue where they went from shop to shop, his mother window shopping and eyeing all of the pastel sundresses and shell-laced jewelry. She pointed and laughed at the ridiculous tourist shirts in the beach shops, poked at him with the swim noodles, made him try on a pair of orange board shorts that featured a cartoon dog with sunglasses, and bought herself a new hoodie. Then mint chocolate chip ice cream cones at the end of the street. Then fried shrimp at Breakers. Then the new Marvel film at the theaters. All while screaming in his head: *This isn't normal. This isn't normal. This isn't fucking normal!*

How dare she act like nothing had happened, all while he felt like dying inside? How dare she pretend they hadn't killed another human being only the day before? His belly was full of snakes, and their babies slithered through his nerves and drank from his heart. He glared at her through most of the movie, daring her to look at him and face the truth. She kept on staring at the screen. But he knew she knew—he *knew* it. The darkness of the theater may have hid her face, but her stiff, robotic breathing gave her away. She may have been saving face for most of the day, but the guilt was eating at her like corpse worms. A tear ran down her cheek, and she reached for his hand on the armrest. He pulled it away.

By the time they got back to the condo, he had had enough. Patrick pulled himself from the swimming pool and dashed into the cabana and into the bathroom. He slammed the stall door shut and collapsed heavily to the floor, letting the tears break free. No matter how much his mother was trying to play it cool, playing the enduring role of the rational adult, it was eating him up inside. At twelve-years-old, he was a murderer. Sure, it may have been self-defense, but he was still responsible for sending someone to their death. He hated Hoyt, more than he ever hated anything in his life, but violence was never the answer. He'd never so much as killed a bug before that. Now? He had blood on his hands, and no matter how hard he scrubbed, the red would never go away.

The bathroom door banged open, and before Patrick could protest, his mother opened the stall door and took him into her arms. He was too scared to fight, too weak to run and never look back. He just cried.

After he emptied himself into her shoulder, he stuttered, "W-what are we going to do?"

She wiped her own tears away. "We move on, hon. We move on."

"But *how*? Won't they find out? Will they find him?"

She shook her head. "No . . . I don't think they will, hon. He's gone, and he's not coming back."

"I'm so sorry, Mom. I'm so . . . "

She pulled him close again. "There's nothing to be sorry about, Patrick. He was hurting me. We had no choice."

"But it was me who—"

"No! It wasn't just you. It was both of us. *We* did it. There was no other way. He would have killed us. We did the right thing . . . the only thing. Don't ever forget that."

"Then why did we lie to the police?"

His mother paused for a moment, contemplating. "It doesn't matter at this point, Patrick. Hoyt is gone forever, and I'm still alive because of you. I still have you." She hugged him harder.

He didn't feel much better, but the snakes inside him had finally gone to sleep.

"Listen," she said. "All we can do now is get on with our week. We ride this out, and by Sunday we'll get to go home and we'll worry about all of that other crap then. Okay? Let's just try to enjoy the rest of the week."

"I don't think I can," he whimpered.

"You know what? I just thought of something. Go get your towel and go upstairs and dry off."

Patrick pulled away. "Why?"

"I have somewhere I want to take you. It's really cool, I promise."

He nodded and wiped his face. "Okay."

She followed him out of the cabana and back out into the sunlit poolside. They gathered their towels and their beach bag and began to walk back to the stairwell when they heard a distant shriek. Slowly, they strolled back to the pool area and across the lawn to the retaining wall above the beach.

Down by the water, a small crowd had gathered. Not able to see, they walked along the wall until they found a break in the circle. Lying in front of them, a beached dolphin whined and trilled, its slick gray body kicking up sand. Several people attempted to lift the creature, and when they finally got a handle and turned it back toward the water, the animal shrieked louder than before. It bucked its body and tail, forcing the good Samaritans to drop it back down onto the sand. They backed away as the dolphin continued to cry, and with a roll and flip of its body, it managed to turn itself back around toward land. The dolphin wriggled forward until it could move no more.

10

AFTER A FEW WRONG turns down several different side streets, Melissa finally found what she was looking for. She steered their SUV onto the sand-blown blacktop and parked in the empty lot. It had been several years since she had been here, and she wasn't even sure if she remembered the park's name, or much less how to find it.

Still red-eyed, Patrick stared out the windshield with a mixture of confusion and exasperation. "You took me to a park?"

She opened her door and grinned. "Let's go."

With a sigh, her son stepped from the vehicle and slammed the door shut behind him. He shoved his hands into the pockets of his board shorts and glanced about the park. It was much smaller than Melissa remembered, but far nicer than the last time she'd been here. Beyond the conjoined bathroom adorned in intricately painted sea life art, a brand new jungle gym sat in the middle of the park, its plastic walls, roofs, and slides molded into every color of the rainbow, and its grounds surrounded by a spongy, child safety rubber surface. Behind it, a green-roofed patio with wooden picnic tables and in-ground charcoal grills. The city had obviously put a lot of money into the park since the last time she was here.

"So . . . what?" Patrick moaned. "Am I supposed to swing my worries away? How old do you think I am?"

"No, I expect you to climb that rope ladder and blister your butt on that hot plastic slide, smart mouth."

"Sounds about right."

She turned to him. "You really don't remember this place?"

He shrugged. "Am I supposed to?"

"I guess not. You were very little the last time you were here. It looked a bit different then. They really cleaned it up quite nice. I like it."

"I guess."

She started forward, nodding him along. "Come on."

"Seriously, I don't want to climb the stupid monkey bars, Mom. I'm twelve, not five."

"Then act like it, little Pattycakes," she called over her shoulder, still grinning.

He jumped after her. "Don't call me that! I hate that!"

She spun around, running backwards. "Listen to your mommy, Pattycakes, or I'm going to spank your little bottom!"

Patrick laughed and ran for her, but she turned back around and fled. Once she ran through the jungle gym and past the sheltered patio, she hopped onto a wooden deck and waited for Patrick to catch up. Together, they walked the bridge path through the saw palmettos and scrub palms and the overhanging limbs of the gumbos. Before the bridge path ended with a sharp left turn, it opened up to a wide view of the Indian River. They both stopped and leaned on the sunbaked wooden ledge.

The mid-day sun glimmered brilliantly over the turquoise waters. Beyond the overhanging dock, miles of untouched swamp lands as far as they could see. Cranes drifted above their heads in the breeze, while tiny, finger-sized fish flitted about in the water below their feet. Two teenagers in a kayak paddled down the river, waving at them.

Patrick leaned forward against the railing and closed his eyes, the wind ruffling his hair. He took a deep breath and smiled. "This is nice. Thanks, Mom."

Melissa swelled with emotion. A smile was all she wanted, and if it was gained this easily, then it was worth the short trip over. She stifled her tears and put her arm around his shoulder. "We're going to get through this."

He dropped his head. "Are we?"

"Yes, we are. Look at me for a second."

He did.

"I really don't want to keep saying his name," she continued, "because, honestly, it tastes like crap on my tongue, but . . . Hoyt deserved it. That scumbag deserved everything we gave him. We did *nothing* wrong."

He nodded, his eyes darting around. "Then why does it hurt so much?"

"Because you're a good person, Patrick. Hoyt . . . Hoyt ran on two emotions: angry and horny. And only one of those were taken out on you. You? You're not like him. You're a great kid. You're smart, funny, intelligent, and thoughtful. You're everything he wasn't, and that's why I love you. It feels pretty darn good to know I raised you right."

He turned back to the water. "What are we going to do after this? I mean, when we get back home?"

She thought about it. "I don't know, kiddo. You'll go back to school in a few weeks and pretend nothing happened. I guess I'll have to find a new job. Gosh, it'll be nice to get back to work again."

They were both silent for a few moments before Patrick said, "I'm really glad you didn't say yes." She turned to look at him. "You know, back on the boat?"

She coughed out a short laugh. "Yeah . . . me, too."

Something below them snorted.

Patrick yelped and stumbled back from the railing. "What was that?"

Melissa grabbed his hand. "*That* is why we came here, my child."

She led him down the wooden bridge until it stopped at another left turn. A small cove lay out before them. Across the way, a massive, white, three-story mansion overlooked the water below, with several other large homes lining the waterway behind it. A sign was bolted against the railing at their knees which read: **You can look, but please don't touch, chase, feed or give water to us.**

Patrick stared into the cove water and beamed with delight. "Wow . . . look at all of them."

The water teemed with life. Dozens of manatees were spread throughout the cove. Their large, bulbous bodies bumbled lazily through the dark water; their wide, fat noses intermittently breaking the surface to snort out a breath. They were clustered in several small groups, and sandwiched in-between were the adolescents still tailing their mothers.

"This is so cool!" Patrick said in awe.

"I thought you'd like this." She pointed to two of them near the dock. "Look, it's Fred and Ethel."

"Who?"

"You know, Fred and Ethel? From *I Love Lucy*?"

He arched an eyebrow and shrugged.

She laughed. "I keep forgetting how young you are. It was a TV show back in the early fifties."

"Geeze, that was like a *hundred* years ago, Mom. How did you watch it?"

"More like seventy years ago. No wonder you got all D's in math. Anyway, back when I was your age, when Nickelodeon would go off for the day, Nick At Night would come on and show all kinds of old programs from back when grandma was a kid."

"They were probably all in black and white, too, huh? That sounds terrible!"

She shook her head. "No way! For the most part they were pretty good. I liked quite a lot of them. *Happy Days*, *Laverne and Shirley*, *Bewitched*, *I Dream of Genie*, *Welcome Back, Kotter* . . . "

"*Welcome Back who*?"

"You know, *Welcome Back, Kotter*. The Sweathogs?"

"Who?"

"Come on, kiddo! Vinnie Barbarino!"

"What?"

"Horshack?"

"Are you speaking English, Mom?"

Laughing, she said, "Whatever, Gen Z kid. Get off my lawn!" She slugged him in the arm. "Anyway, *I*

Love Lucy was a show about a musician and his wife, Ricky and Lucy, and their two best friends, Fred and Ethel. Those two right there look like Fred and Ethel."

Patrick rolled his eyes so hard they may have nearly fallen from his head. "If you say so, weirdo."

"And look over there. There's Lenny and Squiggy! And over there in that group? There's Kevin and Paul and Wendy. And that loner over there by the dock? That's Arthur Fonzarelli—The Fonz. He's over there all by himself because he's the coolest sea cow in the cove."

"Sea cows," he giggled.

They began to walk down the dock toward the playground. When they got back on land, they walked over to the tree line and hunched down to get a better look at the water.

"They're so peaceful, aren't they?"

He nodded thoughtfully. "I wish I could touch one. You know, just to see what they actually feel like. I bet they're all rough, like a rhino or something."

Melissa stood up and glanced around the park. Since they arrived, no one else had visited. She hadn't even seen a car pass down the neighborhood street. Across the water, the three story mansion appeared vacant. "You know . . . if you don't tell, I won't."

Patrick stood up and grinned hard enough to show his back teeth. "*Really?*"

"Yes, really. Just don't make any noise or splash in the water. You don't want to frighten them. Remember, this is their home. You wouldn't want someone breaking into your room at night and scaring you, would you?"

"Definitely not."

CRUEL SUMMER

"Take your shoes off first. Hurry up. We don't want anyone to see us."

Patrick dropped down to the sandy grass and slipped his flip flops off. He put them aside and carefully crawled down the small embankment toward the water. Despite the multiple signs warning park goers to not swim in the water, the two foot drop down between the trees into the half-circle cut hole in the ground showed how much people had taken heed over the years. Melissa added her purse to the ground next to his flip flops and brought her camera phone out to take pictures.

When he dropped to the bottom of the hole, Patrick carefully dipped his toes in the first few inches of water. He turned back to her. "Are you sure this is okay?"

"Absolutely not. But I'm keeping an eye out. Now hurry up, go."

Slowly, he stepped into the water until it came up to his knees. "It's so squishy. Gross." He continued to wade into the water until it reached the bottom of his shorts, then quickly it rose to his stomach. By the time it was to his chest, a large gray shape bobbed up to the surface a few arm's length away.

Patrick turned back to Melissa with wide eyes. She nodded toward him, her phone held high, ready to snap up memories. "Just go very slow," she whispered. "Don't scare it."

He took another couple of small steps toward the great, bulbous mammal. He looked so small compared to the gentle giant, and Melissa took a couple of quick pictures as he closed the gap.

Something struck her as odd. Despite the summer

heat, she shivered. The fine white hair on her bare arms stood straight up. The sun overhead dipped behind a blanket of clouds. The air around her cooled significantly. She looked up across the cove to the three story white mansion. She couldn't be sure but it looked like someone was watching her from a second level window.

"Mom?"

She moved her gaze back down to Patrick.

The floating manatee had turned around to face him, its head fully out of the water. Its beady black eyes were trained at her son. Patrick quickly pulled his arms back toward his body, keeping them bunched up near his throat. "Mom, what do I do? It's looking at me."

She lowered her phone. "Don't touch it. In fact, why don't you come back out, hon? I don't think it's very happy you're there."

Squinting her eyes, she attempted to find the person in the window again. Whoever it was, they were now gone, only to have shown up behind the picture window on the bottom floor. She couldn't make out if it was a man or a woman. Though there was no sun glare obscuring her view, the person appeared blurry, almost shapeless in form. She lifted her arm to wave. The shape did not wave back.

"Uh . . . *Mom?*"

Melissa dropped her eyes to the water.

Patrick had already begun to back away from the manatee, but that wasn't why he was calling her name. Behind the staring manatee, two more had surfaced behind it. They, too, watched Patrick with deliberate stares.

Then another popped up.

Then three more.

Within a few moments, dozens and dozens of sea cows had joined the others. They all stared at Patrick, unblinking and silent.

"Patrick, get out of the water. Now!"

Patrick froze in place. His terrified eyes watching the numerous pairs of sunken black orbs glaring back at him. He whimpered.

One by one they began to swim toward him.

"Get the hell out of the water!"

Breaking his stupor, Patrick finally turned and splashed toward the scooped-out embankment between the trees. Melissa dropped her phone onto the grass and hopped over to the drop down. Panicked, Patrick yelled and pushed his submerged legs through the muck and slime. By the time he reached the embankment he was huffing for breath. He fell to his knees, but Melissa dropped to hers and reached for his outstretched arm. She carefully yanked him up and dragged him over the drop.

Down below, the manatees began to bark. In all her years she had never heard them make noise before, other than their short breaths of air when they broke water. She was certain of it. As they reached the bank, their barking increased in volume until it became a unitized honk. They belted their unnatural cries as they drove their corpulent bodies up onto the sand. Heart racing, Melissa clutched her son's hand and backed them both away.

They watched in horrified fascination as the dozens of manatees undulated their sea born bodies like stout snakes onto the grass above. The mammals continued to honk and bark as they crawled over one another toward them.

Melissa turned and pulled Patrick with her toward the SUV. When they reached the vehicle, she reached for the keys in her purse, quickly realizing it wasn't at her side. They were somewhere with her phone underneath the multitudes of fat gray bodies that crawled toward them a few feet at a time.

"Open the doors!" Patrick cried.

"I don't have the keys!"

"Mom!"

She thought about running toward the street and out of the park, but two manatees had already cut their path at the opening off. Back toward the C-shaped bridge, several more were flopping across the lawn toward them. Like giant grey maggots, they spilled over one another as they came closer to the blacktop.

"Mom! Do something!"

Racing around to the other side of the vehicle, Melissa clasped Patrick's wrist and yanked him toward the restrooms. She prayed they were unlocked.

As they neared the small wooden building, a massive manatee nearly ten feet long abruptly stood up next to them as they passed by a park bench. They both screamed as the creature barked deafeningly over their heads. In a blink, its body came crashing down, smashing the wooden bench in half. She gripped Patrick's wrist harder and pulled him toward the nearest bathroom door.

She swiftly shouldered open the men's room door then slammed it shut behind them. The tiny two-stall restroom was not well ventilated, and several days' worth of one hundred degree plus weather was trapped inside. Melissa gagged for air. She pressed her body weight against the door, while Patrick backed up against the single sink near the back and sank to his knees.

Outside, the barking and honking continued. The terrible noise echoed inside the room, drowning out their own cries. Then the pounding began. While she held the door shut, the manatees slammed their giant bodies against the wood-slatted walls outside. They both screamed as the walls shook and rumbled. The treated wood groaned against the animals' weight.

Patrick hunkered down into a tight ball while Melissa kept herself pressed against the door. The door was smashed into from the outside, pushing her a few feet forward. Melissa yelped and scrambled back into position before the door could fully open. Putting her shoulder into it, she held the door as another crash threatened to send her on her ass.

"*Patrick!* Get over here and help me!"

Still soaking, Patrick stayed where he was, crying into his knees.

"*Patrick! Now!* I can't hold it on my own!"

All at once the building rattled and shook on its foundation. The manatee's cries were deafening. The wooden walls began to splinter. The colossal weight behind the door continued its assault. Melissa screamed as hard as she could—

Then it stopped. Everything stopped.

Trembling, Melissa gasped for breath, continuing to drive every bit of strength she had into the door. For several long minutes, the outside remained silent.

She was terrified to drop away from the door, but the calm beyond the walls stilled her heartbeat. She fell to one knee with a huff and turned to Patrick. He looked up at her with red rimmed eyes. She stood to go hug him—

—and the door began to creak open.

Melissa yelped and threw her body back against the thin wooden door. Patrick finally stood up to join her. They dug their feet into the sandy concrete floor, but as more force was used from the outside, their feet began to slip. They both grunted and pushed hard, but the door at their backs gradually crept open. Melissa whimpered, and when she realized this wasn't going to work, she grabbed her son and ran forward to the back wall.

The door banged open. Harsh sunlight exploded into the dark room. Melissa grabbed her son and held him against her chest as a broad shouldered figure shuffled in.

"What the hell is wrong with you two?" the man cried in a shrill voice.

They both stared at him in confusion.

"Christ Almighty! Some people don't have the ability to hold it in, you jerks! Man, I'm about to shit my damn pants." Without another word, he scrambled into the nearest stall and slammed the door shut behind him.

They both stood there for a few moments in shock before she led them back out through the door. Melissa crept out first, shielding her eyes against the light. Patrick stepped out beside her.

They were all gone.

Beyond the tree line, the waters of the cove remained still.

11

EVEN AFTER PUTTING PATRICK to sleep and taking the longest, hottest shower her skin could possibly stand, Melissa still couldn't stop shaking. Every muscle in her body ached, including ones she didn't know she had. The scalding water helped relax her some, but even the hottest steam in her eyes couldn't erase what they saw today. And she *knew* she saw it.

Despite the lack of giant mammals waiting outside of the bathroom building, she understood what they had seen. The outer walls of the restrooms were caved in and splintered. The grass was still flattened and pulled loose across the lawn. The bench was still smashed in half. Her purse, when she got the nerve to get that close to the bank, was ruined. Her keys were good enough to start the car and drive as quickly away from the park as possible, but her phone was not as lucky. Once she got it to turn back on, the spider-webbed screen was nearly impossible to see. Only a few functions, apps like Message and Facebook, appeared to work. Even if she wanted to, the pictures she had taken at the park would remain unseen until it could be replaced.

After making sure Patrick was fast asleep in his room, she got dressed in a thin T-shirt and shorts, then stepped into her sandals. She left the condo room, locking the door behind her, and headed down the three flights of stairs into the parking lot.

The late night air was cool and salty and instantly roused her gooseflesh. Above her head, the palm leaves shuddered like maracas for the ocean, dancing beyond the beach. She desperately needed to clear her head, and though being near the water brought back a bout of trembles, she knew a walk down the deserted beach would be the best thing for her worried mind.

After crossing the parking lot, she headed down the creaky wooden steps and let the cool sand invade the space between her sandals and feet. With a steady gait, she sauntered down the nearly deserted beach, in no hurry to move toward the moonlit sea. Once she reached the water packed sand, she shook the dry grains from her shoes and walked on into the night, where she passed several roped-off turtle egg mounds. Further down the beach, a single flashlight sliced through the darkness, its owner most likely scouring for washed-up shells.

Her own flashlight in hand, she trudged on.

The nippy wind ripped through her wet hair. Within the week, the humidity and saltwater would ruffle and curl her hair back to its normal, God-given bounciness. The corner of her mouth curved in a smile. It was right then she realized she would never again have to straighten her hair. Hoyt hated her natural curls, always pressing her to keep it long and straight. Something he could grab onto. And pull. The first thing she would do when she got back to the room was throw that goddamn straightening iron he purchased for her right in the wastebasket. To hell with that thing.

She suddenly couldn't stop laughing.

She stopped where she was walking, ankle deep in evening water, and several hotels down the beach from her own. She bent over, the laugher coming out of her so abruptly she couldn't breathe. Sucking in a deep, shuttering gasp, she collapsed into the water and convulsed with hysterical laughter. Had anyone been around to see it, they would have thought she'd gone mad. She didn't care one bit—not about Hoyt, random strangers, the world. It didn't matter anymore. From here on out, she wouldn't have to subscribe to anyone else's opinions but her own. To hell with what anyone thought about her. She would be ridiculed no longer. Quelled no longer. Punished no longer. Hoyt Rainey was gone, never again to tell her he didn't like her hair or the way she ate her food or how she raised her child. She would never have to feel the pain of his unplanned outbursts or the callousness of his hands. Hoyt Rainey was fish food, and that, above all else, made her laugh the hardest.

After a few minutes of purging her deepest regrets, she sat up and stared out into the black water. Tears streamed down her cheeks. They weren't regretful ones, nor were they ones of happiness. They were tears of relief. She wasn't pleased with what they had done. As much pain as Hoyt had caused them, she never, even in her wildest dreams, wished death on the man. In their darkest of shared moments, Melissa knew deep down there was a damaged little boy who needed bandaging. A deep seated problem, with time and a little elbow grease, she could fix. Holy shit, what a living cliché she had become.

Good girl turns bad boy into a prince.
Never. Again.

Melissa vowed right then and there as she stared into the cold, harsh water she would never allow herself to be bullied again. No one would ever lay a hand on her or her son for as long as they both lived. If they did, she would make damn sure, like Hoyt, they would be sitting in pieces inside the belly of a great white.

"You hear that, you miserable bastard?" she growled at the sea. "You'll never get to touch me again. You'll never lay another hand on Patrick. You'll never get to see the sunlight, or eat steak, or breathe, pick your ass anymore. Do you know why, Hoyt?" She slapped the water. "Because I fucking *killed* you! *Me!* I wish it was me who hit you with that bat the second time. I wish I could have felt it bash your skull in."

She paused, closing her eyes in reverie. "I hope you enjoy your new home in that watery prison, because you have no one to blame but yourself. You stole these last few years from us. But now? Now we get our lives back. We're moving on. You reap what you sow, Hoyt. Enjoy Hell, you bastard."

Only the breeze answered, but that was just fine by her. It had only been a few days but his voice was already becoming a vague memory. By Friday it would be forgotten all together. That would truly be the biggest victory.

Her bottom soaked and soggy, she had lost track of time. She became engrossed in her own thoughts, her visions of a perfect life and prospects of what could be in store. There would be questions, maybe even finger pointing, but the week was still young, and their vacation was far from over. Not to mention Patrick's father, Jordan . . .

From here on out, no more excuses. Tomorrow would have to be the day.

Sick of being angry and wet, Melissa reached into the water to grasp her flashlight, finding in her fit of laughter it had been dropped and swallowed by the Atlantic. Its beam was gone, leaving her with only the meager light from the rows of condos lining the beach. Two resorts down another flashlight bobbed in the night, roaming the sands for night critters. Eyelids heavy, she was ready to call it a night and sleep her issues away.

Something swam across her foot.

Melissa jumped, tensing her body as if she'd been shocked. When it didn't repeat, she went to stand, but something else touched her arm. Quickly, she ripped her hand from the water. She immediately felt silly. In the glow of the moonlight, dozens of tiny silver fish darted just below the surface, weaving between her legs, flitting across her submerged hands. She carefully lifted her hand and put her index finger out in the cloudy water. While many of the fish recoiled, one stayed put, floating a few inches from her outstretched digit.

"Come on, little one," she whispered. "I won't hurt you."

The miniscule fish remained in place for several long seconds, and just when she started to lose interest, the creature reacted. In a flash, it flew forward and bit the tip of her finger.

Melissa yelped, "Son of a bitch!" and tore her hand from the water. Blood trickled in one long drip down her finger and arm. She eyed the water with distaste. "Fine, I know when I'm not wanted."

Then came more biting. All down her legs, tiny mouths latched onto her exposed skin. Shrieking, she hurriedly stood, finding the fish still attached to her flesh. She spun and spun, kicking her legs through the several inches of water, feeling every little mouth refusing to let go. Realizing the little bastards wouldn't go on their own, with a shaking hand she swiped at them, knocking them off one at a time. Blood wept down her thighs. She stumbled backwards toward the beach, wanting to get away from the water all together. But the water still wanted her around.

Before she could get too far away, waves lapped at her feet, then lashed. The further she backed away, the higher the waves rose. Panicked, Melissa turned to run, but a waist-high surge crashed into her side and threw her under. The frigid water encased her, chilling more than just her skin. She screamed, retching as briny seawater rushed past her teeth and down her throat. Her eyes burned when she opened them, but she had no other choice. She rolled beneath the surface . . . wherever the surface was. She reached out, her arms moving in slow motion, as she attempted to find the open air above. For a perceived eternity, Melissa floated in a black abyss, lost in space without a safety line. Stars twinkled so close she could touch them. Only they came in close pairs and they blinked. They were everywhere, watching and judging. Admiring her strength, pitying her struggles. She screamed again when they moved closer.

When Melissa was sure she would drown, she felt the air above on her outstretched hand. Without thinking twice, she kicked her legs as hard as she could and pushed up.

The moment her face broke the surface, she gasped for air, taking in as much as possible. But the relief wouldn't last. Before she could fill her lungs, another wave blindsided her, taking her beneath the surface once more. The current grabbed her, shoving and tossing her like a child's toy caught in a tornado. Sand and debris swirled, seaweed sticking to her face and neck. Vertigo conquered her brain. Just when she decided to give up and let the ocean take her away, it spat her out.

Head over feet, she tumbled from the water and landed flat on her back in a dip in the beach. The sitting water splashed, then pooled again around her gasping form. The waves receded, steadied, and within a few moments they resumed their normal breaths. Her own gasps were wracked with coughs as she spat out what water she had unwillingly swallowed down. Shivering, Melissa peeled open her eyes, terrified she might not actually be out and this was only an illusion. She flexed her fingers and took several deep, reassuring breaths.

There was movement off to her right. Two condos down, the singular flashing continued to roam in the darkness.

Melissa slowly rolled onto her side, wheezing. "Help!" she called weakly. Clearing her raw throat, she yelled again. "*Help!* Please, help me!"

The flashlight stopped moving.

"Over here!"

It turned in her direction.

"Yes! Over here! I'm over here!"

When the light found her, its owner began to jog in her direction.

Melissa's chest flushed with relief. Though she had no clue who the stranger was, she was very thankful they were there to help. She was positive she wasn't physically hurt in any way, but help to her feet and assistance back to her condo room would be a God send. Propped on her side, she knew she was shaking too hard to be any good on her own.

"Over here! Please! I'm not sure I can walk."

The flashlight continued toward her, its glow bobbing with its owner's uneven steps.

Melissa waved her hand, squinting to see the person behind the light.

Twenty feet away, the light clicked off.

The beach plunged into darkness, leaving Melissa with a gaping mouth. Eyes wide, she searched the darkness for her help. The moon disappeared behind a bank of clouds.

"He . . . hello? Is anyone there?"

Only the wind responded. The silence was crushing, and the possibility of sudden isolation made her skin crawl.

"Please . . . are you there?"

A tittering noise caught her ear. Trembling, she lifted her head and stared into the black. Something small and low to the earth crawled toward her. A *mass* of something. *What the hell is that?* she thought, squinting. When the clouds drifted past, the moonlight gave her an answer.

From out of the darkness, hundreds of blue crabs

swarmed into the light, scuttling over one another, vying to be the first in line—a line coming straight at her.

Finding a renewed strength, Melissa belted out a scream. She swiftly pushed herself up from the cold puddle and willed her shaking legs to take her back to her condo. When she turned, she pushed forward in a long bound—and stopped short of falling back onto her face. More crabs had migrated toward her, rapidly filling empty spaces of sand surrounding her. Their tiny pincers snapped, segmented legs clicking against the shells of others. The ocean was now calm, and the crabs' cricket-like hissing swelled, coating her skin like saltwater couldn't. Her sandals lost, she hopped around on her toes, spinning, frantically searching for a way around the creatures and finding none. By the time they reached her feet, she had no choice but to go through them.

Squealing, Melissa leapt as far as she could. When her foot came down, she felt the soft *crack* of an exoskeleton give way beneath her. She kept her balance and forced herself, no matter how awful it felt, to keep moving forward. The sand around her disappeared completely, replaced by a crustacean hive mind. They nipped and snapped at her bare feet and ankles, drawing ribbons of blood that speckled their gray bodies from above.

Even though the condos beside her whipped by in a blur, she seemed to be getting nowhere. Her condo was only two more away and yet it could have been miles more down the beach. The horde of crabs appeared as endless as the ocean at her back. As she hopped and skipped over and onto their tiny bodies, she continued to cry for help. As much racket as she was making, someone—*anyone!*—should have been on the way to help. Yet the line of vacation apartments remained quiet and unbothered, their lights kept off and blinds drawn tightly shut. No one was coming, and that made all the more sense to not pause and wait for help.

Her ankle twisted. The writhing beach came up to meet her. Arms splayed, she went down hard and felt dozens of miniscule bodies crunch beneath her weight. Before she could push herself back up on her feet, their pincers bit, finding her arms and fingers with haste. Melissa screamed and went to cover her face. Like a wriggling blanket, they immediately covered her and attacked. She thrashed, kicking and slapping at the swarm. Their hisses drowned her cries, their tittering feet saturating all sound. They weren't very heavy, but their collected mass piled on, and her body seized up from the shock. For a moment, like being beneath water, Melissa believed she was going to die. All she could think about was Patrick.

Then they were gone, replaced by another abrupt weight. Melissa rolled and tumbled as an enormous wave caught them all off guard. Her mouth filled with water, much of it blasting into her eyes and nose. The crabs now gone, she waved her arms through the frigid saltwater, trying to find anything solid to grab on. Her fingers brushed across the ground below, and without a second thought, she dug her fingers into the sand. She gripped with everything she had, forcing her legs down and her toes to match her front half. The raging water pulled her backwards, but she kept her steady grip. Before long, the crisp night air above greeted her once more.

The ocean pulled back and retreated, leaving Melissa mercifully by herself. She gagged for air, then vomited up the water that had stayed behind. Trembling, she lay there for some time, expecting more water or nocturnal creatures to bombard her. When they didn't, she slowly pushed herself up on her elbows. Up ahead, her condo remained still and asleep, as did the others surrounding it. Her fear now gone, she gritted her teeth in anger, pissed off not a single one of her cries for help were answered. But there was no time for resentment. Sopping wet and bleeding, she rose onto her shaking feet, cringing as a blast of air licked her vulnerable body.

"*Meeeelllllyyyyy . . .*"

Melissa froze. Her body shivered, not from the cold but from something deeper. Something beyond fear. Beyond certainty. She told herself to run. To follow her instincts and get as far away as possible. But she had to see. She staggered out a quaking breath and turned her head.

From the black of the ocean, a figure stumbled onto the beach. Its movements shaky and uneven, it fell to its knees and braced itself from falling face-first onto the sand.

Keeping her body facing the other way, Melissa continued her wide-eyed gaze.

The man sucked in deep breaths, water dripping from his naked body. He lifted his head, and the white of his eyes gleamed in the moonlight.

"*Melly.*"

Melissa had never screamed so hard in her life.

Her body reacted, and before she knew it, she took off. The pain forgotten, she dashed across the sodden sand and across the dry grain, then up the wooden steps onto the parking lot, all while her screams echoed in the night. She crossed the blacktop in a heartbeat, disregarding the pebbles and debris beneath her feet, and ran into the condo hallway. She ripped the stairwell door open and collapsed in a heap on the first set of stairs. The metal door slammed against the inner wall before closing behind her. Shaking all over, she sat there for a moment, trying to catch a breath which had already climbed the steps above her.

From beneath the door, water surged into the stairwell. Melissa shrieked and leapt to her feet, unable to comprehend where it was coming from. The water flowed quickly, and before she knew it, it was splashing over the first few steps. She walked backwards up the stairs, not wanting to take her eyes off the impossibility.

This couldn't be happening. She was either dreaming or dead. Maybe she had actually drowned and this was her Hell. She couldn't imagine anything so awful.

The water pushed harder and lapped at her legs, gushing with an unnatural force. No, this was certainly not a hallucination.

Melissa raced up to the second floor landing and reached for the door handle and twisted.

Locked.

"Open the door!" She pounded on the thick metal door with trembling fists. The clamor reverberated through the stairwell. "Please! Someone open up!"

Below her, the saltwater roared like an engine as it continued to fill the concrete tomb.

Tears spilled down her cheeks as she wrenched at the handle. "For the love of God, somebody please open the fucking door!"

Much like her cries outside, they were answered with more water, as it now spilled out from beneath the locked door before her. She tumbled backwards, catching herself on the railing. The water arched up and sprayed right at her, catching her in the chest. Melissa scrambled to catch her footing as the bouquet of water shot harder and added to the pool beneath, which had already reached the second floor landing.

Moving purely on adrenaline, Melissa pulled herself up to the next set of stairs. By the time she reached the third floor, she didn't even get to the door before more water rushed out from beneath the frame to greet her. The water rose, and she continued climbing up, rapidly running out of options.

The final floor was more of the same. Cold water gushed from the door like a broken pipe, spilling out across the last of the landings. The water below was black soup, and within a few breaths it was already up to her ankles. She spun and cried out, begging for anyone who cared to listen. But her cries were lost, and if she didn't figure out something quick, her life would be lost, too.

A small wooden step ladder was folded up on the low ceiling above her. She leapt up and snatched the last rung, then pulled down the set. The stairs unfolded, revealing a small metal hatch leading to the roof. Without testing its sturdiness, Melissa quickly climbed the creaking steps and, with all the strength she could muster, pressed her hands against the hatch.

Locked.

Panicked, she wailed and pounded the metal hatch with her fists. When she couldn't find a handle or a lock, she rose up and pressed her shoulder against the fastened square, but no matter how much she tried it refused her an inch.

The water reached her feet—

She screamed and pushed.

—up to her knees—

Nowhere to go. Her eyes clamped shut.

—filled her belly button—

I'm going to die!

—then stopped at her chest.

The water ceased its surging. It remained still, as did her breathing, as she waited for its inevitable continuation. She stayed there for what seemed like hours, her body quaking with fear. She wondered how long it would take for the water to rescind, if it indeed went away at all. She feared she might be stuck there, forced to swim beneath its black surface and search for a way out. If there was one.

Desperate to not stay locked onto the ladder, she carefully lifted her leg and swept it through the water. She felt nothing below. When she reached out with her arm, she yelped and immediately recoiled—

A head rose from the water before her. His hair and mustache was slick as an otter's pelt, with sea slime dripping from his nostrils. His mouth opened and spat more rancid water right into her face. He sucked in a deep, uneven breath and coughed. Then he opened his milky white eyes.

CRUEL SUMMER

Hoyt croaked, "*Why do you keep running from me, Melly?*"

Melissa filled her own lungs with air before screaming. She splashed at him, backing herself up against the wall while holding onto the top rung of the ladder for dear life. She pounded the concrete, desperately wishing it would collapse around them and save her from facing the nascent revival of the man she helped murder. *Dead. He should be dead . . .*

"*You're not real!*" she cried.

He crept closer. "*Now that's no way to talk to your fiancé.*"

"Stay away! Stay the fuck away from me!"

Water continued to dribble from his mouth like a leaky faucet. "*Where do you think you're going to go, Melly?*"

She continued to scream and thrash, willing this nightmare to go away. It drew closer, and brought with it a briny stench of reality. His words echoed above her splashes. There was truly nowhere to go.

"Please!" she cried, holding her feckless position in the corner. "Don't touch me, you bastard!"

He surged toward her, and in an instant he was mere inches from her face. He growled, "*I see my lessons on how to speak to me never caught on.*"

Head against the wall, she clamped her eyes shut. "W-what do y-you w-want?"

"*Oh, Melly . . . oh, Melly Melly Melly . . . It's not about what I want. Not anymore. It's about what he wants.*"

"You're s-supposed to be d-dead."

He chuckled, moisture dotting her face. "*Yes . . . I should be. You and that pussy boy son of yours saw to that. You tried—you really, really did. I figured you would give it a shot one day. But him? I still can't believe the little fucker had it in him."*

Even his undead words cut her deep. She slowly opened her eyes, hoping he would vanish, but his unseeing judgements held her still. "Please don't hurt him. Do whatever you want to me, but please leave him be. He's just a kid."

"Oh, Melly," he said, grinning. *"In time, as he grows and gives me strength, I will do whatever I damn well please. I won't need your permission or your filthy tears. I'm owed that much, you dumb bitch."*

"H-how is this happening? How are you here?"

Hoyt let his whited-out gaze wander about. *"Because he found me, Melly. He found me, and he chose me. I am his vessel now . . . his perfect candidate."*

She shivered. "Who's he, Hoyt? I don't understand."

He continued to glance around. *"He's me. I'm him and he's me. We are one now. I've never felt so . . . so whole. So complete. I feed him. I give him my hate, and it helps him grow."*

"Hoyt . . . "

"Cetus needs me. And I need him."

"Hoyt, please."

His gaze finally settled on her drenched face. *"But we still need you, Melly."* His arms lifted from the black water. His left hand snaking around her head, his right pressed against her temple. *"We still need the both of you. You feed my hate, and that feeds him."*

She put up a struggle, pulling her head to the side, but he held her in place in an ice cold grip. "Please let me go!"

"*You're going to pay, bitch. You're both going to pay.*" His fingers grazed her cheek, and before she could react, they pushed past her lips, and **DAREMETO** wrapped around her mouth once more. His cold, dead fingers dipped down her throat, and she gagged, the harsh, brackish taste conquering her taste buds. In her pain, she expected him to perform his usual finger fucking her throat, but his slimy digits continued to push deeper, their depth impossibly long. Her eyes rolled into the back of her head, and when she thought his digits couldn't go any deeper, he pressed harder, and they plunged further down. Her body went slack. The wet concrete walls closed in. Just as she began to slip away, he whispered into her ear, "*But not now . . .*"

His grip vanished, his fingers extracted, and Melissa tumbled off the ladder. She collapsed on her side, the breath *whooshing* from her lungs. Expecting to drown, she rolled on her side and gasped for air, realizing the water had already receded. As it drained away, she lay there, sucking in deep, shuddering breaths. Unlike the sea, the tang of dead, waterlogged skin would not go away.

THURSDAY

12

IN THE DARK CORNER of Patrick's bedroom, Melissa shivered uncontrollably, still soaked to the bone. She tried her damnedest to not blink, to keep her burning eyes locked onto her son's sleeping form as his blanket rose and fell with his dreamy breaths. She wondered what he dreamed about: homework or girls or what sort of man he would become in the not so distant future? He would be a good man, she was sure of it, raised to be kind and thoughtful. He would be the type of man any girl would be lucky to have, and the type of son she could always count on. Not a son of a bitch. Not an abuser. Not someone worthy of being thrown off a boat . . . or one to come back to talk about it.

The first thing Melissa did after getting back to her room was check on her son. When he appeared as unharmed as she'd hoped, she gathered several candles spread throughout the condo and lit them inside the room, then sat with her back against the closed bedroom door and waited. For what, she wasn't certain. She wasn't quite sure of anything right now. As she stared at her sleeping child, dabbing at the ribbons of blood on her legs and feet with a towel, tears dribbled down her trembling cheeks. How was this possible? They had killed him. They had beat Hoyt with a baseball bat and threw him overboard, miles out to sea. The bastard should have been chum, halfway digested inside a shark's large intestine, not . . . this. She so badly wanted to believe it was all some hallucination or delusion caused from stress. The waves had taken her under; maybe she knocked herself stupid while drowning, and this is what happens when you fall asleep while concussed. But that wasn't the case, not according to the acrid taste still lingering on her tongue. Cold, briny flesh invaded her throat, souring her senses, blossoming flower-like until it hit her head-on.

Without making a noise, she stumbled into the adjoining bathroom and heaved into the toilet. Nothing solid came out, only thick ropes of spit which dangled from her lips. When her back began to throb, she collapsed to the floor.

He should be dead.
He should . . . be dead.
Her throat ached.

The moment Patrick's eyes opened, the first thing he saw was his mother's face. He yelped and sat up straight, his heart thundering.

"What the hell, Mom? You scared the crap out of me!"

She smiled, her eyes bloodshot. "Time to get up, hon. We've got a big day today."

He dropped back down into the mound of warm blankets. "What time is it?" The clock on the nightstand next to his stack of Magic cards read 6:14 AM. Too damn early to be up and at 'em.

CRUEL SUMMER

Before he could settle back in, the comforter was ripped off his body. "Come on, Patrick. Time to get up. Now."

"Mom! Come on!"

"Patrick, now!"

Noting the tension in her voice, he rolled back over to watch her. She appeared disheveled and tired, her hair wild and frizzy, her face a mask of barely contained stress. "Mom, what's wrong?"

She shot him a forced smile. "Nothing, hon. Nothing at all. I just need you to get out of bed so we can get going."

"Why? Where are we going?"

Grabbing his shirt and pants from the floor, she tossed them onto the bed across his bare legs. She sighed, thinking quickly with her hands held on her hips. "Disney World. We're going to Disney. But we need to leave now in order to beat traffic and lines. Come on."

"Disney?" he asked, yawning. "Why? Rides make me sick."

She opened his bedroom door and stood there, waiting. "Then we'll go to Animal Kingdom—or Epcot, or Universal, or whatever. Just get dressed now."

Slowly, he got out of bed and stretched. After putting on his clothes, he sat on the edge of his bed and watched as she stood in the doorway, glancing side to side in the living room.

"Mom? Is everything okay? You're acting—"

"I said now, Patrick!"

Blinking, he quickly put on his shoes and joined her in the front hallway. Two bulging suitcases sat by the front door. "What's with those?"

She lifted them both and huffed as she handed him one. "You're quite chatty this morning, you know? Come on. Let's get moving. Mickey is waiting."

Patrick held the suitcase out before him in confusion. "Why are we taking our stuff, Mom? Are we leaving? I still have stuff in my room."

"*Stop asking so many questions!*" she shrieked.

They both went silent, her eyes wide and rattled, his squinting with unease.

His mother took a deep breath and gathered herself. She calmly said, "Patrick . . . please do as I tell you. No more questions, no more delays. Just moving feet. Now."

Biting his lower lip, he nodded. While his mother locked the condo door behind them, his heart began to race. He didn't know why. She refused to tell him what was wrong, and he was quite certain they weren't going to Disney, or any theme park for that matter. Her erratic mannerisms, quick to exasperate—she terrified him. But he did as he was told.

When they got to the stairwell, they stopped. Before he could ask why she was shaking so hard, she grasped his free hand and shouldered open the door. Patrick allowed himself to be pulled down the multiple flights, while his feet struggled to stay under him. He yelled, "Mom! Stop! You're hurting me!" but she continued to lead them down. Somewhere in her stuttered breaths, he heard whimpers. In his own deep gasps, he thought the stairwell smelled funny. Wet.

By the time they reached the ground floor and found their SUV, the bags had been tossed in the backseat, and they were off. His mother peeled out of the parking lot, completely ignoring the traffic signal, and sped North down A1A with haste. The engine roared, the line of condominiums rushing by in a pastel blur.

Patrick spun in the passenger seat, watching traffic on all sides. "Mom! Slow down! You might hit someone or get pulled over." When she didn't respond, he gently laid his hand on her arm.

She flinched, taken out of her reverie. "What?"

"You're going to kill us. Slow down. What's the rush?"

Confusion masked her face.

"Disney, right? It'll still be there, even if you drive a little less crazy."

She turned back to the road. "Yeah. Disney. Right. Okay."

The car began to slow, but Patrick's heart rate increased. Something was seriously wrong, and he was quite positive, no matter how much he asked, his mother wasn't going to tell him the truth. They were running, that much was obvious, but from what? The only thing worth running from was sitting at the bottom of the ocean. Maybe the cops? He kept an eye on her, studying her erratic movements, the way she continued to check the rearview mirror, her white knuckles on the wheel. He knew they were on good terms and they could talk about anything, but now was obviously not the time to ask questions. He would play along, hoping it would calm her down enough that once they left town, she would let him in on the reasoning behind their getaway. In truth, he was ready to go home. He loved the beach and the summer heat, but it just wasn't the same anymore. It probably wouldn't be for a very long time. Maybe ever.

Before long, traffic began to thicken, and with only a mile to go before hitting the causeway, it stopped all together. With both lanes unmoving, his mother's anxiety ramped up once more. Patrick opened his window and stuck his head out, unable to see anything beyond the sea of stalled vehicles. His mother did the same, groaning with exasperation. She shook her head and rubbed her bloodshot eyes. *What the hell happened to her?*

After what seemed like an eternity of sitting in the southern heat, traffic began to move, but only at a steady crawl. This only angered his mother more. Patrick could tell she was about to explode, softly beating the wheel with her fists and mumbling to herself, but she kept most of it below the surface. Thankfully she didn't make it worse by adding to the incessant honking outside. Little victories.

At a snail's pace, they continued down A1A, past the condos and restaurants, and after another thirty minutes of inching along they could finally see the causeway . . . and the reason for the long delay. High in the air, the drawbridge in the center of the bridge had been towed up, but not all the way. From where they sat, it appeared to have been in mid-drop, but for whatever reason it had stopped in place. Near the bottom of the bridge, traffic was being directed by uniformed officers toward a two-lane U-turn, away from the stall. When his mother saw this, she growled in frustration and began to punch the car horn in short beeps.

By the time they reached the U-turn, she was ready to explode. She rolled down her window. "What the hell is going on? Why can't we leave?"

Dripping in sweat, the male police officer directing traffic shook his head, just as frustrated as her. "Keep the flow moving, ma'am."

"I'm not moving an inch until you tell me why I can't go over the bridge." She kept her promise by shifting the car into park. Behind them, traffic reacted further with angry horns and yells.

Embarrassed, Patrick lowered in his seat.

The officer huffed and stomped toward the SUV. "Ma'am, I'm not going to ask you again."

"And I'm staying right the hell here until I get an answer."

He shook his head. "The drawbridge is currently down."

"No, it's up."

"You know what I mean."

"What happened?"

"Don't really know yet, ma'am. Some sort of mechanical malfunction. The drawbridge short circuited and lifted on its own. By the time the bridge crew could look at it, it started to descend. Somehow a cluster of sailboats drifted underneath as it was lowering, and the sails all got wedged inside the motor and gears."

It was her turn to now sink into her seat. Her jaw dropped. "How does that even happen?"

The officer shrugged, waving for traffic to go around them. "No clue, ma'am."

"How long's it going to be down?"

"Couldn't say. Few days? A week maybe?"

"A week!" she yelled. "What about the South Causeway? That's still open, right?"

He barked a short, humorless laugh. "You'll never believe it, but the same damn thing happened to the South Causeway. Never seen anything like it in all my years."

"How is this even possible?" She quickly sat up. "Is there any other way off the island? Any other route to leave?"

He shook his head. "As of right now, no. With both causeways out, residents are going to have to stay put—even tourists. I'm sorry, ma'am. Unless it's an absolute emergency or something already pre-approved by the city, only authorized law enforcement are able to access water transportation to get across."

Patrick flinched when she slammed her balled fist on the dashboard. "Fuck! This is a nightmare! We have to leave!"

"Oh, yeah? To where?"

All three of them turned as Detective Holzer strolled up to the car from between traffic. Dressed in gray slacks and a dark blue jacket, she held two sweating water bottles, one of which she handed to other officer. "Thank you, Miles. I'll take this from here." He nodded gratefully and stepped back to the intersection to resume his duties. The woman leaned into the open car window and raised a damp, curious eyebrow. "Hot day, huh? And it isn't even noon yet. Only going to get worse as the day goes, right?"

Patrick awkwardly looked away when her eyes stopped on him.

Holzer asked, "So where are you two heading to in such a hurry?"

His mother shook her head, not meeting the other woman's gaze. "I don't think that's any of your business, detective."

"Oh? It's not? I seem to remember telling you—the both of you—to stay put. To not leave town until I deemed it to be okay. And yet, here I find you, blocking traffic in front of an industrial accident, blatantly ignoring not only *my* orders, but the orders of my fellow officers trying to do their jobs. Now, I'll ask you again, Ms. Braun, and I highly suggest you not lie to me. Where were you both heading to?"

Without moving her head, his mother glared at the detective. "Disney World."

"Ah, the Magic Kingdom. Great place. Haven't been there in while. So that's, what, seventy miles away, give or take? A little out of my jurisdiction, wouldn't you say?"

"I—"

"No no, I'm still speaking. You were told not even two days ago to not leave New Smyrna Beach, and yet I catch you red-handed about to drive seventy miles away from the city—if that's actually where you both were going." She addressed Patrick. "Is that where you were going, hon? To Disney World?"

Despite the air conditioning, beads of sweat dripped down his cheeks. He quickly side-eyed his mother, but she wasn't looking in his direction. He had no idea what to say, so he simply nodded.

Detective Holzer nodded back. "Okay. Maybe you were. I have no reason to distrust you two, right? Unfortunately, you guys won't be going anywhere today. Sorry, folks, the park's closed. The mouse out front should have told you."

His mother rolled her eyes. "How long are the bridges going to be out, detective?"

The woman shrugged. "For city residents and tourists? A few days, maybe. For you two? As long as I see fit."

"We haven't done anything wrong." Tears mixed with sweat on her cheeks. "We don't appreciate being treated like criminals."

"I didn't say you were criminals."

"I lost my boyfriend, detective. He's gone. I'm just trying to take my son away for the day to get his mind off things. He's very upset, as am I."

"I'm sure you are, Ms. Braun."

"And the last time I checked we weren't suspects, correct?"

The detective nodded, taking a gulp of water. "Correct. You are not. For now."

"Then you can't keep us here. You just can't."

"Wrong. I can and I will. Much like everyone behind you, no one without a badge or a serious medical condition is leaving town. The only hospital is just over that bridge, and I need to keep this traffic flowing and clear of obstructions in case medical crews need to get through. Now, do I need to call for assistance and have you forcefully removed from your vehicle, or are you going to leave and stop clogging up my streets?"

His mother sighed, putting the car into drive.

"Good choice, Ms. Braun. Now be good little tourists and head back to your condo. Swim, play in the sand, go get a bite to eat."

As his mother began to drive away, the detective stopped her. "One more thing."

She side-eyed the detective.

"Keep your phone on. And don't try to leave town again. I mean it. Last warning."

Patrick's mother gave her a stiff thumbs up before quickly taking the U-turn and driving away. As she mumbled obscenities under her breath, Patrick watched as the female detective faded in his side mirror. He didn't know why she made him so nervous. Up until then, he had never heard a woman talk like that. Maybe in the movies, but definitely not in person, especially not to his mother. She was only doing her job, to find out what had happened to Hoyt, but that was the last thing either of them wanted. Even though it made him sick, he hoped they never found Hoyt's body, that way, when all of this was over and the bridges were fixed, they could go home in peace. To a new normalcy. *That* was truly something to look forward to.

After several minutes of uneasy silence, they pulled back into the parking lot of their condo. Patrick reached for the door handle, but stopped when he noticed his mother hadn't moved. Still buckled in, she sat there, staring out the windshield. He unbuckled himself, but remained seated.

"Mom? You okay?"

For a moment, she didn't speak, and he was sure she hadn't heard him. Then she said, "Just thinking."

"Yeah? About what?"

She didn't answer.

"Come on, Mom. Remember open communication?"

Finally she turned to him and shot him a sad smile. "I'm just thinking about something I have to do."

"Okay . . . What's that?"

She burrowed through the beach bag, which temporarily acted as her purse, until she found the room keys. "I want you to go upstairs and stay in the room. Make sure to lock the door behind you, and don't open it for anyone but me. Do you understand?"

He shrugged. "Yeah, I guess. Why?"

"Because I have something I have to go do. There's a friend I need to visit."

"You know someone down here?"

She nodded, turning back to stare out the windshield. "Yes. A very old friend."

13

WHILE THE MID-MORNING SUN rose high in the eastern sky over the ocean, baking every inch of uncovered skin it kissed, Jordan Schwartz watched its familiar blaze with a trained eye. Under the treated wooden canopy of his rooftop deck, he studied the scene for several uninterrupted minutes, not taking his eyes away for even a moment. He took in everything: the cloudless, cobalt sky, the shimmering aquamarine below, the slight ruffle of the brushy palms, seagulls crying, the heat sticking to his bare chest. *Everything* mattered. No detail spared.

When the moment felt right, he closed his eyes, took a deep breath, and got to work.

It was the same every time. Choosing his widest brush, he pushed his long, chestnut hair behind his ears and began to prime the blank canvas with a background base, covering the upper half of the white board with what his immediate memory retained. Jordan never cared for glancing back and forth, up and down, as he painted. It took away from his flow, his concentration. He instead preferred to apply his spontaneous nature—a skill he was quite thankful for—and what typically came out of his hands was magic. Like his hero Bob Ross before him, he didn't necessarily have to have the lush woods or a crackling waterfall or the midday sun before him while he worked, but when the day was beautiful and he had nowhere else to be, what else was there to do but stay busy? Bills don't pay themselves.

Peace and quiet. No distractions.

After applying the creamy blue base for the sky, he went to work on the sun. Tangerine was what his mind called for. Taking a clean brush, he carefully mixed his vermillion red and cadmium until the perfect shade of orange began to form on his palette. With his palette knife, he made a small circle of the fresh made mix near the middle of the canvas. He carefully drew the knife out in tiny arcs, and before long he could almost feel the radiant heat from the daylight he created. No, this wasn't his best work—far from it—but it's what the tourists and the local art galleries wanted. Who was he to deny them the ability to overpay for it?

He grinned. *This is the life.*

Down below, dozens of his neighbors' cars wormed their way through the streets, pulling back into their garages and parking spots. Hating to take his eyes away from his work, he quickly glanced at his phone, noticing how early it still was. Despite being late summer, his neighborhood should have been a ghost town by this time of the morning, everyone at work, leaving him the peaceful silence to work in the open. Car doors opened and shut, followed by angry mumbles, and front and side doors slammed in anger. Jordan was confused, but didn't feel like looking into it. He had his own work to worry about.

Among the vehicles traversing the street, one he

didn't immediately recognize drove slowly around the bend. The SUV took its time, creeping past every mailbox before finally pulling up next to his. It sat there for few minutes, and Jordan watched on in annoyance. Probably some lost tourist looking for the manatee park. It happened all the time. He was usually happy to help guide them back to the road, but distractions were piling up, and he was rapidly realizing it was not going to be a productive day. He shook his head and returned to his work.

The front doorbell rang below him.

Jordan dropped his head and sighed. Yep, another lost tourist or a salesman. Either way, he wasn't going to be his usual chipper self. He stood up, put on his faded black Lacuna Coil T-shirt, and headed down the wooden stairs to the side bedroom door. He leaned out over the railing, finding the SUV now parked beside his Prius in the driveway. He couldn't see the license plate, so he had no idea where to tell the owner to fuck back off to.

By the time he got back inside, the doorbell was ringing again. "I'm coming, I'm coming! Hold your horses, man." He hopped down the steps two at time, and by the time he reached the ground floor, the bell was calling out again. "This motherfucker."

He clicked the living room light on and pulled open the front door. "Listen, man—"

Jordan's breath caught in his throat.

In a bright halo of light, a woman he had not seen in over a decade stood meekly behind the glass screen door. She smiled at him, making him do the same, immediately obliterating his anger. He gawked at her, completely taken aback.

"M-Melissa? Is that you?"

She shrugged. "It is! Looks like I found the right place."

"Yeah, you did. Holy crap!" He felt stupid as he stood there staring, unsure of what to say. He had not seen her in so many years, and yet this fully grown woman still looked exactly like the girl he knew all those years ago. He shook his head awkwardly, nostalgia smothering him like a blanket. "Oh hell, I'm so sorry. I'm rude. Come in, come in!"

Holding the door open, she stepped inside, and they quickly embraced. She was so much shorter than he remembered. "Man, it's been so long!"

She nodded. "Yeah, a long time. Almost thirteen years now."

"Wow, thirteen years . . . That's so *crazy!*" He continued staring, feeling like an idiot. "Where are my manners? Come on in and make yourself at home."

"Thank you." She carefully stepped into his cluttered living room, which he immediately cringed at. Dozens of paintings, most his own, littered the hardwood floor like a child's playpen. Though most were piled up against the walls, many lay on their backs as they stared up the at popcorn ceiling. Empty food containers were amassed across the coffee table, joined by half-drunk water bottles. Haphazard socks freckled the open spaces of the floor.

Jordan's face flushed in embarrassment. "I'm so sorry about the mess. I don't—" he caught himself before tripping over a painting "—usually have people over. As you can see, I'm a bit of a slob."

Melissa laughed through her nose. "Some things never change, do they?"

CRUEL SUMMER

He scratched the back of his head. "Yeah, I guess they don't. I mean, you certainly haven't. Look at you! You look great! You look older, but—I mean, you don't look old, just older. Shit, I didn't mean to say you look old."

"I know what you mean." She waved it off. "Thank you, I needed to hear that. You look good, too. So much taller than I remember."

"Yeah, I guess I never stopped growing."

"And that hair! When did you grow *that* out?"

He grabbed a handful. "This? A few years back. I don't know, I guess I just wanted to try something different. Mom and Dad never let me grow it out, so I decided to fight the power in my late twenties."

"I like it. I think it suits you."

He nodded, grinning ear to ear. "Well, thank you. At least someone does. They hate it, of course, but they hardly ever come down to see me, so I don't have to hear about it much. By the way, how did you get my address?"

Melissa glanced around the room, eyeballing his various artwork. "I still get Christmas cards from your parents. Your mom and I talk occasionally, and since I always meant to send you my own holiday card, I got your address from her."

"I don't think I ever got one from you."

"I said I *meant* to send you one. Never said I did."

He smiled so hard it hurt. "Well, either way I'm so happy you're here. Wow, Melissa . . . "

"Braun," she said. "Still Braun."

His heart fluttered a bit. "Melissa Braun is in my house. Man, I never thought I would see my first girlfriend ever again. Such a blast from the past. We were just kids the last time I saw you."

"I wouldn't say kids exactly. We were both adults by then."

"Come on," he laughed. "Eighteen is still kids. I didn't even own a home then. Hell, I still don't, but at least I have my own place now. Can I get you something to drink? A beer? Soda? Water?"

"Water would be great, thanks."

"Absolutely! Just make yourself at home, and I'll get you a bottle." He quickly picked up the few canvases lying on the couch and added them to the nearest pile against the wall. As she sat on the sofa, he hopped into the equally cluttered kitchen. Grabbing a water bottle from the fridge, he leaned in, letting the cool air wash over his prickled skin. *You need to calm down, man*, he scolded himself. He was acting like an animated teenager, and he felt every bit of eighteen all over again. His heart raced, as did his mind. Having to always play the part of a stuffy artist, it felt good to feel like a kid again, if even for a little bit.

"So what brings you to my neck of the woods, Ms. Braun?" he asked, walking back into the living room. He handed her the water, which she uncapped and took two hefty swallows from.

"First off," she teased, "you can knock off the Ms. Braun crap. I hated that back then, and it's still not pleasing now."

He held his hands up. "Sorry. Old habits die hard. But seriously, what are you doing here? On vacation, I take it?"

She nodded slowly. "Yep. Another vacation in the ol' 386."

"Who are you down here with?"

Melissa paused, looking away. "Um, just . . . just my parents. You know, the same old annual trip. Nothing special."

"*Annual?* You mean to tell me you come down here every year and this is the first time you've thought to visit?"

She shrugged. "Sorry. I thought it might be awkward. I didn't want to drop in if you had some girl over or something."

"Ha! Unfortunately, I didn't quite remain the playboy you once knew."

She raised an eyebrow. "You? A playboy? That's not exactly how I remembered you."

Jordan shrugged. "And how exactly do you remember me?"

"Well, for one, I remember a plethora of acne. It was like a minefield across your cheeks."

"Hey!"

"Tell me I'm wrong."

He sighed, crossing his arms. "Go on."

"And I remember all the Star Wars T-shirts. I swear you had enough to last a whole month."

"Still do. What of it?"

"Also, the comic books. *So* many comic books."

"Hey." He pointed. "Those comic books have gotten me to a lot of places in my life. Without them, I would have never wanted to become an artist, and I would have never made literal tens of dollars. Face it, you're talking to a very wealthy man here, Melissa."

They both laughed.

She added, "Once a nerd, always a nerd."

"And yet you dated me. What does that say about you?"

"I never said I didn't like Star Wars."

"Oh, yeah? Then who shot first?"

She pulled a face. "Han, of course. Duh."

He grinned. "Good answer. Very good answer. How are you still single?"

Shifting uncomfortably, Melissa patted her bare legs. "I don't know. Just never found the right sci-fi nerd to stay with, I guess."

"You are single, right?"

She nodded her head quickly. "Yep. Very, very single."

"I don't know how. Any guy would be lucky to be with you. Shit—sorry. That was rude of me to say."

"It's fine. I appreciate you saying it. I needed that. Really. I, uh . . . what about you? How have you not gotten hitched to some beach bunny?"

Realizing he was still standing, Jordan sat on the armrest of the recliner. "That's a damn good question. I don't know. I guess my excuse could be I've been too busy."

She glanced around the room, eyeing his work. "I can see that." She picked up a small, 8X10 canvas from the floor and studied the ocean scene. "Your stuff is amazing, Jordan. It always was. I still can't believe you made it."

"Made it?" he asked.

"Yeah. You know, became an artist. It's all you ever wanted. Hell, it's all you ever talked about when we were together, well, that and Jack Kirby. You were so talented back then." She picked up another one. The painting was of a cluster of blue crabs, huddled together on a sand dune. She quickly placed the painting back on the floor. "You still are."

"Thank you. I really appreciate that."

"Do you do this for a living?"

He nodded, recalling all the times he'd been asked that very question. "Somehow, yes. I'm not exactly rolling in the money from these seascapes, but I do alright. I make enough to get by, with a little extra."

"Do you sell these online?"

"I probably could, but no. A woman named Sharon Lutz owns the local art gallery down off of Flagler, I'm sure you've seen it. Since I keep a steady stream of paintings coming her way, she gave me my own corner at the shop where I get to display my work. It's open all year round, so tourists are always coming and going, looking for something to remember their trip by that's not neon or from the beach store. You'd be surprised what people are willing to spend on this stuff."

She frowned. "You sound like you don't like it."

"No, no." He waved. "I like it alright. Like I said it pays enough to keep gas in the tank and food in the fridge."

"And on the floor and the coffee table," she said with a grin.

Jordan shrugged. "It's the maid's day off."

"What about this place? All this gas and food talk and I haven't heard about the electric or the mortgage."

"That's the beauty of it, my dear. All paid for. After college, I moved down here and found the woman who owned this place was sub-letting the attic. It was cheap, and it gave me the opportunity to save some cash while I was getting myself established. Plus, that rooftop view is something else. You can see most of the way up A1A, and the beach is just across the street. I'll have to take you up and show you. It's pretty stellar."

She smiled sadly and nodded.

"Anyway," he continued, "After a few years, Loraine, the woman who I rented from, passed away. She was quite old. She had moved down here from Missouri after her husband died of a heart attack back in the late nineties. I thought for sure I was going to be homeless—hell, I wasn't going to find a place down here this cheap again, not on my own—but she had a son who took over the house when it was left to him in the will. He was a pretty nice dude, came down to visit from time to time. Well, he didn't want to deal with it, so we cut a deal. The house was long paid off. I could stay for as long as I wanted, all I had to do was keep up on maintenance pay just a little more than what I had been, to cover property taxes. He would take care of the electric, gas, etcetera."

"Sounds like a pretty sweet deal, Jordan."

"Indeed it is."

"And you get to live in the hometown of your hero."

He snickered. "Remember all those weekends we stayed up watching *The Joy of Painting* on PBS?"

"I do, but I also remember trying to do *other* things than watch an old man with an afro paint cottages."

Face flushing red, Jordan smiled at the floor. "Yeah, I remember that, too."

There was a few moments of thick silence between them before Melissa cut it. "Sounds like you're living quite the life, Jordan. You're doing everything you ever wanted. I'm so proud of you." She bit her lip, sighing.

"You okay?"

She nodded, maybe a bit too enthusiastically. "Yeah, yeah, I'm fine. I'm just happy for you, Jordan. So . . . happy."

He stood up, eyeing her. "Melissa, are you sure you're okay? You seem . . . I don't know . . . sad? Upset?"

She continued to bob her head, starting intensely at the dirty floor. Whatever was on her mind, she had to work it out on her own, so he stood over her in awkward silence, not sure what to do. A battle raged behind her eyes, and for a moment Jordan swore she was about to cry.

After several long moments clicked by, Melissa lifted herself from the couch, but then halfway up shook her head and dropped back down. Her eyes glassy and red. She sniffled.

Jordan ripped a tissue from the box on the side table and handed it to her. She nodded her appreciation. "Melissa, what's wrong? If I said anything to upset you—"

"No, no," she spoke into the tissue. "It's not you. I mean, it *is* you, but it's not what you think."

"I don't follow."

Melissa sighed long and hard, shaking her head as if readying herself. "Jordan, I think you need to sit down. We need to talk."

Several long, uncomfortable minutes ticked by in silence, the only noise being Jordan's deep, agitated breaths, as his chest steadily rose and fell. Hands gripping the sides of his head, his eyes never left the floor, and for all Melissa knew he hadn't blinked since she started her story.

I never should have come here, she thought. *This was a massive mistake.* She never should have said a word. Telling him about Patrick, about a son he never knew he had, was like dropping an atomic bomb he never saw coming. The further along in the story she got, the more his cheerful smile dwindled, and before long the brightness that seemed to glow from her presence faded all together. He didn't question her, didn't even speak a single word, as she told him about their child. *I should have just left. Kept him blissfully unaware. Christ Almighty, I think I just ruined the poor guy's life.*

Unable to take the silence, she finally spoke up. "Jordan? Jordan, are you okay?"

He didn't speak, only slowly blinked, as if that were answer enough.

"Jordan?" she repeated, heart racing. "Please . . . say something. Anything. I can't stand not knowing what you're thinking."

Dropping his hands to his lap, Jordan shifted his eyes to her without moving his head. Tears welled in his eyes. "Is . . . Is it true? Everything you said . . . is it true?"

She nodded, tears breaking the dam. "Yes."

"I have . . . we have . . . a son?"

"Yes. He's twelve. And he's beautiful."

He shook his head. "How is this possible?"

"Well, when a boy and a girl love each other very much—"

Jordan stood and angrily waved her away. "No,

damn it, I mean how is this possible? We were always so safe! I always wore a condom!"

She pulled a face. "I mean, not *always*. Especially not toward the end of the relationship."

"Oh, for fuck's sake." Shaking, he paced behind the recliner chair, hands repeatedly running through his long hair as if the answer was hidden in his scalp. "Are you sure it's mine?"

"First off," she snipped, "*He* is not an *it*. *He* is a *he*. And yes, he's yours. You were the only guy I was ever with in high school."

"Are you sure? I mean, who knows? There could have been others after me, or before me—I don't know."

Anger swelled like a busted lip. "There *were* no others, damn it! It was just you. It was only you. Hell . . . my stupid high school heart thought we were going to get married after we graduated. I wanted you to be my one and only."

He blurted out a dry laugh. "Well, lucky me, huh? Your one and only somehow managed to knock you up."

"Jordan, you need to calm down. Please sit and talk to me."

"What is there to talk about, Melissa?" He stopped pacing and leaned over the chair, glaring. "I mean, you show up out of the blue after a decade of no contact, not even a phone call or a text, to tell me about a kid we had when we were eighteen? What were you thinking?"

"I was thinking you deserved to know about our son, Jordan, that's what I was thinking. Please sit down so we can talk."

"But why now? Why not, I don't know . . . tell me thirteen fucking years ago! Why did you not call me?"

"Don't you think I wanted to call?" she cried. "I wanted to call you and tell you every single day since I saw that little plus sign appear on the pregnancy test, but I couldn't."

Jordan threw his jittering hands in the air. "And why the hell not?"

"Because I wanted you to have a life! You have to understand something, Jordan, I didn't find out I was pregnant until the day before you got that letter from Pratt. Do you remember that day? After all these years, I still remember it pretty damn well—how could I not? You were so damn excited by that acceptance, so over the moon, you nearly exploded. Your family, Jesus, they acted like you had just won the lottery. And why wouldn't they? I mean, you had a full ride to one of the top art schools in the country. It was a once in a lifetime chance to get out of town and do something with your life. You have no goddamn idea how badly I wanted to tell you. It absolutely tore me apart. Remember how I spent the next week out of school and we didn't see each other? I told you I was sick, but I shut down, Jordan. I couldn't even physically get out of bed I was so sick with guilt. I lost track of how many times I had to stop my parents from calling you and spilling the beans. My father? Hell, he wanted to march right across town on foot and kill you with his bare hands. But I wouldn't let them. Even if they didn't see it, you were a good guy, and I wasn't going to take away your future like that. I just didn't have the heart. Unlike you, I wasn't going to move to New York. I didn't have the talent or the drive you did."

"That's not fair." He shook his head. "That's not for *you* to decide. What, did you think I wouldn't have helped take care of our child or something? You know I would have. I'm not some shmuck that would abandon a pregnant woman."

Hands over her eyes, she continued to cry. "I know, and that's exactly why I didn't want to tell you. Even back then you would have made a great father. But I didn't want to take you away from the life that was waiting for you."

"That not fair, Melissa. That's not fair at all."

"*I know it's not fucking fair! I know that!* Don't you think the guilt has been eating me up inside for the last decade plus? Don't you think every time I look at Patrick, it isn't a reminder of my failure to include you in raising our child?"

"Patrick?"

She lifted her blurry gaze to his. "Yes. Patrick Evan."

Jordan sighed and dropped his forehead on the back of the chair. "Patrick Evan. I can't believe you named him after our dads."

Melissa wiped her eyes and shrugged. "Seemed like the right thing to do at the time." Mouth dry and stomach roiling, she did everything she could not to throw up. This was going so much worse than she had planned. But how did she really expect this to go? He wasn't going to accept this new truth with a smile and open arms. Maybe she hoped deep down he would be happy at the news, or at the very least curious. All those years of hiding it from him, the long nights lying awake, the guilt, the remorse and shame, was like a ten ton boulder finally snapping from its string to crush her. It was all too much, and it was all her fault. She let it get this way. And with Hoyt's sudden reemergence from the dead, she had no idea where to go next. She was looking for friends in all the wrong places, and right then, when she should have been comforted, she never felt more alone.

A few beats passed before Jordan walked back around the chair and sat down with an exaggerated sigh. "How did you keep this hidden for so long? You had to have seen my parents at some point, right? Aren't they still friends with yours?"

"They were up until the birth. I begged my parents to not tell them. I didn't want you to know. It was so hard, and though I don't think they ever really understood, they kind of cut ties with your folks. Better to keep them away so they couldn't find out they had a grandchild. I know Mom was really crushed to lose a friend like that."

He rolled his eyes. "Believe me, that wouldn't have been the worst thing. They've been bugging me for years to settle down and have kids. I guess now they don't have to wonder anymore. Here." He tossed the small box of tissues toward her, which she caught and extracted a sheet to wipe her eyes.

"Thanks."

"So why now, Melissa? Why come down here now? Is it money? Do you need child support?"

She quickly shook her head. "No, no, no. It's not like that, I swear."

"Then what's it like?"

"Things . . . haven't been too great lately. Things just keep piling up, and I needed a friendly face to talk to. Honestly, I wasn't expecting to say anything about it at all. I . . . I desperately needed to be around someone I could trust and who wouldn't hit me when I needed to unload."

"*Hit* you?"

She waved it off. "Nothing. Look, I guess the time was right. I'm not looking to take anything from you. I don't want your money or anything like that. I only want a little of your time."

Jordan stared at her, swallowing. "Your parents aren't down here, are they?"

She shook her head. "Nope. Just Patrick and I."

"Shit." With a groan, he dropped backwards in the chair, sinking as low as he could go into the cushion.

"He's a good kid, Jordan, he really is. He's smart, funny, handsome. I didn't realize how much he looks like you until right now. Same eyes and mouth. Definitely the same temperament."

He refused to meet her gaze, instead letting his eyes glaze over.

"I think you should meet him."

Blinking rapidly, he shook his head. "I don't know, Mel . . ."

Hoping to break through, Melissa shifted herself down to the other end of the couch until she was nearly touching him. "Come on, I think it's time. Other than Dad, he's never had a real man to look up to, only shitheads who I've come to regret in the recent past." She scooted closer. "Look, I'm not asking you to be a full-time dad. I'm only asking that you be in his life when he wants to talk. He needs someone like you to be there for him when I can't. Can you start with simply meeting him? I swear we won't reveal who you are. We'll start with a simple meeting, just as an old friend of mine—that's who he thinks I'm with right now. Absolutely no telling him who you are. I can't do that to him right now."

He turned to face her. "I don't know."

"Please, Jordan. I haven't asked for anything from you up until this point, and that's okay. But right now I need this *one* thing from you. Can you please do this? If not for me, then for him?"

He sniffed and wiped his eyes. "You're going to have to give me some time. I just don't think I can right now. Maybe soon, but not right now."

She sat back on the couch. "Time is something I don't have right now, Jordan."

"I'm sorry, Mel. It's the best I can do."

Melissa nodded, knowing this was now a complete failure. She stood and gathered her beach bag, then pulled a loose paper from her wallet. She wrote down her cell number and handed it to him. "Listen, we're still going to be in town for a few more days, or at least until the bridges are fixed and working again. If you change your mind, text me—I can't get any calls through right now. We're just down the road. If not, then at least you have my number now."

Jordan took the paper and answered her with a simple nod.

She started to speak again, but decided to leave it at that. Wiping her eyes once more, she stuffed the used tissue into her pocket and without another word, she left out the front door. She put her sunglasses back on and hopped into the SUV, pulling out and away from Jordan's house with haste.

She wanted to cry again, realizing how stupid she was thinking she could make everything right in the world with a run-in with her past. Sweating, she felt drained of emotion, ready to get back to the room and lock herself away from the world that continued to drop boulders.

Her cell dinged inside her bag. She pulled over onto the shoulder and quickly pulled it out. She squinted at the broken screen.

A text message from an unknown number: **Lunch tomorrow**

A moment later: **the three of us**

This time the tears were joyous.

14

IT WAS AFTER 10 PM, and unlike the long-dead sunlight, Patrick's unease had yet to dissipate. No matter how hard he tried he couldn't find sleep. His mind continued to race, heart thumping hard enough to keep his eyes peeled wide open. He rearranged his Magic cards, thumbed through his new Jeff Strand novel, and crushed candy on his phone, but his brain refused to shut down for the night.

He couldn't stop thinking about his mother. Her irrational behavior kept him uneasy for most of the morning, and even though she came back in a much better mood after dropping him back off at the condo, it didn't make him feel any better. He had asked her where she had gone for so long, but her answer of "seeing an old friend" for some reason didn't sit right with him. What old friend? Why was this the first time he was hearing about this person, whoever they were. Not that he really wanted to, but why couldn't he go along? And what about that police woman? Seeing her again so soon after the boat incident made every bad feeling about what they had done resurface like a hideous, white-headed boil. Images flashed in his mind's eye, things that continued to creep back in. And the guilt. So much guilt.

CRUEL SUMMER

When it was apparent he wasn't going to be sleeping tonight, he snuck into the kitchen by the light of his phone and took a bottle of water from the fridge and the half-empty bag of potato chips off the counter. Before returning to his room, he tiptoed into the short hallway by the master bedroom and pressed his ear against the closed door. Soft, muted snores drifted out from the other side. *Good*, he thought. *She needs the sleep.* Somehow she was even more wound up than him. Maybe a good night sleep would help her relax, and they could both try to have a good day tomorrow, despite not being able to leave town. *Disney would have actually been pretty cool . . .*

He returned to his own bedroom and found his streaming stick buried in his luggage. He plugged it into his small TV, then turned on a random episode of *The Office* and snuggled up under the sheets.

After several minutes of familiar humor, Patrick finally began to relax. He still wasn't quite tired enough to sleep, but the bees buzzing in his stomach had one by one gone back up into the hive. Though not always understanding every joke, he smiled, keeping his giggles down to a hush.

Click. The TV went black.

Patrick was startled by the sudden darkness. He pressed the ON button on the remote, but the screen remained off. Activating his cell phone light, he got out of bed and reached around the TV to check the connection on his streaming stick. He pulled it out from the USB and plugged it back in, but the set remained inactive. He angrily jabbed the buttons on the side of the box and received more of the same. Frustrated, he unplugged the stick from the TV and stepped out into the living room to try it on the bigger screen.

"*Help . . .*"

A chill dripped down Patrick's spine as he froze in place. He held his breath. Several long seconds ticked by. Other than the light whistle of the ocean breeze, whatever he had heard didn't repeat. He went to flip on the living room lights but remembered the strict rule against lights after dark. They applied to every condo, to help from scaring the sea turtles away from their nesting in the beach. He waited a few more heartbeats, then shook his head and sat his drink and snacks on the coffee table. He began to crawl around the back of the wooden TV stand when he heard it again.

"*Help . . .*"

Knowing this time he didn't imagine it, he sat his streaming stick on the top of the TV and walked up to the sliding glass doors. Pushing the plastic blinds aside, he cupped his hands around the cool glass and peered out.

"*Heeeelllllpppp . . .*"

The voice was so faint, yet close, like it was right on the other side of the glass. His reflection stared back at him. Unlocking the latch, he pushed the blinds aside and carefully slid the glass door open and stepped outside.

The cool, salty breeze ruffled his shaggy hair as he stepped onto the balcony. In the dark beyond, the ocean murmured evening song, growling against the sodden sand it kissed. A thumbnail clipping of the moon glittered over the black water, and it came and went with the rip tide of clouds surrounding it.

CRUEL SUMMER

Stepping around the deck table and chairs, Patrick walked up to the thin metal railing and peered over.

Three stories below, a nude body was face-down in the sand. Patrick was fairly certain it was a man, but he couldn't be sure. Had the moonlight not been out that very moment, their pale, sickly skin would have disappeared in the dark. Patrick's heart thumped in his chest, his mouth immediately drying out. He leaned forward to get a better look, trying to see if their back rose and fell with breaths. They appeared to be unmoving. His hands shaking, Patrick backed away and reached for the cell phone in his shorts pockets.

"*Heeeeeeeellllllpppp meeeee . . .*"

Patrick stepped back up to the railing. "He . . . hello?"

The body had not moved, but Patrick was convinced the repeated calls for help were definitely coming from it. The moon disappeared, and for a moment so did the body. Patrick squinted, trying hard to keep an eye on the person below. When the moon came back, the prone body had moved, its right arm lifting up in the air.

Patrick gasped. "Sir, do you need help?"

The man's arm stiffened, then dropped limply on the sand. "*Help meeeeeee . . .*"

Staring at the man below, Patrick ran through all of his options. He could wake up his mother, but for some reason he didn't think that was such a good idea. After the way she was acting today, he was quite positive she hadn't slept much the night before. His cell gripped in his palm, he knew he should call the police, but the thought of that police woman being around him again so soon made his stomach turn. Maybe . . . maybe he could go help? It felt stupid to think he wasn't strong enough to do something about this, and though the whole thing made him uneasy, he knew deep down it was the right thing to do. The guy was probably drunk as a skunk and needed help back to his car to sleep it off. At worst, he could go down and flip the guy over so he wasn't eating sand all night. Patrick took a deep breath and nodded to himself. He thought, *Don't be a . . . you know what. Prove that dead jerk wrong and be a man for once. No one will have to know but you.* Determined, Patrick smiled and stepped back inside.

Slipping into his flip-flops, he took a set of keys off the counter and crept into the hall by his mother's closed bedroom door. When he was assured she was still sleeping, he exited the condo room and locked the top and bottom latches in the door behind him. The open outside hall was quiet, and he carefully opened and shut the creaky stairwell door to keep the noise to a minimum. By the time he reached the pool area, his nerves were gone, and he began to actually feel good about his decision. Whether or not anything could be done, Patrick knew this was the right thing to do, and in order to prove to himself he could do things that scared him, this was that first big step to adulthood.

Past the empty lounge chairs and across the shuffleboard courts, Patrick opened the back gate with the four digit passcode on the electronic lock and carefully took the sandy steps one at a time. When he reached the bottom, he looked up to where their balcony was, and then searched for the approximate area the man was lying. The moon had hidden itself once again, forcing Patrick to activate his cell phone flashlight. He walked over to where the man was supposed to be and swept his light across the sand.

The man was gone.

Confused, Patrick called out, "Hello?" Realizing the crashing waves were much louder down here, he yelled, "Uh, Mister, are you still there? Do you need any help?"

He continued to search by the light of his phone. Not only was the man gone, so was any indication he was even there to begin with. Patrick sighed, suddenly feeling very stupid and frustrated. *This was a bad idea.* After being scolded earlier by his mother to not leave the room under *any* circumstances, he was starting to realize she may have been right. Not only did he feel dumb for coming out here, he now felt very, very alone.

Somewhere close he heard digging.

Patrick paused and listened hard. There came the *swick* crumbling sound of sand being tossed through the air, and an intermittent grunting before it hit the ground. Spinning around, Patrick swung his cell phone's light across the barren beach. He slowly moved the LED light over the concrete retaining wall by the edge of the condo. Its wide beam moved across the yellowed beach grass sprouting from the sand dunes, and the few items of loose trash left behind by visitors. A small crab skittered away from the light.

Red flashed in the darkness.

Startled, Patrick leapt back in surprise. Then he felt very stupid. The ocean wind blew, and with it the plastic red ribbon from the turtle egg nest, flapping in the breeze. But it shouldn't have been loose. He moved the light's beam a little further to the left and found the ribbon had been ripped off the opposite wooden stake. Sand flew from inside the roped-off square. Holding his breath, Patrick walked toward the nest. The closer he got, the more his flashlight revealed.

Near the middle of the nest, the naked man was down on his knees. Leaning forward, his back toward Patrick, his hands moved furiously as they dug deep into the ground, tossing the hard-packed sand out behind him like a dog. By the time Patrick reached the outside of the square, the man had stopped and his grunts had turned into satisfied moans. Patrick felt squeamish as he could see the man's shriveled genitals dangling beneath him, but it wasn't the only reason for his apprehension. Though he was positive it was the man from earlier, something appeared very off. In the flashlight's glow, the man's skin was a grayish blue hue, and a slight triangular hump protruded awkwardly just above his shoulder blades. Muscles rippled beneath his flesh, even across his neck and the back of his bald head.

Still shaking, Patrick couldn't stop himself from asking, "Mister . . . is everything . . . alright?"

The man stopped moving and slowly lifted his head.

Patrick swallowed. "D-do you need he—" The words caught in his throat.

Black eyes shimmered like fist-sized marbles as the man turned to greet him. Long, thin slits behind his ear jittered with his deep, harsh breaths. In his gray hands were several white, oblong eggs. Pale, yellow yolk oozed through the dozens of rows of serrated teeth inside his wide mouth. His pointed face curled into a broad grin—a grin Patrick would have recognized from anywhere, no matter what form it took.

"*Hey there, PB,*" Hoyt growled. "*Miss me?*" He squeezed the rest of the eggs in his fist with a slimy *pop*.

Screaming, Patrick fell back on his ass, his cell phone flipping out of his grasp. The beach plunged into darkness. His heart hammering, Patrick scrambled to his feet and ran. He dashed across the sand, guided only by the moonlight, and hopped up the wooden steps two at a time to the pool deck. He leapt over the gate, and within a few breaths was already across the patio and skidding into the downstairs hallway. Flinging the stairwell door open, he raced up the steps, his whimpers echoing off the concrete walls.

This isn't happening this isn't happening this isn't happening!

And yet it was. Even as he burst through the third floor door, he could still see it, could still smell the inside of those turtle eggs like they were rubbed all over his face. He wasn't fully sure what he had just seen down on the beach, but he was fairly certain whatever it was should have been dead.

That couldn't have been Hoyt—it just couldn't! Maybe this was all a dream, and he had fallen asleep hours ago like he had wanted. Even as he reached the condo room door and gripped the handle, it didn't seem real. He frantically twisted the doorknob and it brought him back to his harsh reality. In his panic, he forgot he had locked the door behind him. For a moment he stopped struggling. He held his breath and listened.

The breeze tickled his head, chilling his sweat-stained brow. The ocean spoke in the darkness. A car drove past on the street below. Was it possible he really had imagined it? If he did, he hated he had dropped his phone. Mom was going to kill him . . . but the thought of traipsing around in the dark made his skin crawl even more. It would have to wait until morning.

As he started to calm down, a gush of water splashed across the hallway floor. Patrick spun around as it ran from the side hallway and splashed over the railing to the parking lot below. Something tall stepped around the corner to face him.

"Why are you running, Pussy Boy?"

Patrick whimpered as he frantically searched for his keys.

"Pussy Boy . . . "

When he located them, he combed for the right one of the three and then jabbed it into the handle lock.

Water rushed down the hallway in a wave.

He twisted the knob and put his shoulder into the door. It wouldn't budge.

"No!" he squealed.

He looked up. The deadbolt above stared back at him. He ripped the keys out of the knob and jabbed the first one at the hole.

Another splash, and dark water rushed over his feet. He yelped and dropped the keys. Patrick fell to his knees, terrified he might lose them in the surge.

CRUEL SUMMER

Hoyt's dark, hulking form crept closer.

Patrick swept his hands through the two inch deep water, and though its splashing over the edge of the hallway onto the cars below was a deafening roar, his hammering heart was so much louder. He spun on his knees, keeping an eye on the man sauntering toward him, and continued to feel around. The plastic keychain brushed against his fingers. He went to grab them, but they slipped from his grasp. Not wanting them to slip over the edge, Patrick dove, catching them with a firm grip. In a flash, he got to his feet and threw himself against the door with a huff.

"Little pussy boys shouldn't go out all alone at night . . ."

"Come on, come on!"

When the key finally slipped into the lock, Patrick shoved the door open and threw himself into the air conditioned kitchen. He turned back and ran for the door, throwing it shut and re-locking both locks. Shivering, he dropped to his knees and wept. He wanted it all to go away: Hoyt, the hurt, the regret. He thought he was free from ever having to be called that horrible name again, but it came back, along with the son of a bitch who called him that. Only Hoyt was different—something else entirely.

Head against the front door, Patrick cried, "Mom!"

Water rushed in from underneath the frame.

"*Mom!*" He leapt up, stumbling over his own feet. "*Mom, wake up!*" As the dark fluid continued to pour across the tiled kitchen floor, he scrambled to the side hallway and banged on his mother's door. "*Mom! Mom! He's here!*" He twisted the knob, but the door was locked. "*Mom! Let me in! Mom!*"

His feet were now slipping in puddles of water. When it was obvious she wasn't going to answer, Patrick leapt out of the hallway and through the living room, into his bedroom. He slammed the door shut and locked it behind him. Out of breath, he backed away and listened hard for any sound. For a long while, he huffed through his nose, his eyes never leaving the sliver of space beneath his door. The condo was once again quiet, and for a fleeting moment he wondered if the thing that was once Hoyt had even made it inside at all. He never heard the front door open. He never heard the footsteps of his bully.

I never should have went outside . . . it serves me right . . .

Before he could chastise himself further, more water gushed from beneath the bedroom door. Patrick whimpered miserably and made a beeline for the attached bathroom. He threw himself in and, even though he knew it was moot, he locked the door. Flicking the light on, he searched for anything to protect himself with. The sink was littered with toiletries, but other than a few combs, Q-tips, and his large bottle of hairspray, there was nothing useful to defend himself with. He snatched his toothbrush off the counter and crawled into the tub.

The water never reached the bathroom door gap, but the darkness beyond thickened.

The doorknob jiggled. It turned.

Patrick crouched low inside the tub. "Please," he moaned, "leave me alone."

The doorknob stopped moving.

A sob hitched in his throat.

CRUEL SUMMER

Silence.

A voice whispered, "*Why should I?*"

A thunderous *crack* echoed in the tiny room as someone slammed into the other side of the door. Patrick screamed for his mother—screamed for anyone to hear—but his cries were overpowered by the resonance of heavy fists. The door split down the middle like a lightning bolt. Two sickly gray hands slid in through the hole and in a blink they ripped the door in two.

Hoyt's smooth, slimy form filled the entrance like a door of his own. Bathed in fluorescent light, Patrick could now see the extent of his revived *conversion*. Hoyt's glazed, obsidian eyes were not focused on him, they instead had drifted to the side of his now pointed face. All manner of flattened, needled, and triangular teeth lined the inside of his wide grin, a mouth which now stretched cheek-to-cheek. He stepped into the bathroom. The overwhelming stink of brine immediately filled the tiny space.

DAREMETO gripped the doorframe.

"*Little Pussy Boy . . . hiding . . . cowering . . .*" Hoyt stepped in further. "*So weak. Face me like a man, you little shit!*"

Patrick wept and pressed himself deeper into the porcelain tub. Warm urine soaked his shorts.

The ceiling light disappeared as Hoyt stepped over him. "*Do you know what it's like? Drowning? Choking? Dying all by your lonesome?*"

"Please!" Patrick wept, holding his arms over his head. "Don't hurt me."

Hoyt leaned closer. "It's a little like this—"

He opened his tooth-filled mouth wide, and a

torrent of black, foamy water burst out. The warm liquid splashed over Patrick's head, immediately drenching him, and with it came various fish and sea life. Their slimy bodies tumbled over him and fell into the tub with wet, frantic slaps. They flopped and wriggled as they struggled for air. Dropping the toothbrush, Patrick screamed as the water continued to spray at a steady pace, soaking him to the bone. Something long and heavy fell on his neck. Then another. And another. When their weight became too much, he hefted them off his body and tossed them across the tub. The water abruptly went away, and was replaced by wet gurgles of vindictive laughter. Patrick swept the dripping hair from his eyes, then screamed.

Within the mess of struggling fish, three black speckled eels were slithering toward him. Their snarling barbed mouths snapped at his bare legs. Patrick quickly pulled his feet up against his chest and retreated until his back struck the water spout. He continued to shriek as they crept closer. He reached back and grabbed his bottle of shampoo. Holding it with both hands, he swung the half-full bottle and struck the closest eel. The creature threw its head back and hissed. Patrick swung again, striking it a second time, his blow throwing it back to the other end of the tub.

As he continued to swing at the other two, Hoyt's cackling continued. *"What's it like to feel helpless, Pussy Boy? That no matter where you turn there's no escape?"*

Patrick answered with more tears. He squealed and tried to stand, only to slip on the wriggling fish beneath him. The battered eel, bleeding from its beady eyes, stayed back, but the other two slithered on, hissing at his missed attempts at striking them. Patrick swung once more, and as his arm came back around, one of the eels lashed out, smacking its narrow head against his hand. The bottle went sailing to the back of the bathtub, and before Patrick could react, the second eel struck, sinking its needle teeth into his calf. Patrick screamed and shook his leg, and the eel quickly let go, taking a small sliver of skin with it.

This made Hoyt laugh harder. "*Cetus is pleased! He—*"

Before he could finish, someone other than Patrick screamed. Hoyt nearly fell forward into the tub as two arms circled his thick gray neck.

"*Leave him alone!*" Patrick's mother shrieked.

Terrified, Patrick backed himself into the corner of the tub and stepped up onto the outer rim, keeping a close eye on the two eels glaring him down.

Hoyt gagged and threw his head back, his jagged teeth snapping at her bare arms. Patrick's mother screamed with more rage than fear and yanked Hoyt backwards. Though he was much larger than her, his massive gray body stumbled backwards, slipping on the puddle beneath him. His roar was deafening, rattling Patrick's already racing heartbeat. He split his attention between the tub creatures and the monster his mother was wrestling. He couldn't believe what she was doing. Dread washed over him as he watched her struggle, with not an ounce of trepidation on her face. Teeth gritted and one arm tight around his throat, she continued to beat on Hoyt's pointed head with her free fist, scratching and clawing. Hoyt threw himself backwards and slammed her against the door frame. She grunted but never let go, instead raking her nails over his blackened eyes.

While Patrick observed, the eels drew closer.

Hoyt roared once more. He reached back and seized a fistful of her long brown hair, threatening to pull her over his shoulder. Holding tight, she dug her hands into his gills and sunk her fingers in deep. Hoyt bellowed a painful cry and whipped his large body around. Patrick's mother swung with him. With a vulgar crash, her elbow hit the mirror and shattered glass across the sink and floor. Hoyt's bare feet crunched over the shards.

In a quick strike, one of the eels lashed out, sinking its teeth into Patrick's foot. He howled and immediately kicked his leg. Much like Patrick's mother, the creature refused to let go, driving its needled teeth in deeper. Pain blossomed and burned, making his teeth chatter in response. He grasped the shower head and lifted his body, then kicked his legs simultaneously. After a few solid jerks, the eel released and flew backwards into the tub, joining the other injured creature. The remaining eel hissed and recoiled. The fish lining the tub slowed in their struggles.

Blood flew across the floor. It dripped from his mother's shredded elbow and joined the glitter of light across the floor. Enraged, Hoyt continued to throw his back against the wall. She continued to hold on, but her adrenaline was beginning to fade. The pain was taking effect, and Patrick could see Hoyt recognized it. As her war cries faded into agony, she dropped awkwardly to her feet. She stumbled back and fell against the sink. Hoyt spun to face her.

He growled, "*You stupid bitch!*" and held the bleeding slits on his neck.

Patrick yelled, "Mom! Run!"

Exhausted and out of options, she quickly snatched a can of hairspray from the floor and lifted it over her head. She curled her lips back to scream, but her cry was cut short as Hoyt landed a swift punch into her gut. Wide-eyed, she doubled over and gasped for air. Patrick screamed for her, all while kicking at the advancing eel, as Hoyt seized her throat and lifted her like she was nothing.

"*Worthless!*" Hoyt snapped as he tossed Patrick's mother through the open doorway into the bedroom. Her body hit the floor beyond with a heavy thud. Hate brewing in his filmy black eyes, Hoyt whipped back around to face Patrick. "*You're both so . . . fucking . . . worthless! Can't you see? To him, you're nothing. You're so insignificant, so inconsequential to his plans, destroying you isn't even a blip on his radar. Ants under a giant's foot. Dust among the gods.*"

Patrick whimpered as Hoyt reached into the bathtub past him and grasped the remaining eel around the throat. He lifted the writhing creature, eyeing it as it cautiously eyed him back. "*No,*" Hoyt continued, "*you have no use to Cetus.*" In a quick motion, he opened his wide mouth and shoved the eel inside. He bit down, and a second later he jerked his head, wrenching the eel's body from between his teeth. Hoyt swallowed the creature's head as its decapitated body coiled like a severed worm. He stepped toward Patrick. "*But to me, Patrick . . . to me you both mean everything."* Patrick curled into himself as Hoyt lifted the eel's carcass and let its warm blood dribble onto his head. When that wasn't enough, Hoyt grabbed the eel's tail and, like a tube of toothpaste, gripped the bottom and squeezed its insides out. Bones and viscera spilled over Patrick's shoulders. He wretched, emptying his stomach among the fish that no longer struggled for air.

In a whisper, Hoyt sneered, *"You know, Pussy Boy? I don't think you realize how bad the two of you fucked up. You may have ended your own nightmare, but you unleashed another. Cetus is an ageless hell, and now, because of you, countless millions will suffer. Those stupid enough to cross a god will earn their pain, and those who give their body to him will help deliver it. You gave me to him. You stupid assholes just ended the world and you don't even know it.*

"And for that we must thank you."

Suddenly he cocked his head, confusion plastering his gray face. His black eyes darted around, his head on a swivel. *"No . . . no, you promised!"* He stood up and took a step back, listening to something only he could hear. *"Only them! They're all I want, you can have the rest! I don't care! They're not yours—they're mine!"* A pause. *"Why do you keep calling her that? I don't understand!"* Breathing through his teeth, he eyed Patrick. *"Fine. Take her. I only want him. I deserve him."* He stepped toward the tub, his scowl growing like ruptured earth. *"And he deserves me."*

Gore-soaked and out of options, Patrick cowered in the corner of the tub and cried. He held his trembling arms over his head, curling into himself, as if that would actually do anything. He was too young to die, and though he had no concept of spirituality or religion, he prayed to whoever would hear his words to save him.

The room instantly grew hot. The black behind his clenched eyelids flourished yellow. A moment later Hoyt began to scream.

Patrick opened his eyes as his mother stomped back into the bathroom, her own screams adding to the monster's. In her outstretched hand she gripped the large can of hairspray. Underneath, she held the long neck lighter from his room. Fire bloomed from the nozzle as she sprayed the liquid heat directly into Hoyt's face. Hoyt shrieked in pain as the rubbery gray skin of his face and chest instantly charred black. He reached out to swipe at her, but she jabbed the can closer, scorching his hands and adding more blaze to his vulnerable face. With nowhere to go, he stumbled backwards, and a moment later his legs hit the rim of the tub. Patrick cried out as Hoyt nearly tumbled backwards on top of him. Patrick sidestepped and leapt onto the edge of the tub.

Keeping the fire going, his mother yelled, "Patrick, run! Now!"

Heeding her words, he took his opportunity and scrambled out of the tub. He ran past his mother, and into the dark bedroom, but he stopped himself from going any further. Tears dripping down his cheeks, he turned back toward the bathroom and gazed on as his mother continued to incinerate the monster.

All flailing arms and legs, Hoyt screamed and thrashed as the fire bathed him in orange, yellow, and red. His mother stepped closer and leaned in as close as she could get, aiming the flames directly into Hoyt's screaming mouth.

"Die, motherfucker! Fucking die already!"

Then Hoyt burst.

Like a popped balloon, the monster's charred black body erupted. Foamy sea water exploded from the tub, splashing his mother and everything surrounding her. Patrick backed away as it sloshed over his shoes and ran over the carpet. When the flames burnt out, his mother dropped the can and lighter into the water.

Patrick ran to her side and hugged her hard. Together they watched what was left of Hoyt swirl down the drain.

FRIDAY

15

"**DID YOU KNOW?**"

Melissa flinched. She'd been staring at the scene ahead so intently, unblinking, breath clenched tight in her throat, she had forgotten where they were. Hours ticked by. Swirls of blues and reds from a half a dozen police cars bounced off the walls of their condo and its neighbors. Packs of curious onlookers with long, sleepy faces watched on from their balconies as dozens of uniformed officers milled about the parking lot. Numerous others came and went from the open door of their third floor room. Melissa's tired eyes stung as she watched from the dark interior of their SUV. After hurriedly leaving their condo room, with only their essential belongings, she parked them in the strip mall across the street, in the shadowed alleyway next to the Italian restaurant. She kept low in her seat, not wanting to draw any attention, but wanting to keep an eye on the scene all the same.

Melissa finally blinked and slowly turned around. Curled up in tight ball, Patrick lay beneath a wooly beach towel across the backseat. Two more towels, which they had used to clean themselves off, were in a heap on the floorboard, damp with brine and stained with blood. Though she couldn't see his glare, she knew his eyes were alight with accusatory anger.

She turned back around. Hands tender from the fire, she gripped the steering wheel and sighed. "I don't know what to say."

"Bullshit."

She shook her head, unable to find the strength to correct his language. "I'm sorry," she muttered.

Patrick sat up in a hurry. "*You're sorry?*"

Melissa quickly spun around in her seat. "Keep your voice down!"

"Why? Are you afraid *he's* going to come again, Mom? Are you afraid the guy we *killed* is going to come back and *kill* us? *Again?* Is that it, *Mom?*"

"I said stop yelling!" She pointed out the windshield. "Do you want them to hear us?"

Patrick balled up his blanket towel and chucked it against the door. "I don't know! Would they be able to save us from him?"

In an effort to deescalate, she grabbed his shirt collar and pulled him close. "When I say stop yelling, you stop yelling. Got it? Here's a reminder: I've never laid a hand on you in your life, but I swear to God I will beat your ass if you don't sit back and settle down right this instant."

He stuttered out a breath through his teeth, eyes soaked with trepidation. When a few moments passed without a rebuttal, she slowly let him go, and he dropped backwards in his seat. She blinked rapidly, fighting the oncoming tears.

"What would you have liked me to say, Patrick? What sort of ridiculous, unrealistic explanation should I have given you? That Hoyt—" She swallowed a fat lump in her throat. "That he came back to get us, like some . . . some waterlogged boogeyman? Do you know how insane that sounds?"

Biting his lip, he lifted his hands up and down, showing her his bloodstained clothes.

"Yeah . . . " She nodded. "Yeah, it's just that insane." Melissa pressed her forehead against the leather headrest. "I'm sorry, Patrick. I should have said something. I don't know what, but I should have. Even after the first time, I still somehow thought it was my imagination or something."

"The *first* time? You mean *that* wasn't the first time?"

"I was so scared. Even if it was my mind messing with me like some sort of punishment, I wanted to get you away from here—to get *us* away from here." Her eyes drifted past his head, into the darkness beyond the vehicle. "This place . . . it doesn't feel the same anymore. It doesn't feel like that second home we could always come back to. Now it's always going to feel . . . stained. Tainted. Gross." She turned back around and faced out the front windshield. "Anyway, now that we know we can't leave, I thought maybe . . . shit—"

She immediately ducked down in her seat. Across the street, Detective Holzer stepped out into the condo's parking lot from the downstairs hallway. Holzer stopped to speak to a few other officers, pointing back at the balcony near their room. When they finished talking, the officers followed her finger and walked back toward the stairwell. Hands on her hips, Holzer shook her head and appeared to sigh. She turned her head toward the strip mall.

Melissa sank lower in her seat.

Holzer's glare continued as she swept the mostly empty, lamp-lit parking lot.

Melissa's eyes peaked just over the dashboard. She held her breath, thankful no light was hovering over them.

The detective turned her body fully toward the lot. She took a step toward the street.

Heart pounding, Melissa dropped lower and slowly cocked her head to the side. One eye could still watch, but the top of her head would not be seen.

Holzer took another step. Then another.

Then she stopped. Looking down, she pulled the cell phone from her pocket and answered it. After a few shakes of her head, she stuffed it back into her pocket and turned toward her car. A few more angry curses and she and her unmarked Charger pulled out from the lot and sped off.

When her lungs began to ache, Melissa stuttered a long breath, and with it came hot, embarrassing tears. "I'm sorry, Patrick. This is all my fault. We never should have stayed after we did what we did. I should have gotten us out of town the moment we stepped off that boat. Then none of this would have happened. We could have been back home, and away from all of this . . . this nastiness. But I didn't know— I had no idea he would actually come back again. Even though I needed them, I shouldn't have taken those sleeping aides to help me tonight. That was so very dangerous and selfish of me. I'll never forgive myself. I'm so, so sorry. Will you please forgive me?"

She turned back to face her son, only to find he had pulled the beach towel completely over his body and his head.

CRUEL SUMMER

"Patrick?"

He then turned over and faced the back of the seat, away from her.

Angry with herself, she turned back in her seat and stared at the floating dust moats in her vision. "But Hoyt's dead now," she whispered, unsure if she was still speaking to Patrick or only to herself. "He's right back where he belongs, and he's not coming back. Tomorrow we'll find a way off this island. Somehow. Even if we have to swim to the other side."

Melissa closed her eyes. "I love you. Get some sleep."

She was awakened by the buzz of her phone. It was still dark, and the digital turquoise numbers on her dash read 5:49AM. Dazed, she plucked her phone out of the cup holder and squinted into its shattered screen.

Sorry, couldn't sleep. Haven't since you came over. Could we do breakfast today instead? I just can't wait any longer.

16

JORDAN'S HANDS IMMEDIATELY SHOT to his mouth as they walked into the diner. Melissa's heart raced as they stepped through the front door and it only got worse when she witnessed his reaction. Patrick walked in before her, now hobbling with a limp, so thankfully he couldn't see her swiping her hand across her throat, repeatedly mouthing "Cut it out!" Eyes full of wonder, Jordan's mouth moved with silent words. All in an instant, she could witness his world changing. For better or worse, that was still to be determined.

For as long as she could remember, she had dreaded this very moment. She never thought these two would be introduced, at least not like this. Not over runny eggs and toast in a no name diner on Flagler Street. The entire situation was less than ideal, but at this point there was no other option. They were tired and wounded and neither had showered since the incident. It was only twenty minutes ago they were using a garden hose behind someone's house to rinse the dried gunk from their hair. Not to mention the quick change of unmatched clothing they threw on inside the SUV, both wearing long pants to cover their wounds. Duress was not exactly the best way to introduce father and son, but thankfully they were both in agreement absolutely nothing would be revealed today. It was only breakfast, nothing more. She wasn't sure what he had in mind, but if this was what they had, then she was prepared to make the best of it.

By the time Jordan stood from his corner table, his hands had thankfully dropped to his sides, but the shock on his face was still in plain sight. The poor guy's jaw was nearly against his chest, and his fingers repeatedly flexed like he wasn't quite sure what to do with them. Thankfully Patrick had his face buried in her phone, using hers since he had lost his, not paying attention in the slightest. He had no idea who Jordan was, only that he was a friend of his mother who lived down on the beach. He couldn't have cared less. His anger from the night before was as palpable as the fried potatoes wafting from the kitchen.

Melissa swallowed and nudged Patrick toward the table.

"H-hi!" Jordan stuttered. "Good to see you again!"

She hung her beach bag on the back of the chair diagonal from him, then stepped around the table to hug him. "Good to see you, too."

He shot her an inquisitive eyebrow, fingering the price tag hanging off her sleeve. "What's with the hoodie? Did you just buy this?"

Her bandaged elbow throbbed painfully beneath the thick cotton. "Don't ask."

"Right. Oh here, let me get that." He followed her back around the table and pulled her chair out for her, which she couldn't help but smile at.

"Thank you."

"Absolutely." He turned toward her son—*his* son. "And this . . . this must be Patrick."

"Indeed it is." She poked Patrick in his side. "Hon, put the phone down."

Rolling his eyes, Patrick sighed and put the smashed device on the table.

She added, "No, in your pocket."

This produced a heavier sigh as he then shoved her phone into his jeans pocket.

Jordan put out his open palm. "Patrick, right? It's so nice to meet you."

Without looking up at him, Patrick quickly shook Jordan's hand before slipping it back into his lap. Jordan stood there for a moment longer, rubbing his fingers into his palm, before placing himself back into his chair across from Patrick.

Melissa nearly had her own moment of shock. Her eyes darted back and forth from face to face, and she then found her own hands fidgeting. Jordan's face by itself was so very similar to her son's, but now as they sat there, facing one another, there was no denying the blood running through Patrick's veins. Same nose, same eyes, same deep cleft in their chins. Had Patrick actually been paying attention, he would be looking at his future self. But while his father remained in a stunned trance, his own tired eyes were staring at the floor beneath him.

Melissa shook her head. "Thank you for inviting us out again."

Jordan blinked and turned toward her. "Absolutely! Thank you again for coming out this early. I, uh . . . I couldn't sleep. And I was pretty hungry, so I didn't want to wait until lunch, you know?"

"Yeah, we didn't get much sleep either."

"Oh, I'm sorry. Everything okay?"

She immediately regretted bringing it up. "For the most part, yes. I'll be honest, I nearly forgot about our meet up today. There was an incident at the condo last night. I had lit a candle in the bathroom before I went to bed and forgot about it. Somehow it fell over into the trash can and set the whole thing on fire. It set off all the fire alarms and sprinklers and forced us out of our room. We had to sleep in the SUV last night."

"Oh wow, that's terrible! Are you guys okay?"

"Yeah yeah, we'll live. We had to leave in a hurry and didn't get to grab much of our belongings. Not sure if we'll see any of it again."

"Well, that's just terrible. But I'm glad you both got out unharmed. Geeze, that could have been real bad."

Melissa nodded. "Yeah . . . real bad. But it's been taken care of."

"That's good. That's very good." He turned back to Patrick, running a nervous hand through his long hair. "It really is very nice to meet you, Patrick. Your mother has had nothing but wonderful things to say about you. You're pretty much all we talked about yesterday."

Somehow Patrick had slipped her phone from his pocket and was fiddling with it under the table.

Melissa slapped his arm. "What did I say? Phone in your pocket, or I'm taking it from you. Jordan is talking to you. It's rude to ignore him."

"Whatever," he muttered.

Before he could react, Melissa snatched the phone from his hands and tossed it into her purse.

"Hey!"

"You're being rude. You'll get it back later when I think you deserve it."

An exaggerated huff and Patrick slunk down in his seat with an exasperated scowl. He crossed his arms across, mumbling under his breath.

"What's that?" she asked.

"Nothing."

"That's what I thought."

"It's okay." Jordan smiled. "You guys have been through a crazy night and you're tired. We don't have to talk."

"I'm sorry," she said. "We've been dealing with a lot the last few days, so we're both a little on edge."

"I can imagine."

The waitress approached, and they all quickly made their orders, Melissa ordering for Patrick when he didn't answer, then the three remained in awkward silence for a few long minutes. While Patrick continued to stare at the floor, Jordan watched him with wonder in his eyes. All the fear and trepidation Melissa had felt before was beginning to drain away. Though he still looked nervous, Jordan had no intention of remaining as silent as his miniature. She could tell he was searching for the right words, the right conversation to keep the dialogue moving between them, and that was a great sign. He wasn't closing himself off, ready for the check to get there so he could go back to his tranquil life and forget any of this had happened. She only hoped he wasn't going to blurt out something important too soon.

CRUEL SUMMER

Jordan eventually spoke up. "I like your hair, Patrick. Reminds me of the way I used to wear it at your age."

Patrick's eyes drifted up and finally looked at Jordan. He remained quiet for a little longer, and some irrational part of Melissa believed her son would have a sudden biological revelation. Instead, he mumbled, "I like your hair, too."

Jordan grinned. "Thanks, dude! Took me a long time to grow it out."

"I wish I could, but Mom won't let me. Not until I'm older."

"Well, your mom does know best. I've known her for quite a long time—ever since high school, in fact. She's a very cool person, and from what I can tell she still is. I'm sure you know that."

Patrick rolled his eyes.

"What? You don't think so?"

Patrick shrugged. "Even though she says lying is bad, she likes to lie a lot."

Melissa said, "Patrick—"

Jordan quickly waved his hand, showing her he had it under control. "She lies, huh? Well, sometimes adults lie to protect the people they love, even if it may seem wrong to that person. It's a necessary evil. Do you know what that means?"

Patrick shook his head.

"Okay, how can I explain it? It's like . . . it's like putting mayonnaise on a sandwich. It's gross as heck, but you have to do it to make sure the bites go down smoother."

A small smile cracked across Patrick's lips. "Mayo is so nasty."

Jordan laughed, "That's my boy!" then immediately frowned and shook his head. "I mean, it's nice to meet another mayonnaise hater. There's not many of us left in the world. We have to stick together and fight the power. Fried eggs over egg yolks, am I right?"

Patrick giggled and so did Jordan. The cheery noise made Melissa's heart swell with happiness. As she watched them, she forced herself to contain her emotions, and each passing minute was like running an Olympic obstacle course. At times she couldn't breathe. At times she wanted to run away and not look back. Right then she wanted to embrace them both. This would naturally work itself out. When her assistance was needed, she would step in. For the time being she was going to enjoy their banter.

As the waitress approached, Jordan said, "Speaking of which . . . " She dropped their food off in front of them. With his fork, Jordan poked at his scrambled eggs, then lifted them and looked underneath. "Nope, no mayo. We're all good to dig in."

Patrick laughed once more and then voraciously dug into his bacon and pancakes. Jordan beamed and shot a glance over to Melissa. Her eyes brimmed with tears. She mouthed "Thank you" and he nodded, his own eyes growing glassy. He took a deep breath and went to digging into his own food. Melissa continued to watch them both, trying to steady her full, leaping heart. Though her own food smelled great, she wasn't exactly hungry, but she managed to take a few bites.

While she ate, Jordan and Patrick continued to chat. Jordan asked him about school (he hated it) and his favorite subjects (none), his favorite music (Billie

Eilish and Ed Sheeran), favorite food (chicken nuggets with barbeque sauce from the school cafeteria) and his hobbies.

"Wait—you like Magic the Gathering cards, too?"

Patrick nodded, syrup dripping down his chin. "I've got, like, two hundred cards."

"Two hundred? Dude, I've got like two thousand!"

"No way!"

"Yes way! I've literally got the first two sets of Magic Cards ever made from the early nineties, Alpha and Beta."

"Now *you're* lying to me!"

"Nope! My dude, I even have a mint condition Black Lotus."

Patrick's dropped his fork on his plate, his eyes threatening to leap from his head. "No way! That's, like, the rarest card, like . . . like ever!"

"Indeed! I keep it in a hard-shell plastic case in a lockbox at home. I still remember when your mom got that for me as anniversary present. My eyes looked just like yours did right now."

Patrick's grin immediately wilted. "Anniversary?"

Melissa and Jordan simultaneously grimaced. *No, no, no . . .* While she felt Patrick's eyes on her, she continued to eat her food in silence, not meeting his confused gaze. Instead, she stared at Jordan, who now looked like a cat with a bird shoved in its mouth.

"Like, did you guys date or something?"

Jordan swallowed. "Well, yeah. We did. For a few years."

"When?"

"Oh, back in high school, you know, when we rode dinosaurs instead of school buses."

Patrick didn't respond to his humor. He turned back to Melissa. "So he's an old boyfriend?"

She swallowed her food. "Yes, Patrick, we were once a couple many, many years ago."

"Why are you guys still friends? You can't be friends with ex's."

"Lots of people are friends with their ex's," Jordan interjected. "I'm still friends with many of my ex-girlfriends. As long as you leave on good terms, there's no reason to not be friendly with them."

"You can do that?"

"Absolutely! Maybe you don't do that when you're younger, but the older you get the more you realize how you have to treat people the way you yourself want to be treated. It's the right thing to do."

Patrick eyed him, their fun conversation now skidding into suspicion. "Why did you and Mom break up?" Melissa could hear the protective roadblock beginning to post up.

"Well . . . I don't think we had much of a choice, dude. Your mom was going to go to one college, and I was heading to another one really far away. It just wouldn't work, you know."

"Did you hurt her?"

Melissa sat up straight. "Patrick!"

"No, no," Jordan said, shaking his head. "Quite the opposite. I never laid a hand on her. I really, really like her a lot. Why would you ask something like that?"

"Mom? Who is this guy? Why are we eating with some old boyfriend? This is super weird."

Putting her fork aside, she turned her chair to face them both. "Honey, he's an old friend who I used to date. That's all. He lives down here now, and I thought it would be nice if you met him before we left town."

"But why? I'm never going to see him again. What do I care?"

Melissa sighed as she felt every bit of good vibes fly out the window. "I don't know, Patrick. I figured maybe you two would get along. You both like the same stuff, and I was hoping you two would hit it off."

Patrick pushed his plate away from him, pulling a face. "Why the hell would I care? He's, like, an adult."

"Don't you want someone to talk to about those things?"

"I've got friends, *Mom*. Real friends *my* age."

While Jordan remained silent, Melissa could feel her irritation swelling like a water balloon. It was all going so great, the carpet easing itself naturally into the corners, until the word "boyfriend" was spoken. That seemed to set him into a spiral.

"Damn it, Patrick, I know that. I just want you to have some sort of positive male role model in your life. Is that so wrong?"

Jordan added, "Melissa, really, it's okay. We don't have to do this."

She snapped, "I know what I'm doing, Jordan. He's my son, I know how to do this."

He frowned, pursing his lips. "I'm aware of that, Mel. I'm *very* aware of that now. Maybe don't push him into something he doesn't want to be a part of?"

"What are you both talking about?" Patrick asked.

"This isn't how I wanted this to happen, Jordan. Please stop."

Jordan threw his hands up, frustrated. "What are

you talking about? I'm trying to do the right thing here. I'm doing my best!"

"Well, your best sucks."

"*Stop it!*"

They both ceased their argument and turned to Patrick. He eyed them both with apprehension. His gaze settled on Jordan. It stayed there for several long moments as he stared into his face. Melissa's heart began to thrum. *Not like this*, she kept repeating. *Not like this . . .*

Jordan shifted uncomfortably in his seat as Patrick continued to study his face. Patrick's mouth dropped in a small, tight O. He slowly turned to Melissa. Tears dripped down his cheeks. Before she could open her mouth to speak, Patrick quickly pushed his chair back and stormed away from the table.

Melissa grabbed her purse and ran after him.

Patrick was already out the door and limping past the building before she caught up. She grasped his shoulder and spun him, but he easily shrugged her off.

"Patrick, stop! Stop right this instant!"

He turned around to face her. Anger pinched his features. "Who is he?"

Melissa locked up, her tongue swelling in her mouth. Her arms grew stiff at her sides.

"Mom . . . who is he?"

The morning sun warmed her shaking face. She blinked rapidly.

"Say it," he demanded.

Melissa swallowed.

"Say it."

CRUEL SUMMER

She closed her eyes and whispered, "He's your father, Patrick."

As if his knees had suddenly vanished, Patrick crumpled to the sidewalk and wailed. Melissa grabbed her face and pressed her nails into her cheeks, bit her lips and shut her eyes—anything to keep herself from screaming and punching the nearest brick wall with all her might. How had this gone so wrong? The turn happened like the flick of a switch, and now that switch could never be reversed. Part of her wanted to be relieved. It was finally, after so many years, out in the open, and some small part of her could finally breathe easy. But seeing her son, the only true love of her life, shatter like a glass plate, finally made her realize what a massive mistake this all was. This should have happened years ago, when he was still young enough for it to not affect his life in such a drastic fashion. She would have to live with her decision, but she prayed that somehow she could pick up the broken pieces and make him whole again.

Melissa knelt down to touch him, but he batted her hand away.

"Don't touch me!"

"Patrick, I—"

He leapt back up, facing her with bloodshot eyes. "You're what? You're *sorry*? *Again?* You seem to say 'I'm sorry' a lot these days, Mom!" He wiped his nose with the back of his hand.

She couldn't disagree. "Listen—"

"No, you listen! I'm so tired of you lying to me! This isn't fair anymore!"

"I know it's not, Patrick! I didn't want it to be like this! It's not like we planned it this way!"

He sneered. "How long have you two been planning this?"

Melissa shook her head, knowing what was coming but unable to stop it. "We didn't. This just happened."

"*What?*"

"I only told him yesterday."

Patrick spun like a top and stomped his feet, hands going straight in the air. "*Are you kidding me?* What is wrong with you? Are you crazy? Are you insane?"

She screamed, "Yes, Patrick! I'm all those things! And do you know what else I am? I am your goddamn mother! And that means I have a responsibility to keep you safe, even if that means keeping you from knowing the truth about who your father is. I had to make sure he wasn't just another scumbag like Hoyt, which you can *plainly* see he's not. I wanted you to finally meet him and see if he's someone who you would maybe want in your life. Even if you don't, I would like to keep him in mine in some capacity."

He shook his head, glaring. "I don't trust you anymore."

Melissa wanted to crumble like ash. "Don't say that. That's not fair."

"Neither is putting me in crappy situations like this, over and over!"

The tears were sudden and hot, and she turned away so he couldn't see the hurt his words had caused.

"You guys okay?"

She opened her eyes to find Jordan awkwardly jogging up to them. She waved him away, but he still approached and placed a hand on her shoulder. "I

CRUEL SUMMER

already paid, so that's taken care of. Let's um . . . ." He turned to look at Patrick, who refused to meet his gaze. "Okay. Look, this was . . . not how any of us imagined this would go. We're all upset, some more than others, and that's okay." He paused, thinking. "How about this? There's a cool little place down the road from here toward the water I want to take you both to. It's really neat. We can go for a walk, cool off, and talk. Does that sound alright to everyone?"

Melissa wiped her eyes and nodded.

Patrick, still not facing them, began to trudge down the sidewalk by himself.

17

AS THEY SAUNTERED ALONG the wood-planked pathways which wound through Smyrna Dunes Park, Jordan couldn't stop looking at Patrick. He did his best not to stare and make the boy more uncomfortable than he already was, but he couldn't help it. Everything about him—his hair, his hands, even the way he sulked when he shuffled along ahead of him—was like looking at some home movie his own father would have shot years ago on his prized RCA camcorder. He wanted to reach out and pinch the boy to make sure this was actually real and not some fever dream he'd been having since the day before.

Stop calling him boy, he thought. *Son. He's your son.*

Wow . . . I really do *have a son.*

While Patrick kicked at the dusting of sand across the planks, Jordan continued to take mental pictures. He wanted to savor this moment. With him living down here, and the two of them residing in his old home town, there was an eight hundred and fifty mile barrier between them. Not to mention he rarely ever got back to Indiana for anything outside of the occasional holiday; his parents insisted they come down here during the winter. Who knew if he would ever get a chance like this ever again?

Who else knows? I doubt I have many old friends that still live in that area who might run in Melissa's circles. There's no way in hell Mom and Dad don't know. I'll have to have a long talk with them later.

He turned back to see Melissa tottering a few feet behind him. Whatever words Patrick had fast pitched to her were now a rerun only she could hear, her own personal hell, and it was visibly eating her up. Eyes rimmed in red, her sight was locked onto her feet. She appeared lost and a bit fractured, in only a way a child could make a parent feel. Part of him wanted to comfort her, but the other, reasonable half realized that, though she probably didn't deserve the particular verbal assault she had received, she did deserve a bit of the resentment. And though he had no idea any of this was coming his way before yesterday morning, he realized he was just as guilty. He was equally as responsible for the bewildered, incensed young man before him. But no matter what happened from this day forward, it was *their* responsibility to right the ship and establish the captain once more.

Melissa finally looked up and shot him a sad, tight-lipped smile, which he reciprocated. For a moment it looked as though she wanted to say something, her mouth opening and then quickly snapping shut. She shook her head and looked away, letting her thought blow away with the warm morning breeze. He waved to her, getting her attention. When she looked back, he motioned for her to stay back a few feet, and then pointed forward, showing her he was going to join Patrick. "Are you sure?" she mouthed. He nodded, then turned and took a few long strides toward Patrick.

Other than stepping closer to the railing, Patrick didn't acknowledge his presence. Head, down, he mimicked his mother's stride as the beautiful view of the beach and the naupaka bushes was second to his sneakers.

Jordan finally broke the silence. "I wasn't lying." Patrick continued to look down. "About that card, I mean. I really do still have it, plastic casing and all. I still have all my old cards. I know a lot of collectors usually put them all in those long card boxes, but I actually have all of them individually separated into those binder card sleeves. Heck, I've even got them further separated by color and type, each one getting its own individual binder, which is the color of the cards themselves."

He went silent and wondered if Patrick had even heard a word he had said. He was about to change the subject when he heard, "That's so lame."

Jordan raised an eyebrow and smirked. "Lame?"

Head still down Patrick muttered, "Yeah. That's dorky as hell."

That roused a laugh from Jordan. "Yes, it absolutely is. I've been collecting those cards since I was younger than you. Is Comic Quest still a thing back in Evansville?"

Patrick nodded.

"That's good to hear. When I was maybe just a little older than you, I used to go there on Friday nights with my couple of friends that played, and we would either play each other or we would play some of the older kids that were there, too. And when we got hungry, we would walk next door to the Dollar General and buy Little Debbie snack cakes and soda, and then we would act like crazy fools for the next few hours, all hopped up on sugar. Have you ever done that?"

Shaking his head, Patrick finally glanced up and gave him a side eye. "Kind of. My friend and I get pizza from Covert Una and play at Book Broker sometimes on Saturday."

Jordan grinned. "I see the apple doesn't fall far from the dork tree."

Both grew silent once more as they continued to walk the pathway over the sand. Out beyond, the ocean roared its ancient song as swimmers and sunbathers subscribed to its music. The sun continued to climb the sky overhead, and before long, tourists would begin to flood the town and clog every nook and cranny with various accents and license plates. He truly loved it down here and the life he had made for himself, but all this talk of thin crust pizza and Midwest simplicity made him long for home in a way he hadn't for some time. And now he had this fun-sized version of himself to bring it all back to him like a verbal Polaroid. He decided right then, no matter what happened from now until the time those two went back home, he would keep himself involved in this child's life for as long as he possibly could. If not for Patrick, then for himself. At thirty-two, he needed more direction in his life outside of his sporadic art work and browning his skin like toast. He never knew how bad he needed this until now.

Melissa had drifted a few steps closer, so he

nudged Patrick a little further ahead. "Listen . . . I know you're upset. I one hundred percent get it. I'm a little upset myself at how this all went down. Perhaps I misspoke or crossed some sort of line I wasn't aware of, but you have to know I'm really sorry."

Patrick grumbled. "I've been hearing that a lot lately."

Nodding, Jordan continued. "I get that. Listen, real talk for a moment, okay? You're old enough to where I don't have to talk down to you like I'm some stuffy adult. What you went through a little bit ago? I had that same feeling when your mom came over yesterday and dropped that atom bomb known as Patrick Braun right onto my stupid little life. I was out on my roof painting, minding my own business, and the next thing I knew—*poof!*—I was a dad." He snapped his fingers. "Just like that. It's pretty wild how quickly life can change, isn't it? It's like stepping out of our house one day and the earth disappearing out from under us.

"Just like you, Patrick, I'm feeling all kinds of emotions. I'm scared. I'm excited. I'm nervous as hell. I'm also so very hopeful. But do you know what emotion I don't feel?"

His son looked up at him.

"Hate. And you shouldn't be feeling it either. I know you're feeling all of those others because, for better or worse, you're just like me—hell, you are me. You're a little short, like I was then, but with any luck, you'll hit the same growth spurt and end up being as big as me. But do you know what I don't feel inside my big frame? Hate. And neither can you. You can't go on living like that, and you certainly can't go on with that feeling toward your mom. I get it. Yes, she probably should have told us both forever and a day ago, but she chose not to. She made the decision to protect you because that's what a mother does. That's her whole job. You can be angry with her, sure. I'm a little angry at her for taking this long to tell me about you. But do you know what? I don't hate her. If anything I applaud her. It took a lot of guts to roll up into my house and cave it in on me. It took balls, and your mom's got some big, meaty clackers."

Underneath his shaggy hair, Patrick giggled.

"You see! You can't hate someone when you're laughing. I know it hurts right now, Patrick, and this is all a big whirlwind of craziness, but you know what you got from it?"

Patrick shook his head.

Jordan pointed at his own chest. "You got to meet this cool mofo right here, and as far as I'm concerned that's a big win for both of us. Listen . . . " He paused, stopping them both. Melissa ceased walking, remaining behind them far enough not to overhear. "I don't have to be anything you don't want me to be. If you don't want me to be in your life from this moment on, then you can turn right around with your mom and you guys can wait until the causeways are fixed and then drive back home and forget you ever met my dumb face. Or, and this is totally up to you, I can be in your life from here on out. I'll be honest, Patrick, I really, really like you—a lot—and I want to see you more often after this trip, preferably somewhere a little colder. I miss winter a little bit. So . . . what do you say?"

His nerves buzzing through every inch of his skin, Jordan waited patiently while Patrick went over his options. His son's eyes roamed over the sky blue waters beyond him. While he couldn't read Patrick's thoughts, he certainly had his own, and they swirled around his brain like a washing machine on the heavy cycle. He wasn't a religious man, but right then he found himself praying.

Patrick finally sighed. He continue walking down the wooden pathway.

Jordan stuttered his own sigh of relief. After running his hands through his hair, he turned to Melissa, who was watching them with bated breath. He smiled and shot her a thumbs up, in turn breaking her distress. He waved her forward, and together they followed Patrick down the boardwalk toward the beach.

While the sun made their skin weep, they continued to walk along the winding path, Melissa by his side, and Patrick a step ahead. Instead of his head hanging low, it now stayed up, roaming from side to side on a swivel. Seagulls and pelicans cut through the air above as the sand crabs scrambled and hid beneath the wooden planks. An Eastern Diamondback slithered into a fan palm. Eventually they ran out of walkway and it bled into a few short feet of golden beach. Beyond, the grainy surface opened up into a wide stretch of water.

"What's this?" Patrick asked, pointing.

"That," Jordan answered, "is the Ponce Inlet. This is the body of water that's at the top of the island. Right now we're at the northern most tip. The water runs around us and goes south and becomes the

CRUEL SUMMER

Indian River, which is what the North and South Causeway sit over. It winds in and around all the little islands off to our left. But you absolutely never ever want to swim in this particular water."

Patrick turned back to him. "Why?"

"Well, they don't call New Smyrna Beach the Shark Bite Capital of the World for nothing. I mean, it's a bit of an exaggerated title, but it's there for a reason. For some reason this cove has always had a high concentration of shark activity, which is why the locals call it Shark Cove or The Nest."

"For real?" Melissa asked.

"Absolutely. I mean look out there. I can see at least . . . a half a dozen shapes under the water right now." The other two strained their necks to see, and when they were caught off guard, Jordan clapped his hands and yelled. They both jumped and yelped, turning back to him with laughs. "Sorry, that was way too easy. But seriously, there are always quite a bit of sharks congregating in the cove, that's why you only ever see boats and whatnot drifting though and no swimmers. Not to mention it's a bit rocky not too far down, so they wouldn't allow swimming anyway. But check that out."

They followed his nod to the other side of the water, where not too far off the opposite beach a massive lighthouse jutted from the earth. Its ruddy red shaft stuck out around the various shades of green surrounding it. High above, people walked around the caged top, where they could see miles of land and sea in every direction.

"We've been up there," Melissa squinted. "It's been a long time. I took Patrick when he was very young. Had to carry him up all those steps. I think I lost twenty pounds in sweat by the time I reached the top."

"Tallest lighthouse in the state. Such a beautiful view at the top. I love it. If the Causeways were working, I'd gladly take you both over there to see it again."

Melissa smiled. "That sounds nice."

Jordan smiled, too. He turned his view back to the cove.

Dozens of shark fins were now protruding from the water's surface. They remained perfectly still.

And they were all pointing in their direction.

When they pulled back up to the restaurant, Jordan walked them back to their car. "So what are you guys going to do now?"

Melissa dug into her purse for her keys. She shrugged. "I have no clue. We can't go back to the room."

"Damn, that's right."

"I figured we might just go drive around for a bit. Get some dinner eventually. I don't know." She shuffled in place, her head down as if she were embarrassed.

"You guys don't really have anywhere to go, not with the Causeways still being worked on." He decided to shoot his shot. "You're more than welcome to come stay with me until you can leave town."

She waved him away. "No, no, we wouldn't want to put you out."

"Nonsense! I'm renting a three bedroom house with more room than humanly necessary, and I have a freezer full of enough meat to feed a Kraken. Seriously, just stay with me. I'll grill steaks for dinner and we'll spend the day swimming in the pool."

For the first time all day, she gave a genuine, joyful smile. "That would be lovely. Thank you, Jordan."

"What say you, Patrick? Some beef and shrimp? We'll garlic butter them to death."

Patrick smiled, too, and it warmed Jordan's heart.

"Maybe if we get bored later, we can take some fishing poles and hit up the manatee park—"

"Whoa!" the other two yelled simultaneously.

13

HIS BELLY CHOCK FULL of New York Strip, shrimp scampi, and grilled corn on the cob, Patrick strolled through Jordan's house with mild unease. He was growing more and more comfortable around Jordan, killing the last several hours lounging poolside and helping him cook while Mom sunbathed, but the fact was he had only known the guy for less than a day. His heart told him to relax and enjoy the laughs and the company, but his brain continued to steamroll him with bad thoughts. He desperately wanted to like Jordan—there was absolutely nothing about him he particularly *disliked*—but another man in his life? This soon? After Hoyt, did he really want another man trying to be his dad?

Dad, he thought, staring out the back window at Jordan as he spoke with Patrick's mother. *That guy right there is my dad.* He could think it, but he wasn't sure he could say it out loud yet.

He watched Jordan for a bit longer, wondering what they were talking about. Patrick was sure it was about him. What else would it be about? They weren't looking his way, but both performed plenty of nods and verbal agreements. Another thing he noticed was Jordan's hands. Unlike that other asshole, Jordan kept his hands to himself. He didn't touch her, didn't feel the need to grab her arm or touch her shoulder when they spoke. His hands weren't balled like coiled snakes, ready to strike at the first disagreement. He seemed so laid back and comfortable. So honest. Any other time he would have been protective of his mother, but his internal alarms remained church silent. And for once that felt great.

Patrick continued to explore the main level of the house, and before long he found himself in the spacious living room. Dozens upon dozens of paint canvases were strewn about the floor like dirty clothing. They were in all shapes and sizes, all lying face up. Many others were leaning against the wall, silently observing as he wandered past. They may not have been Patrick's particular taste, but he was still incredibly impressed with the skill nonetheless. Many were of local landscapes, oceans and sunsets, while others were of various animal life and portraits of the beach. He immediately recognized many of the places around town, each precise color a stunning replica of the real thing.

He came across a particularly large stack of canvases. They were all turned the opposite way against the wall, which caught his attention. He carefully pulled them out and, one by one, he turned them around to look.

The first painting was of a large, older man, rippling with huge, veiny muscles, complete with long white hair and a matching beard. He was perched on what appeared to be a mountain top, and in his hand he held a bright, golden lightning bolt, which he held over his shoulder in an attack stance. Below him, menacing-looking fish men with jagged teeth were crawling up the mountain toward him.

The next painting was much darker colored. It looked like the inside of a torch lit cave, gold and crimson illuminating the stone walls. In the back corner, a woman with snakes for hair and long, reptilian body gleamed hideously at several men with her glowing red eyes. Swords in hand, the men appeared to be frozen in place like statues, their half-naked bodies now as grey as the cave walls. Patrick had no idea what he was looking at, but he kind of loved it. They reminded him of those old rock and roll album covers his grandpa loved and hung up on the walls in his basement.

"Pretty cool, huh?"

Patrick spun around and found Jordan leaning against the doorway by the kitchen.

"Stalk much?" Patrick asked.

Jordan shrugged. "Snoop much?" He grinned, nodding toward the paintings. "I see you found my Greek gods."

Patrick carefully placed the paintings back against the wall. "I guess. They're pretty cool."

"Thank you." Jordan joined him in the living room and crouched down by the stack. "Yeah, they're not like the other ones I do. These are just for me, I guess. I probably wouldn't ever sell them."

"You did these all on your own?"

"Every last brush stroke is all mine. Check these out." He carefully pulled them all out and spread them across the floor. "Do you know anything about Greek mythology?"

Patrick shook his head.

"Nothing at all? Have you ever seen *Clash of the Titans*?"

Again, no.

"Jesus, what does your mother make you watch? She's probably still watching all those Kevin Smith films she used to force on me. Anyway, the ancient Greeks believed in these mythological beings who lived among them and controlled the world around them. Gods of love and earth and water. That first guy here, that's Zeus. He's, like, the God of gods. That's him standing on Mount Olympus. That's where many of the gods lived when they weren't screwing around on Earth. Sort of like their version of Heaven or something." He pointed to the next one. "This lovely lady is Medusa. She was pretty nasty. She had venomous snakes for hair, and she could turn any man into stone if they looked into her eyes."

Patrick smiled. "That's pretty cool."

"Right? And I hear that's how my mom met my dad. True story." He flipped another one. In the painting, a younger man stood on the edge of a high cliff overlooking an ocean. His head was a shock of blonde curls, and his bare chest, gleaming with sweat, was lined with row after row of muscle. In one hand was a great glowing sword, dripping with dark, black blood, and in the other, which he held out high, was the severed head of Medusa. A look of determined pride adorned the young man's face.

"Wow," Patrick remarked. "Who's that?"

"That, my boy, is the monster slayer himself, Perseus. That's one of Zeus's many children, but unlike most of Zeus' other children, Perseus was half human. He was quite the bad ass, but he was also very honorable. His mother was human, and he did a lot to protect her from other Gods he didn't feel were worthy of her. Kind of reminds me of you."

Patrick felt his face flush red. He stared at Jordan's interpretation of the Greek demigod, wondering what it would be like to be blessed with that level of strength, to be brimming with that much bravery. To slay the monster. To be the hero.

It was everything he ever wanted.

Jordan flipped the next one, and Patrick's good vibes evaporated.

He couldn't quite figure out why, but what his father revealed sent a current of ice water flowing down his spine. The canvas was splashed in several shades of blue and purple, each one darker than the last, as they grew murkier toward the middle of the painting. In the center, highlighted by two thinly layered white circles, were two obsidian orbs. The eyes, though parked on the side of what he assumed was a long, angular snout, seemed to stare right at him with baleful contempt. Just below, a mouth opened wide, with rows of serrated teeth that appeared to drop down the back of its throat like the dip in a rollercoaster track. Patrick's mouth instantly dried up. His heartbeat kick drummed in his ears. He knew those eyes . . . that smile.

Jordan's voice came to him in a slow wave. "Pretty wicked, right? This big baddie is Cetus. He was this wicked sea monster god, and according to legend—at least, whichever one you subscribe to—he was said to have had many different forms. Some said he looked like a massive sea serpent, like a snake. Others said he appeared as a whale. I've seen paintings that showed him as some sort of dragon, with a big, dog-like head, with short stubby legs with webbed front feet, and a mermaid tail. But the one I've always liked best was the most popular rendering: a massive shark." He pointed at the center of the painting. "I've always thought the idea of this gargantuan shark, some anthropomorphic megalodon, was such an elegant yet terrifying figure in Greek culture and myth."

Patrick whispered, "I don't like it."

Jordan eyed his painting. "Really? I've always really loved this one. I like that you can't quite see what it is, only a hint of what's lurking in the murky deep. But a lot of folks back then didn't care for Cetus either. Legend goes that this Aethiopian princess named Andromeda was tied to a rock by the sea by her own father, King Cepheus, as punishment for his queen, Cassiopeia, for bragging about how much more beautiful their daughter was than Poseidon's daughter. Obviously Poseidon wasn't going to take that crap and he forced the king to either sacrifice his child to Cetus, or he would destroy his kingdom."

Patrick continued to stare, the eyes in the dark water staring back.

"But, like a knight in shining armor, Perseus saved her at the last moment and slayed the great Cetus with his sword. Stuck him in the back, if I remember correctly, and split him wide open. Obviously, there are different legends, depending on which book you read or what experts you speak to, but that's basically the gist of it. It's all pretty neat. I used to love that stuff growing up. I think I first saw the Ray

Harryhausen film when I was about your age. The remake wasn't bad, but it was missing that silly stop-motion animation. I've got both on Blu-ray if you want to watch them."

Patrick slowly shook his head.

Jordan nodded. "Okay. Would you rather take a look at that Magic the Gathering collection I was telling you about?"

Swallowing a lump in his throat, Patrick blinked rapidly, bringing himself back to reality. He turned to Jordan and nodded with a faint smile.

19

AFTER SPENDING AN HOUR in the guest room by herself, then another twenty minutes battling against cold feet and for equal cover space in Patrick's twin bed, Melissa decided drastic measures would have to be taken. She was so tired, so mentally and physically exhausted, she could probably sleep for a week and still want a nap afterward. But sleep refused to overtake her. Lying awake and counting the smattering of cobwebs shivering against the ceiling fan, her mind raced a mile a minute, and she couldn't seem to find the brake pedal. Fire and teeth, threats and impossibility—that kept her eyes peeled wide open. Every sound that clicked or rustled through the unfamiliar house made her heart skip a beat. The hell of Hoyt may have been over, but scars, inside and out, would remain.

With Patrick softly snoring beside her, she carefully crawled out of bed. In the dark, Melissa stood and watched her son with a shaking hand over her mouth. She wouldn't have wished such a day on even her worst enemy and yet she handed it to her child on a silver platter. Thankfully, the day eased into something far more salvageable, because any harder of a left turn and it would have gone right off the cliff. He was such a great kid and didn't deserve the hell she put him through. If the last week had told her anything, now was the time to change the way she operated. She couldn't go on pretending everything would naturally work itself out for the better. Steps would have to be taken, and now that Patrick appeared to accept Jordan for who he was, maybe step number one could now be crossed off that list.

She stepped out of the room and closed the door behind her, letting her fingers linger on the doorknob before turning down the hallway.

After grabbing a pillow from the spare bedroom and taking a couple of ibuprofen for her elbow, she crept up the stairs toward the last bedroom in the house. The hallway walls were completely bare, save for a few random nails jutting from the dry wall. Melissa found herself a little sad for Jordan. No pictures of his family, no friends, not even his own artwork. Before this week, she had not seen him in so long, only remembering him as the homebody, video game enthusiast in high school. She imagined moving to warmer climates brought him out in the sunlight far more often, with no need to stay indoors. He mentioned a rooftop studio. She had enjoyed watching him work in the past, back when he was a novice. Maybe he could show them tomorrow.

When she arrived at Jordan's door, she paused, readjusted the top on her pajamas, took a deep breath, and opened the door.

Jordan immediately sat up in bed. Cell phone in his hand, his eyes were wide with surprise. Melissa froze in the doorway, her own eyes bursting with confusion.

She smirked. "Did I catch you at a bad time?"

Jordan dropped back down on the bed with a sigh. "Holy shit, you scared me! I didn't realize you were still up. Wow . . . I think I can taste my balls."

"Speaking of which . . . what were you doing?"

He grinned and turned his phone around. "I was on Facebook. You caught me red-handed trying to find your profile."

She crossed her arms over the pillow, her face flushing hot. "Yeah . . . I may have blocked you."

"Why?"

She pulled a face.

"Oh, yeah."

"I did it a long time ago. Sorry about that. I'll make sure to lift the ban tomorrow." She shifted uncomfortably. "Listen . . . I, uh . . . I'm having trouble sleeping."

Jordan nodded. "Yeah. Me, too."

"Would you mind?"

His eyes enlarged. "In here? Yeah. Yeah, absolutely." He began to climb out of bed.

Melissa stopped him. "No, no! I didn't mean for you to leave."

In his blue and yellow Indiana Pacers T-shirt and red boxer shorts, Jordan paused and arched an inquisitive eyebrow.

"No!" She waved her hand. "It's not like that. I'm not looking for funny business. I just . . . I'm having trouble sleeping and I think maybe sleeping with someone—*near* someone—might help me relax and fall asleep, you know?"

Jordan nodded vigorously. "Yeah, totally. No problem." He pulled the comforter down and patted the bed. "Hop in."

Smiling, Melissa worked to calm her nerves as she placed her pillow down and crawled into the cool side of the bed. The memory foam beneath her swallowed her back. "Very comfy."

"I don't spend a lot of money on frivolous items, but there are two things I never cheap out on: a good mattress and soft toilet paper. Hey, I can sleep on top of the covers if you'd like."

"Don't be silly. Seriously, it's okay! I trust you." For once, it felt so good to say those words and believe them.

Nodding, Jordan eased himself back into his side of the bed and pulled the comforter over his chest. "I can't even remember the last time I had someone in my bed with me."

"I have a very hard time believing that."

He turned his head toward her. "I'm not sure if you've noticed, but New Smyrna is only a few steps away from being geriatric central. And those who aren't middle aged housewives are probably too young for me anyway."

"You can't tell me you haven't had any hookups since you've lived down here. A guy as handsome as you?"

Blushing, Jordan smiled. "Well, believe it or not, artist groupies do exist. Not so many here—but in Orlando? They don't call it The City Beautiful for nothing."

Melissa rolled her eyes. "Men, all the same."

"Ah, I'm joking. You know I'm not like that."

"To be honest, Jordan, I don't know what you're like anymore." She turned her head to face him. "It's been, like, thirteen years. I don't know how much you've changed."

"I've got longer hair now. That's different."

"As far as I can tell, that's the only thing. You still seem to be the same person you were back in high school."

He pulled a face. "Well, I'd like to think I've changed quite a bit since then."

"No, no, I don't mean that as an insult—far from it! What I mean is I think you're still the same sweet, kind-hearted person you were all those years ago. You still appear to have all the same great qualities that attracted me to you back in our sophomore year. I can't begin to tell you what a relief that is to me." She paused to swallow. "I was absolutely terrified today was going to go so badly. I had to take sleeping pills last night because I was so nervous and antsy. I keep thinking what would have happened had I not woken up, had the . . . fire . . . taken me and Patrick."

"But you guys are okay—"

"Please let me finish. I keep seeing it like a movie, replaying it over and over. We could have died, and you would have never seen your son. You would have gone on your entire life, never knowing him. I would have deprived you of that. I would have died with that on my conscience. And even now that tears me up." Melissa wiped her eyes with the back of her hand.

"But you're not gone." Jordan offered her a tissue from the box on his nightstand. She waved it away. "You're right here, safe and sound."

"Yes, but you don't know how close we were to being killed. We were lucky to get out of there alive." She lifted her bandaged elbow. "Christ, I shredded my elbow trying to leave last night. I guess what I'm trying to say is . . . thank you. Thank you for still being the same genuine person you were all those years ago. Thank you for making today and all this drama so much easier to deal with. I've spent so many years putting Patrick through hell with white lies and terrible ex's and keeping him from knowing where he came from. I don't know how he came out so normal from all this. I love him so *fucking* much. He's such a good kid. And now that I'm seeing him next to you, I can see why. He's so much like you it's not even funny. I mean really, even down to the way he has to touch his food with his tongue before he eats it. I'm just happy he turned out like the less screwed-up one of us."

Jordan shook his head. "You're grossly selling yourself short, Mel. Listen, I've only known Patrick for maybe fifteen hours, but I can tell he has your best attributes, too. He's thoughtful, he's very smart, and the few times he did smile, it was like looking right at you. You didn't screw him up. If anything, you made him into a tough kid. There may be some cracks, but who doesn't have some of those? I don't blame you for anything. You were protecting your child, just like any good parent would do. In your position, I probably would have done the same thing."

She sniffled. "*Probably?*"

"Well, I mean, I probably wouldn't have blocked you on social media. Like, I would have taken a picture of him wearing a shirt with your face on it and waited for you to drunkenly find it one night on Instagram while scrolling for ex-boyfriends."

Smacking his arm, Melissa barked out a laugh. "You're such an ass." She faced him again. "I'm sorry. I've said it a hundred times now, but I am."

CRUEL SUMMER

With glassy eyes, he smiled. "Stop apologizing. We're good. I promise."

She nodded and returned her eyes to the shadowed ceiling. "So what do we do now?"

Jordan sighed. "I don't know. I think we just enjoy the little time we have together and figure it out later. If I keep thinking about you two leaving already, I might . . . "

"Yeah."

A few moments passed in silence. "Let's go to sleep. I think I finally can now." He clicked the lamp off, and the room plunged into darkness.

Suddenly Melissa began to giggle.

"What's so funny?" Jordan asked.

"Of course you have tissues by your bed. Of course you do."

Jordan's grin shined in the dark. "Shut up."

Before long, Jordan began to snore softly, and soon after, Melissa found sleep nibbling at her eyes. She closed them, and for once she found herself drifting off without a knot in her stomach . . .

SATURDAY

20

. . . AND THEN WAKING IN a sea of black. Unsure of how long she'd been asleep, Melissa slowly fluttered open her eyes, expecting to see a dark bedroom ceiling or feel the relaxed breath of the oscillating floor fan on her face. What she received was the sudden sting of ice cold water. And it wasn't just in her eyes—it was everywhere. In her ears, up her nose, coating her naked flesh. Her eyes stung as she kept them open. Gloomy shadows and thin shafts of moonlight, all slow dancing in the ebb and flow. She lifted her head, petite bubbles escaping her nostrils. No surface. No bottom. Only water. Lifting her hand, she snapped her fingers, listening to the hollow whisk her digits made.

This had to be a dream. She closed her eyes once more, willing herself to wake up and reach out to Jordan, to feel his warmth. Melissa yawned.

Water immediately filled her mouth.

Her eyes snapped open—a swift, sobering realization this wasn't a dream. She attempted to scream, which only added to the icy liquid grasping her taste buds. She exhaled, pushing it all out, and set to thrashing her arms. She worked her upper body, kicking her legs like a frog. Her arms in sync with her lower half, she willed herself to propel upward. Her body refused to move. Rapid movements got her nowhere. She stretched her feet out, hoping to touch something below her, something to give her a better understanding of where she was or how deep she could have been, but her reach was as effective as her ability to surface. That's when she really began to panic.

Her failure to comprehend how this was happening came second to the need to breathe. The more she struggled, the more she spun and filled her murky world with bubbles, and the more her lungs burned with fire. Seconds trudged past, each one full of panic and flurry. She watched as the bubbles rose and rose, higher and higher, never hitting the top. Melissa's brain screamed, and her mouth craved to do the same.

Something flashed through the water.

Her panic halted. The water around her instantly chilled. When the flash repeated, this time off to her left, her movements slowed, the water transmuting to mud.

Another flash, this time closer. A thick, gray body slipped through the shadows.

Her chest felt ready to burst, her heart hammering away.

No no no no! she frantically thought. *I killed you! You're dead!*

The shape darted around her like a fleshy knife. Her body growing weak, Melissa tried to keep up, but the white, pillowy fuzz around her vision expanded. Her tired limbs grew frigid and stiff.

He whispered, "*And yet . . . here you are . . .* "
Another flash. Closer. Colder.
"*. . . a willing participant . . .* "
Her chin drifted down to her chest.
"*. . . a Queen's vanity . . .* "
Hands curled like wilting flowers.
"*. . . a King's scapegoat . . .* "
Melissa's eyelids drifted shut.
"*. . . and wouldn't you know it, Princess . . . .it's my mealtime . . .* "
Another flash, this time with teeth.

Water be damned, she jerked awake with a yelp, and her cry was answered with a mouthful of black water. Before she could fight, Hoyt shot forward and sank his massive mouth onto her chest. In that split second, Melissa felt hordes of jagged teeth sink around the soft meat of her right breast. Dark blood flooded the water. Adrenaline surging, she screamed with all her heart, but her pain was as trapped as she was. Liquid rushed down her throat, filling her stomach and lungs. Through the mud, she reached out to grab Hoyt's head. Her fingers slipped over his smooth, bald cranium, and ran across the half dozen long gill slits along his neck. She met a narrow black eye, which had now fully shifted to the side of his head. The eye winked. Her lungs drowning, Melissa attempted to close her mouth, but a large, webbed gray fist darted toward her face. Two thick, tattooed fingers jutted down her throat.

As the world faded away, Melissa only had one thought: *Please don't let him hurt my baby*.

Another flash ripped through the dark water. Hoyt roared, sending a shock wave through Melissa's body.

She instantly came to. A second flash, and the serrated teeth left her chest. His fingers ripped from her mouth, taking a front tooth with it. The pain was instantaneous, drawing more blood from both her wounds. Melissa fully opened her eyes.

A long metal pole jabbed through the water and repeatedly stabbed at Hoyt's long, angular skull. The pole disappeared and in a blink it came back down into the water and sank right into the dense, black orb of his left eye. Hoyt howled, his gray body spinning madly. Before he could grasp the pole, it was yanked from his eye, spraying thick black blood throughout the already clouded water.

Melissa kicked her legs and tried to back away, but the pain in her chest was too great to ignore. Chemicals in the water crept into the bites, causing her to scream in agony. The mud cleared, and she continued to kick. Eventually her back hit a hard, flat surface, startling her.

With one good eye, Hoyt spun toward her and grimaced, his mouth full of angry blades.

In a blink, he shot toward her.

Two hands dipped in front of her face and grasped ahold of her arm pits. Before she could protest, Melissa was pulled upward.

Cold, night air accosted her as she was lifted from the water and drug backwards across a smooth pad of concrete. Melissa gasped for air, then immediately vomited the water in her throat. Quick hands spun her onto her side, allowing the water to drain from her mouth and lungs.

"Melissa, breathe!" Jordan yelled, patting her back. "Breathe in deep, in and out, in and out."

CRUEL SUMMER

She did so, spitting out the last of the chlorine water from her mouth. Panting, she tried to form words, but her tongue was seized with shock, her breath unable to find her. Blood continued to drip down her chest and lips.

Behind them, water exploded from the pool and across the deck. Melissa shrieked and threw herself backwards, grunting as the broken skin on her chest stretched and opened wider. Jordan leapt to his feet and faced the pool.

Hoyt bellowed a vicious roar as his upper body splashed out from the water. His massive, balled fists beat at the swaying surface.

Jordan stumbled back and cried, *"What in the fuck?"*

Grabbing onto the lip of the pool, Hoyt began to lift himself out of the water. His body was so much larger now, his hulking gray torso heaving with raw, untamed strength. He glared resentfully at them both. *"Andromeda! Come back to me! You're mine!"*

Growing white with shock, Melissa continued to crawl away toward the house, covering her naked body with her arms. Frozen in place, Jordan gazed upon the creature pulling itself from his pool. The shrill music of crickets rose and fell like a heartbeat.

"Jordan, run!" Melissa cried.

Jordan did not run. Instead, he took a defiant step forward and, reaching back into the waistband of his shorts, produced a pistol. He lifted the firearm at Hoyt. Now noticing the weapon, Hoyt growled. He slammed his fist into the concrete deck, shattering the block pad, and then threw himself backwards. Water splashed over the edge of the pool, covering them both and soaking much of the mesh screen walls surrounding them. Jordan marched toward the water, the pistol held out before him. Shaking, he stood there for several seconds, aiming.

When the crickets were the only remaining sound, Jordan turned back to her. His face was now as white as hers. "What . . . in . . . *the fuck* . . . was that?"

21

AFTER COVERING MELISSA WITH a couple of pool towels they had left out to dry earlier that day, Jordan helped her back inside, keeping one balled-up towel pressed firmly against her chest wound. Melissa wanted to hold the makeshift bandage herself, but her arms remained weak and stiff, and despite being covered up, her nudeness make her skin prickle with embarrassment. Since escaping the pool, she hadn't bothered to speculate how she even got there in the first place. At the moment, all she cared about was getting her wounds and body dressed.

Her arm around his shoulder, Jordan carefully carried her into the house. They stopped at Patrick's bedroom door, and Melissa quickly checked on her son, relieved to find him still sleeping. When they passed through the kitchen, Jordan stopped briefly to sit his gun down and to reach for the digital phone sitting in its cradle on the counter.

"What are you doing?" she asked, cringing at the waves of pain in her chest and mouth.

Jordan tapped at the dial pad. "What do you think? I'm calling the police and an ambulance."

Melissa quickly lashed out and slapped the phone from his grip. It hit the linoleum floor and slid beneath the dinner table.

"What the hell are you doing?" he yelled.

"No cops, please. And no ambulance."

He stared in confusion. "Excuse me? You were just attacked and you're hurt! What do you mean—"

"I said no!" she shrieked. Jordan stiffened beside her. The silence grew heavy and uncomfortable. She swallowed and said, "You can't. *I* can't."

Sighing, Jordan shook his head. "Melissa, why? You're bleeding all over the place. For Christ's sake, can I at least drive you to the hospital?"

"The hospital is on the other side of the causeway. And even if we could get there, I just . . . can't."

The silence returning, Jordan stared at her for several long moments. She refused to meet his eyes. Finally, he asked, "Mel . . . what are you not telling me?"

The towel still held tight against her chest, she bit her tongue, instead focusing on the consistent, rhythmic throbs of pain.

"Who—or *what*—was that in my pool?"

Melissa swallowed the lump in her throat. It was slow to descend. "Do you have a first aid kit?"

"I have antiseptics and some gauze, yes."

She nodded toward the bathroom. "I need to sit."

~

While she sat on the toilet, Jordan was on his knees, gingerly dabbing hydrogen peroxide-soaked cotton balls on her bites. They were not nearly as deep as she originally feared, but nevertheless the ache still hissed through the new gap in her teeth. She hated that her bare breast was exposed, but there was no way to properly cover herself. She attempted to keep her hand over her breast, but Jordan was unable to work around her arm.

"You can stop being embarrassed," he said. "We're both adults, and it's not like I haven't seen it before."

Dropping her hand, she nodded sadly, still looking at the floor.

He continued to work on her wounds. While one hand applied medicine, the other wiped the tears of blood that wept down her chest. "This isn't going to help. It might stop infection for now, but these cuts are only going to open up the more you move. Plus, I don't have anything to sew them up with."

He leaned forward, getting a better look. He gazed up to her. "They're bites, aren't they?"

She nodded.

Jordan stopped talking and went back to work. After cleaning her wounds the best he could with what little he had in his cabinet, he rolled out a length of white gauze and cut several pieces, then carefully taped them over the individual openings. Realizing her hair was still a dripping mess, he handed her a fresh towel from the closet.

"Alright, now that I've done my part, it's time to do yours. I need an explanation of what the fuck is happening."

While drying her hair, she glanced up to him. "All these years, and this is the first time I've heard you say 'fuck' this many times in one night."

"It's a fucked-up kind of night." He put his hands on his hips. "Stop changing the subject."

"Can you please get me some clothes to wear first? Please?"

Jordan sighed. "Yeah, absolutely. I probably should have grabbed them earlier." The moment he slipped out of the bathroom, Melissa felt short of breath. Her heart began to thunder, her nerves like lightning strikes beneath her skin. By the time Jordan returned, she was hyperventilating. Tears streamed down her face, and her hands struggled to cover her face. "Jesus, Melissa?" He dropped the clothes on the floor and knelt down to hug her, careful not to squeeze too hard. "Calm down. Seriously, breathe. Breathe."

Melissa sucked in deep, wavering breaths as she tried to steady the sudden outburst of emotion. She had not been expecting it, and though her body was wracked with guilt, she refused to hide it any longer. She was sick of burying it deep down where it ate her away like a cancer. She was actually glad this was happening now, with someone she really trusted. It was time to let it out.

"We killed him."

Keeping his hands on her shoulders, Jordan backed away. "Come again?"

Melissa wiped her eyes. "Patrick and I . . . we killed him."

Jordan cocked his head. "What? You . . . *what*?"

"Hoyt. My boyfriend."

Jordan let go of her shoulders and stood up. "Your *boyfriend*? Why am I just now hearing about a *boyfriend*?"

"Because I didn't think it was necessary to bring him up."

"Not necessary? I think it's a pretty big thing to not bring up to me when you're crashing back into my life like the Kool-Aid Man, saying '*Oh, yeah! You have a son!*'"

Melissa screamed, "I didn't think it was necessary because we fucking killed him, you insensitive asshole!"

Jordan remained silent. He backed away until his back hit the wall.

Angry and sick of being embarrassed, Melissa stood, dropping the towels at her feet. She then snatched her clothes and quickly put them on. When she was dressed, she pushed her hair behind her ears and sat back down on the toilet. "Patrick and I didn't come down here alone. We brought my boyfriend, Hoyt, with us. Hoyt . . . he was a son of a bitch—a *real* son of a bitch—but I wasn't much better myself. I spent years being this prototypical cliché, thinking I could tame the wild animal, instead of dumping his abusive ass after the first time he hit me."

Jordan went to speak, but Melissa stopped him. "I'm still speaking."

He nodded, obviously biting his tongue.

She continued. "I thought this trip was going to be a last ditch effort to salvage our relationship, but over and over he continued to prove me wrong. On Tuesday morning, Hoyt took the three of us on a fishing trip a few miles out at sea." Melissa ground her teeth together. "The bastard started abusing Patrick again and then, in a last ditch effort to save his skin, he tried to propose to me. Naturally I turned him down, and naturally he got violent again. So we fought back."

She slammed her fist on the porcelain sink next to her. "We took a baseball bat and we hit him—" When that didn't satisfy her, she snatched the metal toilet paper stand off the floor and bashed it on the corner of the tub. "—and we hit him and we hit him and we hit him—" The stand snapped in half and crashed into the empty tub. She dropped the other half on the floor. "—and then we tossed his cheating, woman beating, child abusing ass off the boat and left him for fucking dead! And he deserved every goddamn hit we gave him! Every ounce of saltwater he swallowed on the way down! He deserved to die!" Melissa sucked in a deep breath. "Yet . . . he didn't."

Jordan continued to stare as his back slid down the wall. He dropped to the floor and remained there, silent, as she continued to spill her guts.

"I don't know what happened, Jordan, but I can tell you this: he didn't stay down. I can't even begin to imagine what happened after he went under . . . but he keeps coming back. Teasing us. Taunting us. Then attacking us. And every time he does, he changes. It's like, I don't know, he's becoming an animal—literally. I mean, you saw it! He's nearly unrecognizable now. He looks like a monster. Like—like a—"

"A shark."

Melissa met Jordan's bewildered gaze. "Yeah . . . like a shark."

He ran a hand down his dazed face. "I . . . This is all so . . . shit. I don't know what to say, Mel."

"Say you'll help us get the hell off this island. Say you'll help get us as far away from him as possible. He's keeping us here. I know it was him that broke the bridges on the causeways. It sounds insane, I know, but he's got *powers* now or something. He's able to control things like water—"

"*What?*"

"—and other animals! We were at the park up the street, and the manatees came out of the water and attacked us—"

"Oh fucking come on, Melissa! Now you're sounding like a crazy person."

Melissa angrily pointed to light bloodstains spreading underneath her shirt. "As crazy as a shark man pulling me into your pool and trying to bite my tit off? Crazy like *that*, Jordan? You know what? You're right. You're absolutely right. I'm a crazy person. All these years of letting Hoyt abuse us, and I probably should have let him kill Patrick and I on that goddamn boat! It would have saved you all this trouble, right? You could have just went on living your perfect little surfer boy, goody goody, artist life here in Florida, and we would have never forced ourselves into your house and ruined your whole week. Is that right?"

"Damn it, Mel, you know that's not what I meant!"

"Then what exactly did you mean?"

"Well, shit, just listen to yourself. Let's shelve the fact for a moment that you admitted to murder."

"It was self-defense."

"Second degree, whatever." He waved her off. "Regardless, you're now telling me that said boyfriend came back from the dead and is—what?—out to eat your flesh? Exact revenge? Tell me, if this situation was reversed, and you were sitting here looking at you, exactly how would you feel?"

Frustrated and full of adrenaline, Melissa sighed and ran her shaking hands through her drying hair. She could understand where he was coming from, could absolutely sympathize, but she hadn't even told him everything. Jordan wasn't there for the fear, for the desperation—didn't have the lingering taste of the bastard's fingers in the back of her mouth.

No, he didn't know the half of it.

"Jordan . . . whether you choose to believe any of it or not, I really don't care. *I* know it's true. Our son knows it's true. And whether your brain chooses to acknowledge it, your own eyes saw what they saw. Hoyt's going to keep coming back until he kills us. After that? Who knows? He could continue to alter and get bigger and stronger and take out this entire island—hell, maybe even the whole state? Are you going to believe then, Jordan? Are you going to believe in Cetus then?"

Jordan immediately pulled a face. "What did you say?"

"What?"

"That name. What was that name again?"

She shrugged, waving her hand. "Cetus? When he attacked us in our condo room two nights ago, he mentioned that name. I think he said, 'Cetus was an ageless hell' and 'it was all our fault he was here.' The first time he revealed himself, he said something like, 'Cetus needs me.' I have absolutely no clue what any of it means."

Jordan audibly swallowed. "He called you Andromeda."

"What?"

"When he was pulling himself up out of the pool, he called you Andromeda. You heard that, right?"

"I honestly don't remember. It's all such a blur right now."

Jordan got to his feet before pacing the tiny bathroom. He ran a hand over the nape of his neck. "Yeah, I thought maybe, I don't know, I imagined it or something. I mean, shit, some giant animal was attacking you. I guess I wasn't even thinking of anything other than getting you away from it. It spoke, right? I didn't just imagine that?"

Melissa stared at him, then shook her head.

"He—*Hoyt*—called you *Andromeda*. I can hear it clear as day now. He yelled, 'Andromeda' and then said, 'You're mine.'"

"I don't understand. What does that even mean?"

He continued to pace. "Andromeda . . . he called you that. And you said he called himself Cetus? Jesus, this is unreal."

"Jordan, are you going to slow down and explain what you're thinking?"

Finally Jordan stopped, but his eyes were still staring off into the distance, where his thoughts appeared to be piecing themselves together. "Christ, it feels like déjà vu. Come on." He exited the bathroom.

"What are you talking about?"

"Just come here!"

With a huff, she stood and followed him out of the bathroom and through the hallway into the living room. Jordan flipped on the light and then stepped over to his bookshelf against the far wall. When he found what he was looking for, he pulled out an oversized hardcover book and stepped up beside her. Rapidly thumbing through, her eyes followed each picture-filled page. Despite the medicine and bandages, the bites on her chest throbbed with her heartbeat, and the feeling made her lightheaded and woozy. Mixed with the continuous surges of excitement and the lack of sleep, she was having trouble focusing. By the time Jordan found what he was looking for, a bout of nausea was taking hold.

"It wasn't even twelve hours ago I was talking to Patrick about this."

Her blurred eyes followed his finger as it pointed to an image on the glossy page. An alarmingly detailed painting of a cliff side, looking over a vast ocean. At the edge of the outcropping, a beautiful woman was chained by the arms and legs to a boulder twice her size. Next to her, standing proudly at the edge of the cliff was a tall, shirtless, muscular man, holding a great sword that gleamed in the brilliant sunlight. His stance suggested he was waiting, if not beckoning, for something to test his strength. Below them both, a massive fin had risen from the blue glass of the water. Just beneath that, an even bigger shape, one that suggested its full immensity would dwarf them both, appeared ready to break the surface and wreak havoc.

Jordan pointed at the ominous shape beneath the waves. "Cetus." He moved his finger up to the cliff and to the captive woman. "Andromeda."

Melissa's eyes crossed, her breath coming short. "How do we . . . fight him?"

"Well, short of having a Greek God on our side—" His finger moved to the sword-clad warrior standing defiant and ready to fight. "—I have no damn clue."

As her eyes landed on the chained woman—Andromeda—Melissa's knees buckled. She collapsed to the floor with a huff.

"Melissa!" Jordan tossed the book to the side and dropped to his knees, cupping her head so it wouldn't fully hit the carpeted floor. Carefully, he tapped her cheek. "Jesus, Melissa, are you okay? Mel, open your eyes."

"Ye . . . yes."

Jordan sighed. "You just scared the shit out of me!"

"I don't feel well."

"You're faint from blood loss, hon. Here." Ever so gently, he helped Melissa to her feet and guided her over to the couch. She laid her head against the back cushion. "You're probably dehydrated, too." He leaned over and examined her shirt. "You're seeping through your bandages. I'm going to get more gauze from the bathroom and I'll be right back with a bottle of water, okay?" He took off with long strides toward the back hallway.

Her eyes closed, she nodded. The waves of nausea were gone, but the dizziness remained, making her feel like she was descending a never-ending twirly slide. She continued to breathe in deep, hoping it would calm her heart. Of all the muscles being overused lately, it deserved the rest.

"Mel?"

"Yes?"

"*Mel?*"

Her heart began to thump again. Her eyes shot open. His tone sent violent shivers running down her spine. Despite the weakness, Melissa pushed herself up to her feet and stumbled down toward the hallway. When she reached Jordan's side, she followed his terrified gaze to the floor.

Pools of scummy black water had gathered across the bare wooden floorboards, leading from the back sliding door down the whole length of the hallway, past the downstairs guest bedrooms to the kitchen. Water dripped from the ceiling and down the walls as if a silent storm had raged through only moments before. A salty brine permeated the air.

Jordan asked, "You weren't dripping this badly, were you?"

"*Patrick!*"

The pain and dizziness forgotten, Melissa raced across the sopping wet floor until she reached the bedroom she had left her son in hours before. Water dribbled off and around the doorknob. Not wanting to put her hand on it, she shouldered open the door, sending it crashing against the inner wall. She flicked up the light switch.

The room, now bathed in light, was not quite what she feared. Unlike the hallway, it appeared dry and unbothered, exactly how she left it before joining Jordan upstairs. Jordan stepped into the room beside her. Together they moved toward the bed.

"Patrick?"

Though she couldn't physically see her son's body, she could see his outline underneath the comforter, which had been pulled up fully over the top of the bed.

"Patrick, hon?"

"Patrick?"

Something squirmed underneath the comforter. Something slimy and wet.

Jordan leapt forward and tore the comforter from the bed.

Melissa screamed and collapsed to her knees.

CRUEL SUMMER

Beneath the heavy blanket, Jordan exposed a mattress teaming with glistening sea life, roughly in the shape of a young boy. Fish of all shapes and sizes flipped and flopped as they struggled mightily for oxygen. Crabs and shrimp skittered about the sopping sheets, crawling over elongated bodies of eels, who curled up and hissed at the sudden exposure to light. At the head of the bed, placed just so on the pillow, was a blob fish who stared at them helplessly. Its frowning lips opened and closed, as if mouthing its apology.

Melissa cried out once more, reaching for the bed. Jordan pulled her away, leading her out of the room and away from the wriggling nightmare.

"Jordan, he has Patrick! He has our son!"

"Listen, they couldn't have gone far. We were just in the hallway not five minutes ago. He has to be close. Come on."

She followed Jordan back to the kitchen, where he snatched the pistol from the countertop. For the next several minutes, they ran from room to room, screaming Patrick's name, tearing open every door, looking under and into every empty space. After a quick search of the back patio and pool came up empty, they rushed upstairs and searched Jordan's bedroom.

He slammed the closet door shut. "Fuck!"

Melissa stood up from looking underneath the bed. Tears rushed down her cheeks. She was shocked to find she even had enough moisture left in her to cry out. "Jordan, where is he? *Where is he?*"

"Shit, shit, shit!" Jordan turned toward the side window. "Come on!" He unlocked the side door and threw it open, leading them out to the wooden staircase attached to the side of the house. "Let's see if we can spot them from above."

Melissa followed him up the steps and soon she found herself looking out over the neighborhood. It was still early, but the morning sun was beginning to rise, kissing the roof and treetops with the lightest touch of shimmering gold. A warm, gentle breeze whipped past them, cooling the sweat collecting on her brow. Despite the still calm of the early hours, she was anything but.

Jordan pushed aside his easels and paint table and leaned over the side. "See anything?"

Melissa shook her head, fighting the screams wanting to burst from her throat. She raced from side to side, unable to see anything but the vinyl siding of the surrounding houses. No Patrick. No Hoyt.

"Here." Jordan handed her a pair of binoculars, which he had stored on a small shelf against the wall.

Pressing them to her eyes, she adjusted the focus wheel and then swept her vision across the neighborhood and beyond. The slightest movement caused her heart to leap, but each time it turned into a car or an early morning jogger, it sank. She lifted the binoculars higher, toward the ocean.

Beyond the one lane highway, a yacht raced across the water. Upon closer inspection, the boat appeared to be unmanned, zipping through the water like a freshly discharged bullet. Melissa moved the binoculars to the right. A long, braided rope was stretched taut as it dragged something heavy through the water behind it.

The boat hit a wave, causing it to leap into the air.

CRUEL SUMMER

The rope pulled tight with the weight and lifted out of the water. Patrick's body flew out with it.

22

THERE WERE ONLY A few instances in Jordan's thirty-two years of life where he had felt absolute terror.

The first time was when he was eleven years old, in the midst of sixth grade and desperately awaiting Christmas break. His parents were visiting his aunt and uncle in Terre Haute over Thanksgiving weekend, and his cousin, Samantha, then a budding sixteen year old, couldn't wait to show off her new car. Based on its tremendous length, the teal Dodge Intrepid reminded a young Jordan of a party boat he had seen floating in the summertime on the backwaters of the Ohio River, and he didn't hesitate to call it a pontoon. This got him a swift punch to the arm, but one with love, as Samantha, after a few moments of thought, decided to deem her new ride Ponty.

Looking up to his cousin like the older sister he never had, Jordan desperately wanted to take a ride in Ponty. He himself couldn't wait to get older, to be able to shave like his Dad, to watch rated R movies without supervision (which he did with the assistance of Joe Bob Briggs late on Saturday nights with Monster Vision, long after his parents fell asleep), and to be able to drive himself to St. Louis to watch baseball or hockey games all on his own. But right then, all he wanted was a joy ride with his cousin. When her parents asked her to drive down to the grocery store for eggs for the cookies they were baking, Samantha begged them to let Jordan come along. After initial protests, both sets of adults allowed it, and instructed them to travel very slow, mind the snow and ice, and only drive when Jordan was buckled up in the backseat. Being children, they unquestionably agreed and then took off, but being children, they straightaway ignored the strict rules with a hearty laugh. The moment they left the driveway, Jordan unbuckled and crawled into the front seat. Samantha also unlatched herself and displayed just how far the gas pedal could be pressed down to the floor.

While they fumbled with the tape deck adapter and argued over which CD to jam out to, their childish quarreling took their eyes away from the road . . . and the black ice spread across it. The car spun. The children screamed. A Bradford pear tree rushed out from the woods to greet them. In a flash, the driver's side struck the tree's thick trunk. Glass exploded across their laps. Jordan was thrown from his seat into his cousin's side. At the exact same time, her window burst, cracking in half. The force of his body threw her toward the door. By the time the car had stopped moving, Jordan tumbled back into his own seat. He had no idea what had happened. When he realized two of his fingers on his right hand were broken, both bent in opposite directions, he screamed wildly for his cousin. She didn't respond. He leaned over to see why.

A thick sheet of shattered glass had nearly scalped his older cousin. The foot-long, blood-covered glass had slid up the side of her head, scraping against her skull, though thankfully not penetrating the bone, and had exited the top of her head like a gleaming horn. Jordan watched in mute horror as her scalp slowly slid away from her head and down her cheek. His own pain forgotten, Jordan quickly exited the car and sat on the side of the unfamiliar road and wept. Twenty minutes later, a car stopped and found them.

Samantha survived the whole ordeal, but she was never the same. She immediately withdrew from school and remained with her parents to be taught from home. She never went to college. Never married. She eventually moved from her parent's, living alone in a tiny apartment in Fort Wayne, where she worked from home and rarely left the house. Being that his aunt and uncle weren't wealthy and couldn't afford the full plastic surgery required to fix her injury, she remained a shut-in and refused to attend any family functions from that point on. Jordan hadn't seen her since that night at the hospital. He tried to keep in contact with her, even now, but his letters, texts and emails remained unanswered. He remained hopeful she would someday find happiness.

His other test in extreme fear was much more recent and far more personal. Though he was no celebrity, he had garnered a few fans in the art community who desired to know Jordan outside of an art gallery. Once such case was a young woman named Camilla who he met at a small show of his in Tampa. She had taken a liking to him and spent several weeks private messaging him through every social media account he had. Being quite lonely most of the time, Jordan relented and finally invited her over for a night. A night became a weekend. A weekend became a week. By the following Saturday she had left, and Jordan, a little sore, felt a bit less lonely. Hookups didn't happen often, but he relished them when they did.

What he didn't relish was the text he received two months later.

Jordan spent the next several days on pins and needles, waiting to hear back from his doctor about his test results. He couldn't sleep. Couldn't eat. At times he forgot how to breathe. Ready for his life to be over, he split his time between staring at the wall and dry heaving into the toilet. After getting the negative test results back, it took him another two days before he moved his sleeping place from the bathroom floor back into his bed. It was another three days before he could finally stop shaking. He swore to himself he would never be so careless again.

As terrible as those two instances were, he would re-live them every day for the rest of his life over having to witness his child in mortal danger.

It only took a quick look through the binoculars to show what had Melissa violently screaming. The small yacht, which could comfortably hold around five or six people, currently held none as it tore wildly through the Atlantic waters. Jordan felt his stomach drop like an elevator cab down a shaft when he saw Patrick's flailing body rise fifteen feet into the air before crashing back down into the endless blue. Even in that moment of sheer terror and confusion, he was thankful his son was somehow still alive.

Before he could add to Melissa's parental, nightmarish shrieks, she had already taken off down the stairs. He ran after her, then stopped. A horrible thought washed over him. One more look into the binoculars and his fear was becoming a reality.

Despite being unmanned, the boat had corrected itself and was running parallel to the beach. A long direct line north. Toward the Inlet.

Toward Shark Cove.

Jordan dropped the binoculars and dashed after Melissa.

By the time he reached the bottom of the stairs and shouldered open the door, she was already down the inside steps and into the kitchen. Jordan followed hastily, pausing only long enough to grab his keys from the bowl on the counter near the stove. When he ran outside, Melissa had already started her SUV and was throwing it into reverse. Jordan ripped open the passenger door and leapt inside, dropping his pistol into the cup holder in the middle console.

"Melissa, where are you going?"

After backing into the street, Melissa jerked the car into drive and hit the gas, sending the vehicle roaring forward. "Where do you think I'm going? That's my son out there!"

"I don't mean that! What—are you going to drive us into the water?"

"*If I fucking have to!*"

"Listen, my homeowner has a small speed boat he leaves docked at the marina a few miles down the road, behind us on the river side. I have the keys. Let's take that and get to him quickly. Take a right up here."

"How are we going to get to him quickly if we're

on the river side? It'll take us forever to get around to the ocean."

Jordan paused. "The yacht . . . it's heading right for the cove."

Melissa turned to him with wide, horrified eyes.

"Jesus, Mel—eyes on the road! Slow down and take a left up here."

"Don't tell me to calm down, Jordan!"

"I didn't tell you to calm down, damn it, I told you to slow down! *Slow down.* You're going to hit another car or a jogger or something!" Visions of his cousin flashed through his memory as he held tight to the dashboard and arm rest. "We're not going to be any good to Patrick if we're lying upside down in a ditch."

Melissa growled in frustration, letting up on the gas as she pulled out of his residential neighborhood and onto A1A South. When they saw the coast was relatively clear of any traffic, Melissa gunned the engine once more and raced down the highway. Though he couldn't see the ocean past the rows of houses lining the other side of the street, it was nauseating to be driving in the opposite direction.

Hold on, Patrick. Just hold on . . .

Jordan's hand instinctively went to his gun. He wasn't much of a shot and he certainly didn't believe in the supernatural, but if this Hoyt-Cetus was a real thing, then Jordan planned to empty the pistol's magazine right between bastard's eyes. Melissa started to cry again, and it only added to his anger. Nobody—*nobody*—was going to hurt his son or their mother.

"Right up here."

They took a hard turn into the marina parking lot.

A moment later an unmarked police car pulled in behind them, lights flashing. Jordan and Melissa swiftly exited the SUV. Jordan carefully stuck the pistol in the back of his shorts.

A woman in a dark suit leapt out of her car, her gun drawn. Her long brown hair was a tangled mess, sweat-soaked locks escaping her ponytail. Her firm, bloodshot eyes gave away her lack of sleep. "Both of you, down on the ground! Now!"

Heart racing, Jordan threw his hands up, keeping his eyes on the detective's weapon.

On the other side of the SUV, Melissa slammed her door shut. "Fuck off, Holzer!"

"Ms. Braun, I will only ask you one more time. I mean it. Put your hands up, slowly drop to your knees, and lie face down on the ground. You too, mister. Now!"

While Jordan did as she asked, Melissa yelled, "Come on, Jordan! We don't have the time for this!"

Gun still raised, the detective—Holzer—took an assertive, unblinking step toward Melissa. "Goddamn it, Braun, don't make me shoot you! We've been searching for you for the last thirty-six hours, and I will not hesitate to take you down, with force if I must."

"Leave us alone! He's going to die!"

She craned her head to look into the SUV's back window. "Where's the kid?"

Face blood red, Melissa screamed, *"That's what I'm trying to tell you, you stupid bitch!* Patrick is out there in the water! He's going to fucking die if we don't get to him!"

Holzer eyed them both, sweat dripping down her face in rivulets. "What the hell are you talking about?"

"It's true," Jordan said, hands still held up. "Patrick is out there in serious danger, and if we don't get to my boat to go help him, he could die." *If he already hasn't.*

The double-fisted gun swung toward him. "Who are you again?"

"I'm Jordan Schwartz. I'm the boy's father."

Holzer pulled a face. "His father?" She turned to Melissa. "I thought your missing boyfriend was his—"

"*We don't have time for this shit!*" Melissa slammed her fist into the side panel of her SUV. "The longer we fucking stand here and talk, the more likely Patrick is going to drown! If you have to ask questions, then follow us out to the boat and I'll tell you everything. Every-fucking-thing! But we cannot stand here another minute!"

Confusion swept across the exhausted detective's face. Just as she was about to reply, the radio in her unmarked car squawked. "*Holzer? You got a copy? This is urgent. I repeat this is urgent. Please answer.*"

Holzer hesitated, then said, "You two, don't move." Without turning, she walked backwards and, keeping the gun pointed toward them, leaned into her car and grabbed the microphone. "This is Holzer. Go ahead."

"*All hands are needed immediately. Boat loose in the bay. Unmanned. Appears to have a person tied to the back in the water, pulling them along. Eyewitnesses say it's a child.*"

Jordan turned to look at Melissa who, hand on hips, paced anxiously back and forth. She looked like a caged animal, ready to break loose the moment her cage door opened. Jordan was right there with her.

Every second that ticked by was a moment Patrick drew closer to the cove. Jordan's knees bounced nervously, his stomach tying itself into knots.

"Come again, dispatch? You said there's a child tied to the back of a boat?"

"*Affirmative. Coast guard is following the yacht, but they're going to need any assistance they can get. Do you have immediate access to a boat?*"

Melissa screamed, "Yes! We have a boat! Now do you believe us?"

The detective eyed them both, her face a mask of bewilderment.

"Come on!"

Holzer nodded and sighed. "Dispatch? Can confirm that I have access to a boat. Taking off immediately. Contact me on my cell from this point on. Out." She tossed the microphone back into her car and slammed the door shut. "You two have a lot of explaining to do. Let's go."

23

WHILE JORDAN RACED HIS landlord's tiny speedboat through the river canal, Melissa did her best to explain to Detective Holzer everything that had transpired, yelling over the roaring engine. The trip down to Florida, the abuse, the fishing excursion, Hoyt's reemergence, the condo fire. Everything. It took all Melissa had to not shove the smug bitch right off the boat. The faces she made as Melissa spilled her guts, the interruptions, the obvious questions and answers, not to mention the precious moments lost back on the dock waiting for her to decide whether or not to arrest them both. Melissa could tell the woman didn't believe a word she had said past throwing Hoyt into the sea. Holzer's law enforcement predisposition latched onto that aspect the moment it left Melissa's lips and she declined to move past it. Refusing to listen to the claim of Hoyt's miraculous unrest, the detective kept a firm grip on her service weapon, while the other held tight to the hand rail on the side of the boat.

After several minutes of getting nowhere with Holzer, Melissa turned her frantic attention to the front of the boat, as Jordan piloted them through the

Mosquito Lagoon Aquatic Reserve and up the Indian River. Dozens of three story mansions raced past in a blur. Roped-up yachts bounced in the water as they sped past. Old men in Panama Jack hats waved as their disturbed fishing lines bobbed in the water. Kayakers rowed past in the opposite direction. Families enjoyed their vacations. Locals bronzed their bare flesh. They all seemed so normal, and Melissa hated every single one of them for it. All she ever wanted was a normal, rejuvenating vacation with her son and her boyfriend, and it only took twenty-four quick, bruising hours for it to all go to hell. Never, for as long as she continued to breathe, would she forgive herself for letting this happen. Though she had no way of knowing how *unnatural* the circumstances would come out, she put her and Patrick, his father, and possibly countless others in immediate danger. But while pity was what her brain wanted to feel, her heart told her to buck up and be strong. She intended to listen.

Across from her, Detective Holzer answered her cell phone. The boat continued to roar along, making it nearly impossible to hear what she was saying. She yelled, "Okay! We'll be there shortly!" She hung up and pocketed the phone, then turned to Melissa. "We have two different groups following the unmanned yacht. One is coast guard, and one is carrying three of my local officers."

"What are they doing?" Melissa yelled back.

"They're keeping as close as they can to the boat, but its movements are erratic and unpredictable. Every time they get close, the boat spins sideways and they have to move away, that way they don't hit your son!"

"Can they see him? Is he . . . "

For the first time, Holzer appeared genuinely concerned. She shrugged. "Can't say. All I know is he's still attached to the rope."

Melissa grit her teeth so hard her gums throbbed. "Jordan! Drive faster!"

Jordan turned back to her. "Going as fast as I can."

Holzer asked, "Do you know where you're going?"

He nodded. "Unfortunately yes."

A few minutes later, they faced the massive bridge of the South Causeway. The mechanism appeared to still be damaged, its roadway sticking up in the air like a giant middle finger from Melissa's ex-boyfriend. A few smaller vessels worked directly underneath as their crews continued to clear the wreckage caused by the errant sailboat lodged in its gears. Their boat sped past, earning them dirty looks from the workers.

Once they exited the other side they took an immediate right. The boat raced past both Bouchelles and Chicken Island, and the water space tightened. Dozens of personal yachts and deep sea fishing boats from the nearby marina clogged the waterway. Taking a note from Holzer, Melissa held tight to the hand rail as Jordan carefully traversed the traffic.

"Get the fuck out of the way!" he screamed. Several other boats honked their displeasure.

Holzer waved her badge in the air to the others as they passed, which quickly ended their horn blowing.

When the islands were behind them, they hurried under the smaller, equally-damaged North Causeway and pushed north. His aim steady, Jordan remained calm as he weaved in and out of the other transports as they moved toward the cove and into the ocean beyond. The closer they got, the harder Melissa's heart beat inside her chest. Her breath came in short gasps, eyes burned from the tears she fought back. She glanced across the boat toward Holzer. The woman seemed oddly calm, as if she'd done this a million times. Even though she wanted to be hateful toward her, Melissa found herself thankful for her calm demeanor.

Just as they rounded the Smyrna Dune Park, and the cove finally opened up before them like a yawning blue mouth, they spotted the yacht racing straight towards them. Behind it, the tight rope cut the water.

Melissa leapt up from her seat. "Jordan! There it is!"

Behind the boat, the two pursuing ships raced up along its side. The red-rimmed Coast Guard ship drew near, and, keeping parallel to its side, two men in life vests carefully leapt off the port side. The moment they hit the inside of the yacht, they raced up to the captain's seat and took hold of the wheel. Within seconds, they managed to steady the craft, and a few blinks later the boat slowed to a halt. The other two boats swung around until they, too, came to a stop.

Jordan cautiously drifted their boat until it knocked against the hull of the craft. Both Holzer and Melissa stood.

"You two stay here."

"Try and fucking stop me!" Melissa pushed past her and joined Jordan as they carefully eased themselves over the side of their boat and onto the other. Two more coast guards leapt onto the boat with them. The boat carrying the other police officers remained beside them.

CRUEL SUMMER

"Patrick!" Together, they joined the two coast guards at the rear of the boat, where the thick length of rope was still tied to the fishing chair facing the stern. "Please help him! Pull him up!"

Face covered in sweat, Jordan leapt into action, helping the two uniformed men as they began to pull their son from the waters below.

If Patrick could actually form a thought, he probably would have wondered where he was . . . or how he got there . . . or where his parents were. But he had no thoughts. He only knew water. Cold, harsh, unforgiving water that filled his nose, mouth, and lungs, wrapping him in a salty blanket of thrashing surf. As the gruff voice had said just before he woke, the ocean was now his only blood relative, and it had the power to give life and to take it. Patrick kept his eyes shut and accepted his new family.

After an eternity of flying, he felt his body no longer rushing forward. Instead, he came to a light drift and slowed. When the rope pulled tight, he stopped, his arms hanging limp over his head.

Patrick opened his eyes.

A mass of black eyes stared back.

In the gloomy depths beneath the surface, a multitude of long, grey-blue bodies circled Patrick as he dangled like a worm on a hook. As if vertigo had already taken hold, their vortex dizzied him, forcing his eyes to cross and roll back into his head.

With teeth and purpose, they circled closer. And closer. And closer.

The rope pulled tight above him. Patrick felt his body being hauled up.

Sensing his exit, the sharks ceased their rotation and darted toward him.

The water abruptly chilled.

Patrick closed his eyes.

Waves whipped around him, swinging his body.

The water grew ice cold.

He slowly opened his eyes again. The sharks were gone. Retreating. The rope continued to pull him up. Patrick looked down.

A ghostly white hand reached up from the deep and took his hand.

24

WITH BREATH CAUGHT IN her throat, Melissa watched while the two men lifted Patrick from the dark waters of the Atlantic. As carefully as they could, they grabbed his non-tied-up leg and pulled. When his upper body exited the water, the bigger of the two coast guards grasped Patrick's sopping wet T-shirt and yanked him the rest of the way up over the stern and onto the boat.

Melissa screamed.

Though her son was fully intact, his body was pale and lifeless, arms hanging limp under him as they lifted him over the lip of the boat. They carefully laid him on his back. His head flopped to the side, water draining from his nose.

"*Is he alive?*" she shrieked. "*Patrick! Is he still alive?*"

Jordan knelt down to help, but the other coast guard, an older man with a slick bald head, pushed him away. "Stay back, sir. We'll take it from here. We're trained for this."

"Are you sure?" Jordan was visibly shaken, his entire body quaking with shock.

The older man nodded. "Positive. Both of you take a step back and we'll handle it."

Melissa grasped onto Jordan's shirt and pressed her face into his chest. Her shaking added to his as she fought to stay on her feet.

The two men before them went to work. After checking Patrick's pulse, the taller, younger man flipped him over and, with his first two fingers, pried open the boy's mouth. More water drained from his lips, running across the deck.

"Careful with setting him back down," the older one said.

"Airway's cleared," the other answered.

When Patrick's mouth and nose were emptied, they gently flipped him back onto his backside. With both hands, the older man grabbed Patrick's shirt and ripped it right down the middle. The moment his hands left, the other man immediately started chest compressions. After several pumps, he leaned in and breathed into Patrick's mouth. He repeated the process several times.

The older man gently ran his hands down Patrick's tied up leg. He carefully pulled up the leg of the boy's pants and untied the thick rope from his body. "Looks like multiple fractures in the ankle. His hip might be dislocated, as well. Damn it, keep his neck straight, chin up!"

"Sorry, sir." The other man continued his switching from chest to mouth.

Through burning, teary eyes Melissa took a moment to glance around. The passengers of the other two boats watched on in silence, their faces dour. Several other boats in the cove had stopped in their leisure to watch what was transpiring. Dozens of onlookers had their cell phones held high, capturing the scene from a distance.

"*What are you looking at?*" she screamed across the water.

Their phones rose higher in the air.

At some point Detective Holzer had climbed onto the craft. She stood behind them in silence, watching as the two coast guards continued their efforts to revive Patrick. She cupped a hand around her mouth and shouted, "Have you guys called in an EVAC?"

The guards on the other boat tossed her a thumbs up. "Already on their way!"

She turned to Melissa. "The airlift is on the way, Ms. Braun."

Melissa's focus remained on her child as the men persisted in their work. Back and forth they switched, each one taking turns on compressions while the other performed CPR, keeping Patrick's face pointing straight up. No matter what they did, no matter how hard Melissa prayed to any god that would listen, Patrick didn't respond. His lifeless body remained splayed out in the morning sun, his flat, bone white chest unmoving under the guiding hands of his rescuers. She focused on his eyes, waiting for any sign of movement underneath their lids. She willed them to flutter, to roll, to do something. But they remained closed, frozen in place. Jordan caught her as she sunk to her knees.

"Come on, little guy," the older man said, pressing his chest. "Show me something. Show me anything."

Off in the distance, the sound of helicopter blades roared through the air.

"Come on, kid, give me something. Give me anything."

Losing his grip on her shoulders, Jordan joined Melissa as she collapsed onto her legs.

Please, Patrick, honey . . . Please don't do this . . .

Patrick abruptly began to cough. Melissa yelped with joy, sitting straight up in surprise. The men backed away as the boy turned his head. A torrent of black water rushed from his mouth and sprayed across the hull.

"There we go!" the older man praised. "Get it all out, kid."

Another gush of water spewed from his lips. A few moments later, Patrick's head flopped back into place. His eyes remained shut.

Melissa screamed, "Patrick!" and fought against Jordan, who continued to hold her back.

"Patrick?" the older coast guard asked. "Come on, buddy! Wake up!"

"Let me go!" Melissa pushed Jordan, but he held her tight. "He needs me!"

Tears drained from Jordan's eyes. "He needs them, Mel! Let them do their job."

"No! No . . ." *Take me, please . . . Not him.*

The air grew cold and quiet. The gulls above ceased their cries. The surrounding water stilled. The only sound was the approach of the helicopter. Melissa sat up and glanced around. Judging by the wandering eyes above, they all felt it, too.

Something heavy slammed into the hull underneath. Everyone screamed, grabbing onto something anchored for support. The crash repeated, this time rocking the boat to one side. Losing his footing, Jordan tumbled sideways and landed on top of Melissa. They both fell into Holzer as they rolled into the side of the boat. The two coast guards manning Patrick grabbed the boy and covered him with their bodies. Keeping their balance, they pressed their feet firmly against the sides of the boat, maintaining their hold on the child. The boat rocked back and forth until it settled back down in place. The crashes didn't repeat.

With the help of Detective Holzer, Melissa and Jordan stood back up cautiously, glancing about with wide, terrified eyes. Beyond their boat, the occupants of the other vessels watched on in surprised confusion.

"What the hell was that?" one of the officers yelled.

Jordan answered with a shrug, still eyeing the surrounding water.

Holzer called out, "Do we have an ETA on the airlift?"

"Five minutes! Maybe less?"

The two guards watching over Patrick stood and glanced around. The older man said, "We need that airlift now!"

Melissa cried, "No, please! Keep trying!"

"Ma'am, we will, but—"

A large shape leapt from the water. The five of them ducked as a ten foot marlin cut through the air over their heads and dove into the water on the port side of the yacht.

"Jesus jumping fuck!" the older man yelled.

Jordan asked, "What the hell was that?"

The younger man spun toward Jordan. "A big ass fish, that's what! Holy hell, I've never seen one that cl—"

Before he could finish, another marlin, one even longer and sleeker, rocketed out from the starboard side and pierced its massive bill through the man's back. Its long point ruptured through his chest. Blood sprayed across the deck, splashing over the other four and across Patrick's bare chest. The others screamed and backed away. Confusion swept across the young man's face as he collapsed to his knees and then onto his side. The massive fish wriggled its black, lacquered body as it struggled to tear itself free from the man's prone body.

Holzer shouted, "Hit the deck!"

A half a dozen more of the sleek, sworded fish broke water on all sides of the boat and soared through the air above them. Loads more leapt into the other two manned boats, causing a swell of shouts and screams from those onboard. The remaining coast guards still on their vessel ducked into the shaded overhang, but the uniformed officers on the opposite boat did not have the same luxury. Three marlins leapt into the police boat, all stabbing into the officer standing near the back. Over all the commotion, they heard his garbled shouts, and a moment later a splash as his skewered body hit the water below. Arms splashed and blood gushed as the blue waters immediately flushed red. Sharks swarmed the scene, adding to the chaos.

From underneath, the shark's banging into the hull continued, forcing the boat to rock back and forth in place. While Holzer ducked near the captain's seat and the older coast guard protected Patrick's unconscious body, Jordan had laid his body on top of Melissa's like a shield. "Stay down!" he yelled, keeping his arms wrapped around her head.

Something huge and heavy landed on Jordan's

back, crushing them both. They screamed as water soaked right through them. Jordan pushed up and rolled the massive marlin off of him, letting the creature flop to the deck of the boat. Jordan stood and pulled Melissa backwards as the fish flopped and bucked, its bill swishing through the air like a frantic fencer. Holzer backed away from the creature, pressing herself against the gunwale siding. The marlin bucked up, nearly standing on its fins, and shrieked. Melissa had never heard a sound like that before, from man or beast, and it brought her back to the manatee park, where the bloated creatures had them cornered in the bathroom. These were peaceful creatures, not meant to attack unprovoked or anything above the water—yet here they were, at the mercy of an ancient being, using their bodies in ways God never intended. Though they were being assaulted, Melissa felt undeniable guilt for bringing this upon them.

Both Detective Holzer and Jordan took out their pistols and simultaneously opened fire. Three bullets ripped through the beast and exited the other side, spraying dark blood across the boat's chrome railing. The marlin cried out, its body going rigid, before collapsing to the deck with a *splat*.

Holzer yelled, "Would you mind telling me where that goddamn gun came from?"

"Is that really your first concern, lady?" Jordan, still huffing, rolled his eyes. "It's the fucking South—everyone has a gun."

Shaking her head, the detective re-holstered her weapon. "Maybe a warning next time, yeah?"

Jordan clicked the safety and stuck the pistol back

into his waistband. "Just help me get this damn thing off the boat." Together, they approached the fish and carefully wriggled their arms underneath to lift.

Wary of more flying projectiles, Melissa turned her attention back to the older man hovering over her child. Keeping low, she crawled on her hands and knees toward them both. Eyes brimming with terror, the coast guard sat on his legs, swiveling his gaze around the waters beyond. Sweat poured down his slick, sunburned scalp. They both dropped as another massive marlin leapt over them. Its tail struck the boat railing before it tumbled back into the water.

Soaring high above, pelicans croaked and honked as they dove toward the boats. Dozens of the large, white birds swarmed the coast guard boat, covering nearly every square inch of the surface. The men and women on board screamed as they swatted and swung at the influenced creatures. Gunshots rang out over the cove. The screams rose higher until each one extinguished.

The banging underneath their boat continued.

While Jordan and Detective Holzer lifted the marlin's corpse over the railing, Melissa continued crawling towards her son. She had to be near him, to touch him, to feel for herself if any life remained inside him. Sea life be damned, she would get to him.

A slick, squishing sound filled the air.

Over the older man's shoulder, several reddish brown tentacles squirmed over the railing. Then several more . . . then several more. Melissa pointed and screamed. The coast guard turned around as a mass of octopods crawled up the side of the yacht and over the railing. The man yelped as one leapt off the side and onto his face. Its thick tentacles immediately wrapped around his face, covering his eyes and mouth, smothering his bald head. Underneath the mollusk's rubbery flesh, the man shrieked. He stood, swinging his arms wildly as the creature grew tighter around his face and throat, cutting off his breathing.

Behind her, Jordan yelled, "Melissa? What's going on?"

She turned back to them to say—but a massive gray shape ruptured from the water near them. Jordan yelped and let go of the marlin, Holzer doing the same, as a giant, tooth-filled mouth shot straight up into the air on the port side. The shark clamped onto the dead marlin carcass and ripped it from the boat. As quickly as it came, the shark disappeared back into the deep.

"Jesus fucking Christ!" Jordan yelled.

Holzer cried out as several octopods swarmed her, undulating up her arms and legs with an unnatural speed. Jordan pulled out his pistol and took aim, but Holzer waved him off. "Don't fucking shoot them, you idiot! You'll hit me or someone else! Just get them off me!"

Jordan leapt into action, grabbing their slippery, blob-like bodies and tearing them off her clothing. He kicked at the ones by his feet and tossed the others back overboard. Still suffocating, the coast guard spun above Melissa, nearly tripping over Patrick's body. She dove for her son, shielding him. Head pressed against his bare chest, she felt the steady rise and fall of his slow, shallow breaths. Amidst the anarchy and blood, relief washed over her frightened heart. For a moment, everything went away and it was just the two of them.

"Patrick," she whispered, "honey, wake for Mommy. Wake up, please."

Above her, Patrick's eyes slowly fluttered open.

Melissa sighed and smiled.

Patrick coughed and a gush of water gurgled out from his mouth. He closed his eyes once more and lay still.

"Patrick! No! Wake up!"

Something crawled up Melissa's leg, surging her back to reality. She turned over on her back as two octopods squirmed along her pants. She felt another drag its tentacles through her hair. Squealing, Melissa spun on the ground, kicking them off towards the others undulating in her direction. Above her, the older coast guard was a hive of mollusks as they had swarmed over his body, covering him like a new, heaving skin. Somewhere beneath, the man roared in pain. Before Melissa could move from his path, he tripped over her legs and went tumbling toward the back of the boat. Pulling the squirming octopus from her hair, she leapt for the man, grabbing his covered legs and keeping him from falling.

"I've got you!" she yelled. "Push back!"

Just as he responded, water gushed over the stern as a massive great white shark emerged from the water. In a blink, the man's upper half disappeared into the shark's maw. Stunned, Melissa threw herself backwards onto Patrick's body. The shark's giant gray form rose up and slammed into the back railing, half of it landing inside the boat. Behind her, Jordan and Holzer yelled as the yacht's bow tipped up into the air. Holzer grasped for the steering wheel to keep balance. While reaching out to grasp Holzer, the gun slipped from Jordan's grasp and tumbled down the boat. Grabbing her son's unconscious body, Melissa pushed her feet against the back of the boat in an attempt to keep away. The shark's giant mouth snapped over and over as it wriggled back and forth. The beast roared unnaturally and snapped at her feet. Holding tight to Patrick, Melissa grasped for the metal bracing pole underneath the fishing chair and, with all her strength, pulled them both up and away. The shark responded by wriggling further up the stern onto the boat.

Jordan screamed, "Melissa! Take my hand!"

She lifted her head, finding his outstretched arm only a foot away. Next to him, face full of panic, Detective Holzer struggled to keep hold of the steering wheel.

The boat bobbed and groaned. Something gleamed in the sun and slid toward her, striking the back of her head. Instead of grabbing Jordan's hand, Melissa grasped his gun, and took aim at the beast. Mouth frothing with foamy blood, the shark roared, snapping its jagged teeth at her dangling feet. Patrick began to slip from her grasp. The shark turned toward him and its snapping doubled.

"Melissa, take my goddamn hand!"

Gritting her teeth, she aimed the gun and squeezed the trigger.

It wouldn't budge.

"Click the safety off!" Holzer yelled.

Finding the safety with her thumb, she clicked it and then squeezed the trigger once more.

The pistol bucked in her grip. A second later, a fist-sized hole ruptured on the shark's nose, and a plume of blood spread across its face. The great white threw its head back. Melissa squeezed off four more shots. The first one hit the water behind it, but the next three entered the shark's head and mouth. The shark bucked, and the boat responded by bouncing up and down. Water splashed from both sides, dousing the other three boats. The pelicans cawed and rose back into the air, leaving gore-soaked decks behind.

Slowing its movement, the shark turned its head. Melissa met its eye. She said, "I'm so sorry," before taking one more shot.

The shark's eye exploded, and a pinkish-gray pulp sprayed across the deck. The shark dropped its head, and a moment later its fifteen foot body slid off the stern. When the last of it fell off and into the water, the boat dropped back into place. The speedboat they had driven out into the cove drifted away from the yacht.

Melissa dropped the gun and exhaled.

25

MELISSA WAS TIRED OF crying. Tired of screaming. Tired of feeling like her heart was going to burst out from her chest at any given moment. She didn't want to hurt anymore. Didn't want to fear for her life, for her son's or his father's. She was tired of being afraid.

Mostly, she was sick of it all.

What really drove her over the edge was the idea she had killed her only child, who remained unresponsive to her voice. No matter how loud she yelled, or how much air she gifted his lungs, his only response was the constant drip of water from his mouth and nostrils. While Jordan checked his pulse, Melissa lifted the boy's eyelids. Only the whites of his eyes stared up into the morning sun.

Kicking away the remaining octopods, Holzer yelled, "You! Jordan! Get this boat started—now!"

Leaving her alone with Patrick, Jordan leapt to his feet and joined the detective at the wheel. He sat down and started up the motor. The engine whined in protest, then roared to life with a plume of smoke from the exhaust.

Holzer asked, "Does it have enough gas to get us back to the dock?"

"Looks like it. But which—*shit!*"

A massive crash hit the starboard side of the boat, sending Melissa and Holzer tumbling toward the port. When they regained their footing, Melissa rushed back to Patrick, who had rolled onto his side. After carefully rolling him onto his back, she leaned over the side of the boat.

Beneath the water, a combined school of dolphins and tuna were swimming back around in an arch toward the boat. When they crashed into the starboard again, blood-soaked water splashed up the side of the boat. The sea creatures repeated the process, pushing through the bodies of their dead brethren in their attempt to capsize the yacht.

"*Jordan, go!*"

Jordan responded by pushing the hand throttle down into the control board. The yacht leapt forward, throwing Melissa and Holzer backwards. The detective held onto the back of Jordan's seat, while Melissa held the side railing with one hand and another on Patrick's ripped shirt. The boat spun in place as Jordan fought to straighten the wheel. Unable to immediately right it, the bow swung into the small police boat. The remaining officer's pelican-shredded body rolled out and hit the water. The sharks hurried to it and fed. Jordan swung the wheel the other way, back toward the river.

Holzer yelled, "No, no! Turn around! Now!"

Melissa scanned the river's opening. The teal water ahead was now dark and murky, crammed as far as her eyes could see with the waiting bodies of uncountable sea life. As Jordan spun the boat back to the other direction, the black mass pushed toward them as one.

CRUEL SUMMER

The ocean opened up before them, and with it the possibility of anything. Even though they couldn't go back toward the river side, the idea of being out on the open water, with nothing to protect them but a couple of half-emptied pistols, terrified Melissa more than anything. Somewhere, out in that vast, cold blue hell, was Hoyt . . . or whatever he had become. Ancient god or not, he could control anything that called the ocean its home, and there was no telling what else he could do with that unrestrained power.

As Jordan nudged the yacht north toward Daytona Beach and beyond, another black mass beneath the surface straightaway cut them off. Panicked, Jordan swung the yacht to the right, back down south, as the black mass drew further out into the sea beyond. Keeping a steady grip on the wheel, he led them away as fast as the clunky yacht could carry them.

The wind rushing through her hair, Melissa gazed at the beach, of which they ran parallel. Hotel after hotel, condo after condo swept by in a red and tan blur. Thousands of people stood in the sand, watching their frenzied flight with rapt interest. Melissa waved them away, urging them to get away from the beach. They responded by waving back.

"Where the hell am I supposed to go?" Jordan asked. "I don't think there's a dock anywhere down here on this side."

Holzer kept a steady grip on his shoulder. "I don't know. Just keep driving."

Keeping a firm hand on Patrick's chest to make sure his heart was still beating, Melissa leaned over the starboard railing and kept her windswept view on the water ahead. She narrowed her eyes.

"You guys!"

"Damn it!" Jordan yelled back. "I see it, too!"

All three stared ahead. Another black mass swelled beneath the water a couple of hundred feet ahead. With the rest of the throng coming in from the back and to their side, they were completely cut off. The boat continued to race ahead toward it.

"Jordan, do something!"

"Fuck! I don't know what to do!" Melissa could see his shoulders itching to spin the boat and race out into the open water.

The mass on their left had reached out and merged with the rest of the sea life. They were now completely cut off.

Holzer took out her phone and punched in a number. Plugging her other ear, she yelled, "Geoff, is that you? Yes! Yes, it's Danielle! Where are you right now? Yes, right now!" She paused and listened. "Okay! We're right near there! They have a walk down off to the side of the building! Meet us on the beach pronto!"

Jordan pulled a face and turned to her. "Are you fucking kidding me?"

"We have an ambulance waiting for us, ready to take care of your son. If you have another option, I'm all ears."

He shook his head, sucking in deep breaths.

"That's what I thought." She pointed out toward the beach. "Up there. Misty Sands. The tall one with the pool on the roof. That's where we're heading."

"And you want me to just—"

Melissa screamed, "*Just do it, Jordan!*"

Pinching his mouth into a tight O, Jordan nodded.

To Holzer he added, "Then buckle into that seat." To Melissa he called out, "Mel, hon, you buckle in, too!"

"I can't! I have Patrick!"

Jordan glanced back to them both. His arms were visibly shaking. "Then hold on real fucking tight."

Melissa hunkered down and pressed her quivering body over her son's. She leaned into his ear. "Hold on, baby. Mommy's got you."

Water continued to leak from his nose and mouth.

Holzer said, "Alright, Jordan. Go at an angle and drive right toward that condo there."

Jordan didn't respond.

"Now, goddamn it!"

He then jerked the wheel, and the yacht cut forty-five degrees to the right. Melissa held tight to Patrick's body. Holzer screamed toward the beach, "Get out of the way! Out of the way now!" The beach goers watched on, fascinated, but when they realized the yacht was driving right toward them, they scrambled, falling over one another to move out of the way. Holzer pulled out her gun and fired a shot into the air. "I said move away! Go!"

When the last of the rubberneckers fled, Jordan let off the throttle, and the whine of the engine lessened with it. Not wanting to be surprised, Melissa sat up high enough to look over the railing. Behind them, the black mass closed in. Ahead, the beach rushed forward to greet them.

Jordan cried, *"Hold on!"*

When they were thirty feet from the sand, Melissa ducked back down and regained her grip on her son.

The crash was so much louder than she expected. The moment the hull hit the beach, dry sand erupted all around them like an explosion. The engine roared, and a massive *crack* detonated near Melissa's ear. She was thrown forward against the back fishing seat, striking the top of her head against its metal post. Patrick's legs swung up into the air. Feet over head, his body flipped up limply and hit the seat above. He dropped on top of Melissa, and she tightly wrapped both arms around his chest. Ahead of them, Jordan shouted something unintelligible. Holzer screamed, "Keep her steady!" The boat, now tilted on its side, continued to rocket forward toward the condo. Before long, the roar of the beach below died off, and the yacht slowed. Fifteen feet from the retaining wall below the condo's back yard, the boat skidded to a stop. Keeping her eyes clamped shut, Melissa held onto Patrick with everything she had left inside.

"Mel! Melissa! Are you okay?" Jordan climbed over the seats and found her huddled in the back.

A moment later Holzer joined them. "Ms. Braun? Melissa? You still with us?"

Eyes still closed, Melissa could nod.

"Mel, the paramedics are here. Come on, let's get Patrick down to them and get out of here."

The sun above burned her eyes as she gradually opened them. Jordan smiled sadly as he leaned in. "Anything broken?"

"I don't think so," she croaked.

"Good. Come on. Help me with Patrick."

Standing with a groan, Melissa helped lift Patrick's limp form and handed him off to Jordan, mindful of his leg and hips. Two paramedics, one male and one female, stood on the beach below, with a gurney board already waiting. Carefully, he and

CRUEL SUMMER

Holzer handed Patrick's body down to them and they quickly laid him across the board and strapped him up. Melissa glanced around. Hundreds of people stood on the beach, slowly approaching the wreckage. While most appeared as if they wanted to help, others stood by, recording everything on their phones for social media.

Jordan offered her his hand. "Come on. We need to go."

She took it and together they climbed down the side of the broken yacht. Her knees weak and wobbly, Jordan took her under the arms and helped keep her on her feet. She looked up to him with a weak smile. "Thank you." She handed him his gun, which he placed back into his waistband.

"Don't thank me yet. Come on. Let's go help our boy." Hot sand brushed over their feet as they followed behind the paramedics and Detective Holzer.

"Andromeda!"

Both Melissa and Jordan froze. The curious onlookers spread across the beach gasped, while many screamed and ran away. The two paramedics stopped to look.

Holzer spun around and drew her pistol. "What . . . in the actual . . . *fuck*?"

Fifty feet away, Hoyt stumbled onto the beach from the water. His humongous body was a tower of hardened meat, his gray skin a slick muscle ready to strike. His arms were long and lean, nearly dragging against the sand below. A large, forked tail whipped behind him, striking the sand. The beast grimaced with an impossibly large mouth, each razored tooth gleaming in the sun. He lifted an arm and extended a webbed finger right at Melissa. "*Andromeda! I have come for you. You will not deny me any longer.*"

"Leave us alone, Hoyt!" Melissa cried.

The beast cackled a dry, humorless laugh. "*The man is gone, my dear princess. No more to this world or the next. There is only Cetus. Only payment.*"

Fuming, Melissa shrugged off Jordan and took an uneasy step toward the beast. "I am not Andromeda! Leave us the hell alone, you bastard!"

The beast growled, all teeth and ire. "*Get over here, woman! You're mine!*"

Jordan reached for her. "Melissa, get back!"

She rolled away from him, keeping her shoulders square to the monster. "No!"

Cetus cocked his angular head to the side like a dog. "*Well then . . . If you won't come to me . . . then I shall come to you.*"

The air grew still. The beach went quiet. Cetus didn't move, only remained focused on Melissa as the two stared each other down like gunslingers. In her peripherals, several beach goers backed away, and then turned and ran. Screams erupted all around. Behind her, she heard Jordan mutter, "My God . . . " Breaking their stare, Melissa slowly averted her eyes toward the water.

The beach before them lengthened as the water withdrew into the horizon. It continued to retreat, soon emptying the beach completely of all moisture. Moments later, an enormous silhouette formed a few miles out. Building and building, it rose higher until it appeared to touch the sky. When it seemed to grow no higher, the wave surged forward toward them and the city below.

Melissa stumbled backwards until she ran into Jordan. "*Run!*"

26

IT STARTED WITH A quiet gush of wind, only strong enough to whisper sweet nothings like a gentle lover, but as the tsunami approached, the crash of the white-capped break converted to more like the growl of a cornered tiger. The closer it rushed to the beach, the more it howled—a thousand screams right into Melissa's ears. Just like the cacophony itself, the wave rose higher and higher. Those who shook off their stupor ran as fast as they could, stumbling over one another, shrieking and crying, pushing and stumbling. Death advanced and bedlam retreated.

Hearts hammering, Melissa, Jordan, and Holzer turned and ran with them. All three helped with Patrick, each taking a grip onto his gurney. Carrying his board, the five of them raced as fast as they could across the blazing hot sand toward the wooden steps near the edge of the condo. Holzer and the paramedics screamed for people to move and clear the stairs, but their own lives took precedent as they continued to flood the shaking steps. Those who couldn't access them attempted to crawl up the concrete barrier, climbing over other's backs and shoulders like frightened animals.

CRUEL SUMMER

Letting go of the gurney, Jordan pulled his pistol out and shot it twice into the air. "Clear out or I'll open fire!"

The frightened crowd responded by scattering. Those who were already on the stairs raced up and cleared the path, while the others turned and fled for other nearby exits.

"Are you crazy?" Holzer yelled.

Melissa snapped, "Shut up and move!"

By the time they reached the steps, they had completely cleared, and two police officers were standing at the top, waiting for them. Their eyes went wide when they looked out over beach and beyond.

The male paramedic yelled, "Stop fucking staring and help us!"

The officers nodded and hopped down a few steps. The five below grunted as they lifted Patrick's gurney over their heads and, with the help of the two in front, they carefully climbed up toward the parking lot. When they reached the top, the gurney was hustled toward the open back doors of an awaiting ambulance. Melissa paused for a moment and turned back toward the water.

Cetus had already disappeared, but his colossal wave had drawn closer, only a couple of hundred feet out.

"Melissa! What are you doing?"

Somewhere she heard Jordan's voice calling to her, but it paled in comparison to the ruin that crept toward them. The wind picked up, smashing into her like a car meeting a brick wall. The sky darkened, and rain began to pelt the world around her.

"Goddamn it, Mel! Come on!"

Finally she turned and ran. She took Jordan's outstretched hand, and he yanked her up into the back of the ambulance. He slammed the doors shut behind them, and a second later they were racing across the parking lot toward the highway, with two flashing police cars in tow.

A1A was in near pandemonium. Cars raced like scurrying mice, dashing between one another to avoid the hungry cat on their tail. Dozens of vehicles had already crashed, leaving their occupants to scramble along the highway on foot. Others took to the opposite side of the road to drive North. All three emergency vehicles had their lights spinning and the sirens blaring, but self-preservation was strong and took precedent over all.

In the back of the swerving ambulance, the male paramedic went to work on Patrick, strapping a foam neck brace around his throat and checking his eyes with a pen flashlight. Holzer sat in the front passenger seat, keeping in touch with the officers behind them with the CB radio in the center console. Jordan sat on the other side of the gurney from the paramedic, holding Patrick's hand, while Melissa sat hunched in the back near the doors.

"Please help him," Melissa muttered. "Please save my baby."

Frantically going through his supplies, the male paramedic glanced up with panic in his eyes. "Under the circumstances, lady, I'm doing my fucking best!"

"Hey!"

The man, still shaking, looked over at Jordan.

"Calm down, breathe, and do your best, man. We're *all* not having a great day, you dig?" Jordan continued to hold Patrick's right hand with both of his, stroking his palm with his thumbs, warming him.

Sighing, the man nodded and wiped his face. "I'm sorry. What happened to him?"

"He was dragged behind a boat by the ankle. He's been unconscious for a while. We haven't been able revive him."

"Jesus Christ . . . Okay, from the sounds of it he's got fluid in his lungs. With this much bruising, his ankle appears to be fractured, and if what you told me was correct, his hip might also be displaced. We'll have to get that wrapped up. His temperature is critically low, might be hypothermia. I don't know how you're doing it, kid, but keep holding on." He spun around and opened up several drawers behind him, not finding what he was looking for. "Liz? Where are those blankets and the hot packs, and the—"

A massive crash boomed across the road behind them. Melissa flinched and stood to look out the back windows.

Nearly as tall as the condos themselves, the first wave hit land. The giant torrent of water smashed into the line of condos they had just left. While two of them remained standing, the four surrounding them crumbled and collapsed into the rush of water below. By the time the wave reached the highway, the stray vehicles racing behind them were gone in a blink. Green and yellow earth instantly became a deluge of chunky brown soup. Rain pelted the roof like baseballs, obscuring the windshield.

"Oh, my God!" the driver cried.

Melissa screamed, "Drive faster! Drive faster!"

The gas pedal hitting the floor, the ambulance

leapt forward and continued to swerve around other panicked vehicles. The three in the back held tight onto the gurney, keeping it in place. Up front, Holzer yelled into the CB microphone. "Keep up behind us! Do whatever is necessary to keep up!"

The waves continued to surge, toppling the line of condos one after another. Their debris tumbled into the street, bulldozing vehicles right off the road and flipping them as the water did the rest of the work. The buildings continued to disappear. The waves drew closer.

Jordan leaned toward the front of the cabin. "It's right on our ass!"

"I can only get this rig to go so fast!" the driver growled. "Sit back and hold on!"

Holzer added, "Get back and strap in! All of you!"

Black water gushed from Patrick's mouth and splattered across the back of the ambulance.

"Patrick!" Melissa cried, reaching out for him. "Wake up, honey! Wake up for Mommy!"

More water coughed out from his lips. Opening his eyes, Patrick rolled his head up, straining against his neck brace, and groaned. He fought against his restraints, balling his fists, knuckles white and popping. Jordan leaned across his legs as he lashed out with his bare feet.

"Patrick, calm down! Stop moving!"

"Patrick, baby! You're going to hurt yourself. Stop kicking."

Another groan escaped his mouth, followed by another rush of water.

"Help him!" she cried.

"I'm trying!" Keeping a steady arm across the

boy's chest, the paramedic carefully rolled Patrick onto his side and let the water drain from his mouth onto the floorboard. After a few moments, Patrick sighed and ceased his movements, then laid still.

"Patrick! Is he . . . "

The paramedic shook his head. "No, he's still breathing. How the hell is he still breathing?"

Behind the ambulance, the waves roared their fury as the world behind them flushed away. The water was nearly touching them.

Holzer squeezed the microphone. "Both of you, go around! Hurry!"

"*It's right behind—*" And then there was static.

Melissa watched as a wave rushed across the street directly behind them. In a blink, the two police cars vanished beneath the foul water.

Jordan screamed, "*Go, go, go!*"

Water smashed into the side of the ambulance, causing it to skid sideways into the median. Everyone inside screamed and held on tight. The driver yelped and allowed the vehicle to drift to the left. Then she hit the gas and cut the wheel, pulling the vehicle into the left lane. The road on the opposite side was much clearer, and from what Melissa could see the road was an unblemished shot out of town. The rain continued to pound the world outside. The sky flashed and blackened.

As they rounded the left-leaning curve in the highway to drive toward the mainland, an enormous wave collapsed into the road from behind the last of the condos. The water struck the road and leapt up, washing over the ambulance and nearly submerging them.

Holzer pressed her palms against the dashboard. "Don't stop! Keep turning!"

The driver screamed and frantically spun the wheel, and a moment later they broke the water. The bulky vehicle whined as it swerved and nearly spun, but the driver quickly corrected them and kept them on the forward path. Melissa wanted to sigh in relief. They were finally no longer driving parallel to the ocean, now speeding away from the waves, but the storm continued to rage on. She remained glued to the windows.

"You guys . . . it's still coming!"

Jordan joined her at the back. "Fuck me . . . "

Though the waves were no more, the black, debris-filled ocean water surged down the highway toward them. Everything behind them—businesses, houses, innocent lives—vanished instantly, adding to the steady current eating its way toward the ambulance.

The driver stared into her outside mirrors. Tears burst from her eyes. "I don't know where to go! The hospital is on the other side of the causeway!"

The male paramedic crumpled to the floorboard. "We're all going to fucking die!"

Jordan stepped over him and lifted him by the shirt collar. "Get back to work on my son, you motherfucker, or I'm going to throw your ass out the back doors and *give you something to cry about!*" He dropped the flustered man back onto his ass and then stepped up to the front of the cabin. "Keep driving."

The driver turned toward him. "To where, damn it! It's going to keep following us! There's nowhere to go!"

Jordan grasped her shoulder. "You keep driving straight on. Don't stop for anything, you hear me?"

She arched an eyebrow. "What?"

"We have to get as high as possible."

Holzer turned her gaze up to him. "This is a really stupid idea. You know that, right? You're literally going to corner us up there."

"What other choice do we have, Detective? You got a better idea? Let's hear it?"

She turned her gaze back to the rain-soaked road ahead. After a few moments of silence, she pointed out the window. "Keep going, Liz. Don't stop unless I say so."

The driver continued to whimper as she drove them forward.

The beach disappeared behind them, along with the bright, pastel paints and sunburnt architecture Melissa had come to know and love over her many years of visiting. As they drove on, the raging waters ate her memories away, consuming them like photos placed on a fire. Her second home—Jordan's only home—had vanished. Everything was gone. The water continued to spread out, widening its reach, covering the swamps and swarming the high end apartment complexes beyond like a plague. The road rose up above the ground, allowing the current to surge past and fill the wetlands on both sides.

Up ahead, the road rose higher, and just beyond was the high rise of the South Causeway. Its outstretched bridge remained elevated, touching the swirling black sky above with its tip.

"Detective?" The driver pointed to the barriers across the road.

Holzer shook her head. "Did I not say keep driving until I say otherwise?"

The driver nodded. "God help us. Hold on!"

While the other paramedic worked on Patrick, Melissa and Jordan strapped themselves into the back bench. The ambulance roared, and a moment later the front bumper smashed through the wooden barriers, sending dozens of pieces flying out into the rain. Several other cars beside them followed suit and raced up the causeway with them, crashing into one another as they fought for road space. The water rushed up the concrete bridge behind them.

They drove for another forty or fifty feet before the lifted bridge loomed before them, forcing them to stop. As they slowed to stop, a pickup truck slammed into the rear of the ambulance at full speed. The ambulance swung sideways, throwing them against the lifted bridge. Everyone inside screamed. The ambulance skidded to a stop, the driver's side crushing into the vertical rise. The other vehicles slowed to a stop before they could run into them.

Jordan shook his head, holding it with one hand. "Everyone okay?"

"Okay up here," Holzer called out.

The male paramedic in the back nodded, keeping a grip on Patrick's gurney.

Melissa opened her eyes and shot him a thumbs up.

They sat there for a moment, catching their breath, listening to the rain beat against the roof and the cries of those outside in their cars. Melissa expected the water to rise to the top of the bridge and overtake them at any moment, but the rain was the only water reaching them.

"What do we do now?" the male paramedic asked.

Melissa unbuckled and, taking Jordan's pistol from the back of his shorts, unlocked and pushed open the double back doors.

"Mel, what the fuck are you doing? Get back in here!"

She ignored Jordan's request and lowered herself out of the vehicle. Outside, the rain immediately drenched her hair and worked its way through her clothes in a hurry. It had cooled the summer heat, which made her shiver and hold her arms over her chest. Dozens of others had joined her outside of their cars, and she, too, shared their horror as they stared down the path of the road.

The water, still and black as night, had stopped fifteen feet up the ramp. Beyond that, the road, the town, the beach . . . .gone. All gone. The few remaining condos and hotels stood up out of the water like stone and stucco islands. On both sides of the bridge, the islands were gone, blanketed over, along with the yachts and luxury homes which docked them. With what little light that peaked through the clouds, she could see bodies floating in the soup, along with the remains of their lives, destined to drift away into the sea. The people around her held onto their loved ones and wept. Water peppering her face, Melissa stood there, numb and broken. She could no longer cry, and even if she could, she would not waste her energy on that which she could not change. She knew she had to save her strength.

He was coming.

From out of water below, Cetus rose like the god he claimed to be. He was positively gargantuan, his body now a pillar of hate and reckoning. Though his face remained that of a shark, his neck had elongated, giving him the extra length of a ten foot long serpent. He leisurely crawled on all fours from the water, then stood and trudged up the roadway toward her.

Jordan leapt out from the back of the van. "Melissa, get back in here!"

Detective Holzer exited the passenger side of the ambulance and un-holstered her weapon. "Ms. Braun . . . Melissa . . . I suggest you step back toward the vehicle. Now!"

Melissa did the opposite, taking a few indomitable steps forward. The pistol shook in her grip.

"*Andromeda!*" The beast that called itself Cetus continued to march up the bridge. The closer he got, the bigger he seemed to grow, his body swelling larger with every step.

The people remaining on the bridge screamed and ducked back into their cars. Melissa remained steadfast.

"*Andromeda, stop this running and hiding!*"

"I'm not running anymore, you bastard!" she called back, continuing her march. "And I'm not hiding!"

His massive mouth pulled up into a hideous grin. "*This ends now, sweet princess. There's a price to pay, and I'm afraid you're my prize. You will not continue to deny me your flesh, my right.*"

She howled, "I am not Andromeda! This isn't Greece—this isn't even your time! Leave us alone!"

He snapped, "*Silence, bitch!*" Reaching out to the nearest vehicle, he tore the car's door off its hinges and yanked the driver out from their seat. The man screamed in Cetus's massive, webbed paw.

CRUEL SUMMER

"I know Hoyt is still in there somewhere. Deep down inside. He was once a good man." Melissa cupped her hands around her mouth. "Hoyt, if you can hear me, please turn around! Take this creature back into the water and keep him there!"

Cetus cackled and lifted the squirming man in his grip. With both hands he effortlessly tore the man in half. He tossed both bleeding halves into the water on opposite sides of the bridge. "*The man inside is gone. His flesh is no longer borrowed, but gifted, his soul but scattered dust across the ocean of history.*"

Behind her, both of the paramedics hopped out the car and crawled over the side of the bridge. A moment later, they splashed into the water below.

"*Nothing remains of the man but . . .*" Cetus lifted his arm and observed his giant paws. There, stretched across his knuckles in faded black ink: **DAREMETO**.

A fuse lit in Melissa's brain. She snapped. Lifting the pistol, she ran forward and pulled the trigger. Over and over the gun bucked in her hand, but she kept her grip tight and her aim on target. She roared, willing her anger to coat every bullet that exited the barrel. When the gun emptied, she continued to squeeze the trigger. Frustrated, she tossed the gun to the ground.

When the smoke cleared from her eyes, she hoped to see the giant's body, bloodied and unmoving, on the roadway.

In the rainfall, Cetus's unmarked body continued to stroll up the roadway. The beast cackled repulsively as his eyes ruptured and burst from the sides of his angular head in two long, thick, fleshy plates. He swung his hammerhead, keeping his black eyes trained on her.

Melissa dropped to her knees, letting her chin drop to her chest. "What do you want?"

The beast neared. *"Now? Only you. After . . . "* His eyes swept over the land beneath them, his new waterlogged kingdom. *"Who knows? I am alive and free. The world is my oyster. All I need is to pluck the first pearl."* Cetus stopped twenty feet away and gazed upon her. *"Will you be my pearl, sweet princess?"*

Melissa lifted her head. Rain pelted her eyes. "You don't scare me anymore."

"Is that so, little one?"

Jordan ran up beside her and attempted to pull her back. "What are you doing? Get back!"

She brushed him off and glared up at the beast. "You hear me, Hoyt? I'm stronger than you! It doesn't matter what shape you take! Patrick and I will *always* be stronger!"

Something changed in Cetus's face. The black eyes on his stalks narrowed. Familiar anger swept over his face. His lips twitched, pulling up over his teeth. *"You should have just taken the ring, bitch."*

Melissa stood up on shaking legs. She squared up her shoulders. "I wish it was me that hit you in the face with that fucking bat."

Beneath the beast's skin, Hoyt growled viciously and continued forward.

Jordan hugged her around the shoulders and whispered. "Hold me, Mel."

Melissa stood her ground.

Gunshots rang out behind them as Holzer popped round after round into Cetus. The bullets bounced off his thick, rubbery flesh.

The people inside their cars screamed.

CRUEL SUMMER

Jordan screamed.

Melissa held her chin high.

Suddenly it went quiet. The rain slowed to a drizzle. Ten feet away, Cetus stopped his advance. Behind them, Melissa heard Holzer mumble, "What the hell . . ."

Taking a deep breath, she turned back to the ambulance.

From out the back of the cab, Patrick leapt down onto the wet cement. Melissa froze as she stared into the milky whites of his eyes. Hip popping as he walked, the boy stumbled on his broken ankle toward them.

"Patrick, baby!" Melissa screamed. "Get back in the ambulance!"

Jordan turned to face him. "Patrick, son, please go back—"

Before he could finish his sentence, Patrick grabbed Jordan by the shirt and flung him back toward the vehicle. Jordan yelped and tumbled head over feet, landing awkwardly on his back with a thump. Eyes wide with fright, Melissa watched her son stumble right by her and walk toward the enormous beast.

"Patrick, what—"

Without looking, her son placed a hand on his mother's chest and shoved. Melissa cried out and she toppled backwards, sliding several feet backwards on her rear end. After Jordan stood back up, he ran to her and pulled her to her feet. "Patrick! Stop!"

Cetus grinned down at the boy. *"Ah, yes, I've heard of you. Pussy Boy . . . Are you here, too, to claim your fearlessness, young one?"*

His stare blank and unseeing, Patrick's mouth fell open as if he were going to answer. Instead, dark water surged, gushing between his pale lips with the force of a tsunami. The water roared as it lifted up and spun around his body like a cyclone. Before long, the water fully encapsulated his broken frame.

Melissa's jaw dropped. She stumbled backwards, nearly fainting. Jordan caught her, his face matching hers line for line.

Within a matter seconds, Patrick was a column of swirling water that reached higher and higher, matching the height of the beast. Soon, the spinning slowed, and from out of the top a ghostly white head formed. Two long, muscular, watery arms grew out from the sides, soon joined by a pair of legs beneath. As the contained hurricane continued to swirl, the watery, translucent body of a man now stood before Cetus.

The great beast snapped its teeth. "*Perseus . . .* "

The water man lifted its right arm out from his side, and the water swirled downward into his wrist. The arm stretched and grew to twice its length, the end eventually curving into a wicked, sharp point. The man's head glanced down at the water sword and then back up to the beast.

Cetus growled and leapt forward.

Melissa screamed, "*Patrick!*"

The watery man reacted and swung his sword. The beast was quicker. It ducked its long neck and slid underneath the blade's arc. When it skidded past, Cetus racked his massive paw up the man's back. Water flew across the bridge, splashing over everyone near the ambulance. The man turned and swung his sword once more. Cetus roared and batted the sword away with his tail. The sword hit the bridge and burst into the water. Lunging, Cetus overtook the giant man, grasping him by the throat with both webbed paws. He swept his leg behind the man's, and a moment later they tumbled to the ground. Water burst from the man's back as Cetus landed on top of his massive frame.

"Patrick!" Jordan kept his grip around Melissa's midsection and held her in place. "Leave him alone, you bastard!"

Pressing the watery man to the ground, Cetus kept one paw around his throat, while the other was wrapped around his right arm. The watery man struggled, bucking his legs and rear end, but he seemed unable to beat the creature off of him.

"*Not this time, demigod!*" Cetus roared. "*She's mine! She's mine! Not even you will deny me!*"

In their struggle, the watery man turned his head toward Melissa. Though she could not see his eyes, she could sense Patrick within, could feel the goodness and purity fighting its way to the surface. They stared at one another for an eternity, and for a fleeting moment she saw Patrick's grateful smile, happy and unburdened. He was strong, indomitable. He was free. Melissa ceased her struggling and collapsed back into Jordan's lap. She let out a breath and nodded. The watery man nodded back.

Perseus turned his head back to face the beast. "*Not . . . this . . . time!*"

With his free hand, he stretched it out beyond Cetus's control. A moment later another sword grew from his hand. Unperturbed, Perseus reached behind the beast and ran the watery sword over the back of his elongated neck. Cetus roared and threw his head back in pain. Taking the opportunity, Perseus bucked the beast off his body and sat back up on his knees. Cetus crashed into a tangle of cars, then quickly got back on his feet. Blood gushed from the back of the beast's long neck. He turned back to Perseus and snarled. Fuming, the beast leapt toward him. Perseus ducked and lashed out with his sword. Dark blood gushed from the stump of the beast's leg. Cetus collapsed onto his chest, howling in agony, his cries echoing across the land. Taking his time, Perseus spun the water blade in his hand and stood over the downed beast. Squatting, he sat on Cetus's back, then grabbed the beast around the long neck. He pulled back, snapping the back bones of the beast. Cetus squealed and beat his fists against the ground.

In a deep, booming voice, Perseus leaned into Cetus's upturned face and proclaimed, "*Not . . . this . . . time. Not . . . ever!*"

He lifted his sword and drove it into the beast's spine. Blood ruptured from the beast's chest, spraying across the wet bridge in thick, bubbly blasts. Still holding Cetus's neck, Perseus stood and lifted the giant beast with his sword. Using the beast's own weight, Perseus allowed Cetus to slip down until his back hit the sword's hilt. Satisfied, Perseus dropped the beast to its feet and then swiftly ripped the sword upwards into the sky. Blood rained across the bridge.

Cetus stood there for a moment longer, his great, black eyes blinking confusion, before his two halves tore the rest of the way down the middle and fell in opposite directions. Steam rose as his innards splashed across the concrete.

Perseus loomed above the corpse, staring down at the great beast he once again slayed. He lifted his head high and howled into the sky. The bridge rumbled beneath them. The watery body of Perseus lifted his arms and howled once more in victory.

Then he exploded.

A frigid wave of water dropped over the bridge and splashed across the sides, adding to the water below. Covering themselves, Melissa and Jordan took the brunt of it, throwing them backwards against the ambulance. Holzer ducked and used the passenger door as a shield. When the water stopped falling and the world drew silent, Melissa took her arm away from her face.

The sky broke. The sun bled through the clouds. Beneath its rays, Patrick sat on his legs. Water dripped from his hair and down his face, his head drooping against his neck brace. His eyelids heavy, he turned toward his parents.

"M . . . Mom? Dad?"

"Patrick? Patrick!" Jordan let her go, and Melissa stood and stumbled toward her son. She collapsed against him and hugged him hard. Jordan joined them and threw his arms over them both. Together, they shivered into one another, waiting for the summer heat to return to warm them.

27

JORDAN BLINKED BEHIND HIS cheap sunglasses at the blazing Georgia sun overhead. He had no idea how long he'd been driving, hadn't even bothered to keep track of time. After spending the last three months in the hospital with Melissa and Patrick while they healed up, he was ready to hit the road and get the hell out of Florida and all of its dismal memories.

But they weren't all bad. Even though it took nearly everything he owned, he gained something far more precious in return.

Before leaving the state, Jordan called in a favor from Detective Holzer. Though she wasn't happy about it, she escorted him back to the remains of his house and let him salvage any belongings that weren't ruined by water. He took everything he wanted, with a few extras, and left his ruined paintings behind. That was okay. They weren't important to him anymore. He could paint anywhere. He no longer needed the sun or the ocean to keep him inspired.

Letting his mind wander, Jordan kept the rental car at a steady pace going up I-75 North past Valdosta. In the passenger seat, Melissa slept with her head curled up against the window. Her soft snores wheezed in and out, only slightly louder than the air conditioning. Propped up in the back seat, Patrick shuffled through the boxes of Jordan's Magic the Gathering cards he had sitting across his leg and hip casts. Patrick caught Jordan staring at him in the rearview mirror.

The boy smiled. Jordan smiled back.

Yes, there were other things to inspire him these days.

AUTHOR'S NOTE:

The beautiful city of New Smyrna Beach, Florida is a very real place, as is nearly every single location I have written about in this book. But, as many writers do, I have taken fictional liberties with most of these areas to fit the narrative of the story. The real city is a warm, welcoming place, and a vacation spot my family and I have been frequenting for decades. I promise it's not as scary as I have made it seem. Definitely go check out the manatee park!

ACKNOWLEDGEMENTS

They say writing is a solitary act, but no one writes their work alone. I would like to thank the following individuals for their help, love, friendship, and encouragement: Kelli Owen, Robert Ford, Brian Keene, Mary SanGiovanni, Mike Lombardo, Somer and Jessie Canon, Wile E. Young and Emily Rice, Chris Enterline, Kristopher Triana, Stephen Kozeniewski, John Boden, Lynne Hansen and Jeff Strand, Kenzie Jennings, Jonathan Janz, Tim Meyer, Aaron Dries, John Wayne Comunale, Christine Morgan, the entire No*Con crew, Matt Wildasin, Deena Dib and Dave Thomas, and my in-laws and extended PA family.

To Mom, Dad, and sis, for so many great memories at the beach. But no more fish stew for you, Dad. That stuff is gross.

A hearty thank you to Sadie Hartmann, Jamie Goecker, Ron Dickie, Tod Clark, and Kyle Lybeck, for their eyes and their help on the final drafts.

To Alex McVey for bringing Hoyt to life.
To Katie. I love you forever.

And to Paul Goblirsch, Jarord Barbee, and Patrick C. Harrison III for taking this book on. You all are the best!

ABOUT THE AUTHOR

Wesley Southard is the Splatterpunk Award-Winning author of *The Betrayed, Closing Costs, One For The Road, Resisting Madness, Slaves to Gravity* (with Somer Canon), and *Cruel Summer*, some of which has been translated into Italian, and has had short stories appear in outlets such as *Cover of Darkness Magazine, Eulogies II: Tales from the Cellar* and *Clickers Forever: A Tribute to J.F. Gonzalez*. He is a graduate of the Atlanta Institute of Music, and he currently lives in South Central Pennsylvania with his wife and their cavalcade of animals. Visit him online at www.wesleysouthard.com.

Made in the USA
Columbia, SC
14 March 2021